Praise for *THERE WILL BE OTHER SUMMERS:*

"Curious, contemplative, and heart-achingly tender, *There Will Be Other Summers* is a poignant snapshot of being understood. With thoughtful disability, queer, and mental health rep, Anderson shows the myriad ways we can be there for each other when it seems the world is shutting us out."
Cass Biehn, author of *Vesuvius*

"To be known is to be loved, and *There Will Be Other Summers* neatly fills the need in the market for more platonic love stories. It's also a thoughtful entry in the canon of coming-of-age novels, perfect for fans of Nina LaCour and John Green."
Emma Saska, author of *March & Feather*

THERE WILL BE OTHER SUMMERS

Also by
TEGAN ANDERSON

Beauty in the Breakdown

Paper Forests

There Will Be Other Summers

THERE WILL BE OTHER SUMMERS

Tegan Anderson

First published in Great Britain by
Little Oaks Independent Publishing

First paperback edition September 2025

The text for this book was set in Palatino Linotype.

A CIP catalogue record for this book is available from the British Library.

Paperback: 9781739170639
Ebook: 9781739170646
Large print: 9798294600013

Independently published

www.tandewrites.com

*To Bonnie, who loved me so hard I finally started to
believe that I was worthy of it.
And for making me better at GeoGuessr.*

A NOTE FROM THE AUTHOR

Please note that this book depicts issues of: mental illness, including anxiety and depression; suicidal ideation; blood and imagery reminiscent of self-harm; voluntary hospitalisation; and discussions of ableism and transphobia

I have done my best to approach these topics with sensitivity, but if you feel this kind of content may be triggering for you, please be aware.

MAY

ONE

There are over seven thousand songs on Ryn's phone, yet he can't find one that fits his mood. From the bench at the peak of the cliff, wind tears at his jacket while pop singers croon love in his ear and rockers disguise their anguish with contagious guitar riffs that he will never learn to play. Out of seven thousand songs, not one of them manages to portray the overwhelming emptiness that he feels. Not one song can replicate the feeling of being numb.

Eventually, Ryn commands Siri through his earphone microphone to shuffle all the songs, turning the volume down until the music serves as backing vocals to the howling whale song of the wind. The weather serenades him as he tries to conjure an image of his location in his mind.

Throughout his childhood, Ryn visited a similar salt-choked shoreline just to admire how the peak of the cliff was in the centre of an upside-down V, so anyone standing near the edge could see the beach curving back either side of them, and how there was nothing but endless water in front. It felt as if he was at the edge of the world. Ryn can remember feeling like he was infinite back then, back when his biggest concern was if his mother would be late home from work that night.

But his visual memory faded soon after the bulk of his eyesight, and now his mother doesn't come home at all.

Now, when he stands near the edge of a different cliff and looks around, he sees an immense blackness that taunts him even when his eyes are open, disrupted by the occasional glint of sunlight reflecting off the waves. The scene his father once described to him remains a list of facts rather than a clear picture in his head, and Ryn will stare at the horizon and pretend that he has seen something other than light and shadows for the past few years.

But he'll still try. He tries every time he winds his way up the weatherworn path, rain or shine.

He unfolds his white cane from where it lays abandoned beside him, stands up, and tentatively taps his way to a spot a few feet back from the cliff edge, marked by a large, smooth rock. The distant sound of waves a couple of hundred feet or so below replaces his music as they crash relentlessly upon the beach, and Ryn tries to convince himself that it's the force of the wind that causes tears to drip down his cheeks. It's been too long to fall back into the pit of self-misery that served as his home after he lost the ability to see colours or anything in the dark. After he turned fourteen and he had to relearn how to pour a glass of water without help. After he lost almost all of his remaining vision.

Some days, he's not convinced that he ever left the pit.

When he was thirteen years old, a condition with his eyesight became something else, something that could not be held at bay by a childhood full of prescriptions and glasses and surgeries. His vision decayed rapidly over the next year, and one of his eyes was removed after contracting an infection during what was supposed to be a routine procedure. He was told there was no other option, and why would he question that?

The eye had to go, and the surgeon attempted to salvage the socket in the hopes that a prosthetic might fit, but it was such a mess that nobody gave Ryn a straight answer as to whether it'd be possible, and he eventually became so afraid of leaving the house that he never went back. Now, almost four years later, he wears sunglasses to cover the scar tissue that guards the eye socket without the eye, and his mother convinced him over a phone call to use a white cane to help him go to places he could navigate in his sleep.

On the plus side, his cane has a new curved tip, so he's prepared for all terrain.

After a few minutes, Ryn's phone rings, the sound cutting through his music and taunting him as he fumbles for the zipped pocket inside of his jacket. The sound mutes itself before he can respond and stays quiet, so he decides it was only an alarm. If it was either of his parents, they would call until he answered.

He questions Siri about his day as he guides himself down the cliff path and to the car park at the bottom. He pauses his music long enough to hear the response. "Siri, what time is it?"

"It's thirteen twenty-seven, Ryn." Siri—set to have the voice of an Australian man—pronounces his name as 'Rhine,' like the river. It's difficult to hear the voice over the howl of the wind, but he will always notice when his chosen name is mispronounced. It never fails to bring back memories of school days with teachers ticking names off the attendance list, making several stuttering attempts to read the name when they got halfway down the list, concluding in a pronunciation that was often far from correct.

His name is only three letters long, pronounced like 'win' but with an *R*. How hard can it be?

"Is therapy today?" he asks when he's finished circling through the memories, confirming that the sound was an alarm and not a concerned parent. Beneath his feet, the crunch of cliff path gravel gives way to the smooth asphalt of the car park. The wind isn't any less strong down here.

There's a brief pause before Siri replies, "You have eighteen events this month, Ryn. That's a lot."

Ryn lets out a frustrated sigh, not caring that someone could be around to witness him arguing with his phone. "Read out the events for today, please."

"I don't understand, Ryn."

Sighing again, he locks his phone and wedges it into the front pocket of his jeans. It's time for him to go.

Asher slumps into the passenger seat of a second-hand Volvo, waiting for her mother to put down her phone long enough to remember that being behind the steering wheel is more than a change of location for her online life. Asher opens her music app, pauses the song that was playing on mute, and scrolls down to reveal the lyrics.

Her mother taps in furious silence at her shattered phone screen with a freshly manicured nail. She mouths words in a fashion that appears to be angry, and Asher can't decipher the exact words that are being said—she hasn't got around to replacing the batteries in her hearing aids, and every voice sounds like it's underwater until she does—but she assumes they're most likely directed at her mother's newest boyfriend. Asher doesn't remember his name, just that he graduated university a handful of years before she's due to start.

She sinks into the seat with her feet tucked beneath until her spine resembles something that should be a medical concern. She stops reading for a few moments to examine the world outside of the car.

In this late spring, the weather is unpredictable. Earlier in the week, Asher left the house under a blue sky, broken only by a spatter of picture-book clouds, barely moving in the breeze. Today, the air is cold, and last month's frigid rain threatens to return, cumuli blocking out the sun.

After she's consumed the lyrics of a song that was topping the charts a few decades before her birth, Asher notices the time. It's passed half-past one. Accompanied by an eye roll, she skips to the next song, pauses it, and reads the lyrics in time to a melody she invents. She pretends not to care that her mother is making her run late to something that wasn't her idea. In fact, she pretends not to care so hard that she chews through the sore spot on her lip until it bleeds. Again.

But Asher isn't that good at pretending that something doesn't matter to her, so after another song, she says, "Mum, I can't be late. It's my first session."

The time is twenty minutes to two, and group therapy, beginning in ten minutes time, is a fifteen-minute drive to the other side of town. Her mother's head snaps up, and she spouts what Asher can only assume are profanities as her eyes land on the dashboard clock. She frantically buckles her seatbelt, releases the handbrake, and sends the car screeching into the road, narrowly missing the neighbour's recycling bins.

Asher sighs and rubs her temples between her forefingers. Maybe, one day, her mother will pay more attention to her than the other life that exists solely inside her phone.

"Have a good time, kid. I'll be waiting here a little before three in case you finish early."

Or in case Ryn decides to leave early, but neither he nor his father will acknowledge that.

Ryn nods in the vague direction of his father, knowing that the man will be unlikely to leave the car park for the next hour. Ever since his wife packed her things and never came home three years earlier, he has become increasingly protective of his son, willing to spend all of his time waiting outside of meetings and appointments and activities, guaranteeing that he is always available to be by Ryn's side at a moment's notice, whether or not it is wanted.

And it is rarely wanted, but Ryn doesn't have the heart to tell him that.

As Ryn unbuckles his seatbelt and reaches for the door, his father leans over and holds the handle shut. A lingering scent of paint fumes clings to his father's shirtsleeves, alongside something bitter and familiar—coffee, perhaps—and Ryn wonders what has been repainted around the house.

"Can you at least try to make some friends today?" his father asks, knowing his son's preference for straying away from any form of discovered human life.

If Ryn still had two fully functioning eyes, he would

roll them. "Don't set your sights too high, Dad. It's so quiet in there that I could be sitting in an empty room for all I care."

"But you should, Ryn. You *should* care."

Ryn inserts another hypothetical eye roll into the conversation. "If I talk to someone this week, will you stop bothering me?"

"Why don't you see for yourself?"

Ryn restrains a half-hearted laugh at the word choice, pushing his hair back from where it falls behind his sunglasses and irritates the scar tissue engulfing his eye socket. "There may be a slight issue there."

Before his father has a chance to respond, Ryn wins the fight over the door handle and guides himself toward the youth centre, an apparent concrete monstrosity of a building that was constructed in the past five years in the name of 'urban development,' more commonly known as bulldozing a perfectly fine abandoned garage for teenagers to smoke behind after school. He's soon accompanied by a young woman and her cloud of perfume, who his father described as someone who could've stepped straight out of the pages of a magazine, but one of the ones Ryn remembered seeing on the top shelf in the corner shop.

Reluctantly, he tucks his hand into the crook of her elbow. She's wearing velour again, and he curls his fingers into a fist at the texture.

"How are you today, Ryn?" the woman asks in a voice like treacle. She speaks as if she's reading from a script, making a point to say Ryn's name after each line. It's more likely that she's fresh out of training and hasn't found her stride yet, but Ryn tends to assume the worst from people.

"Average," he replies, nudging his sunglasses further up his nose with the handle of his cane. He's twenty steps from the car, so he has a smooth stretch of thirty steps where there are no potholes or cracks in the pavement, and he could walk unaided as long as he kept count if anyone let him. "I'd be better if I could see past my problems."

The woman supplies a polite laugh, and Ryn realises he's known her for weeks and he was never told her name. Or he was told, but he never remembered. Or he simply never asked. Not like it matters to him anymore: he's shown he doesn't intend to build a friendship with her in the few minutes they are forced to share as they cross the car park together on either side of therapy sessions. Those attempts mainly consist of jokes about his lack of one fully functioning sense. Sometimes, after realising what he's doing, the woman tries to retaliate. Now is one of those times.

"Joking about people's disabilities—even your own—does more harm than good, Ryn. Didn't anyone ever teach you that?"

There's a pause as they reach the front doors of the building. Ryn waits until he hears her groan as she tugs one of the heavy doors open, takes a few steps forward and hesitates, looking directly at the place where he heard her voice. "To be honest, I didn't think I saw anyone laughing."

TWO

"Is there anyone here who would like to share with us today?"

Jonathon, a man in his early forties with a haircut belonging to someone at least two decades younger, stands in the middle of a circle formed by plastic chairs and a dozen teenagers who don't want to be there, let alone share with the group on a weekend afternoon. The room is out of place in the newly built youth centre, with tall windows to let the light swarm in and paint-splattered, refurbished wood surfaces adorned with drying acrylic pieces from the morning art sessions. Asher considered signing up earlier in the year under the guise of expanding her university applications, but really, it would've been an excuse to leave the house.

Asher chooses the last chair available—spotlighted by a direct beam of sunlight—but at least her eyes can fix on the clock above the door, counting down the minutes until she can escape from behind the curtain of fried pink hair that she uses as a barricade. If she observes the session from behind her hair, maybe Jonathon won't try to get her to open up to the group of people she's just met. And, if she hides, she won't have to force herself to read anyone's lips and pretend that they all have the same grasp on the discussion.

As she peers around the circle, she can't help but notice how different she looks from everyone else. Not just the fashion sense—she's mistakenly dressed as if she wants to be noticed, a patchwork of colours like her favourite fairytale characters—or the non-functional hearing aids that remind her that she's disabled, and visibly, too. And she can try to chemically fry the spiral texture out of her hair as much as she wants and bleach it brightly to match the cool girls in her class, but she can't change her dark eyes or wide nose or deep brown skin to blend in with the hoard of light-skinned, light-haired teenagers that surround her.

For the second time today, she shrinks into her seat.

A feather-haired boy wearing oversized sunglasses sits a couple of seats away from Asher, his legs outstretched and crossed at the ankles as if he's lounging on a deck chair beside a swimming pool. He's a picture-perfect postcard of calm that Asher wishes she could pocket.

"No one?" Jonathon says eventually, mostly to himself, visibly deflating as he realises his efforts are wasted. Asher wonders how many consecutive sessions he's spent desperate for someone to engage. "There is no one in a group therapy session who is willing to participate?"

A pair of girls who sit out of his sight line hide smiles behind their ring-clad hands, the jewellery silver and sparkling and scattering light around the room like a disco ball. Asher glances up to acknowledge the minute hand's journey around the clock. The feather-haired boy does nothing to disguise the grin on his face, only leans further back into his chair and folds his arms behind his head, something that Jonathon notices with a look of disgust sweeping across his features. A target has been identified. "Ryn, please share with the group."

The boy's smile doesn't falter as he stands, dragging out the process, reaching for the white cane beneath his chair and adjusting his sunglasses, revealing a glimpse of what could be a scar beneath. Jonathon turns toward him, and Asher would pay to have a clear view of the look on his face.

"What do you want me to say?" Ryn asks, slipping his free hand into his jacket pocket and shrugging. Asher admires the collection of pin badges that adorn his lapels: a lot of flowers, a few colourful stripes that could be pride flags, something that may be a pronoun pin, but Asher can't tell from this distance. The largest adornment is a stickered nametag, curling at the edges and clearly hiding an identical sticker beneath.

"Just reintroduce yourself, Ryn. Tell us how your week is going. This is the first time you've ever volunteered yourself. It will be nice for the group to get to know you a little better, especially as there are some fresh faces here today."

He gives another smile that doesn't reach his cheeks, followed by an amused shake of his head. There's something about an arrogant demeanour—unconditional confidence—that attracts Asher's attention, for better or for worse.

"Hi, I'm Ryn. Nice to meet you all." He gestures at his sticker, and Asher now clearly sees his name written in blocky handwriting, followed by a lopsided smiley face.

Jonathon's face crumples in a way that makes Asher assume he's groaning. His hands twitch impatiently. "Tell everyone why you're here, Ryn."

"What, tell everyone why I'm screwed?" Ryn's expression suggests that he's reluctant to explain the indoor sunglasses and the cane, not like everyone in the room has already guessed. Asher saw him escorted across the car park as her mother struggled to fit into a parking space.

Jonathon folds his arms across his chest and says nothing. Ryn interprets his silence as a prompt to continue. Asher has never been more relieved that someone interesting is both facing her and speaking clearly enough for her to lip-read. "Well, I've had problems with my eyes since I was a kid. I knew I was screwed when I was thirteen and I couldn't see past sunset anymore. I knew I was *really* screwed when a doctor dug my eyeball out of my head."

Without another word, he slumps back into his

chair and Jonathon handpicks another unwilling victim. "Asher, how about you?"

Asher thinks of the worst swear words she knows and curses herself for not turning away the second Jonathon thought about looking in her direction. Her skin is damp with a sweaty sheen, and it's not just the repercussion of sitting in direct sunlight. She pushes herself out of her chair, silently praying that moving slowly will disguise how her body is behaving as if it is her first day on earth.

"Uh, I'm Asher," she begins, uncertain of how much of her anxiety is being released in her shaky voice, growing croaky from disuse. She hasn't felt the urge to engage in long conversations since her batteries died, not like she has anyone to talk to except her parents. The faces of the bored teenagers surrounding her remain blank. The giggling pair across from her continue giggling. For a moment, Asher wishes she could be the blind boy, wishes that she doesn't have to see the eyes drifting aimlessly around the room before returning to dissect her appearance. Her cheeks burn red, and she looks at her battered white Vans—the pair where the original white laces have been replaced with neon ones re-tied in a fun design. She stares at the bright colours and tries to force an equally bright smile onto her face. She fails.

"How are you feeling today, Asher?" Jonathon prompts impatiently as if he gets paid by the patient rather than the hour. Luckily for Asher, she hasn't quite mastered the art of distinguishing tones of voice by lip-reading.

She takes a moment to think about the question, eyes drifting to the windows as she turns emotions over in her head, holding them up to the light until she finds one that fits. She's too hopeful for disdain, too cautious for optimistic. Not sad enough for depressed. Sometimes happy. Never content. She chooses the most suitable feeling. "Alone."

Jonathon waves his hands wildly to capture Asher's attention, making sure that she'll read his lips to save himself from making a half-hearted attempt at signing out the words for her. (He's been taking classes—Asher's mother made sure of it, even though she knows Asher has not and can barely fingerspell her name.) "Would you like to take that thought further? I'm sure that there's someone else here who is feeling the same but isn't comfortable enough to voice their emotions."

Asher sinks her nails into her palms and regrets that she didn't wear her patchwork hoodie with the big front pocket to hide her restless hands. "I feel like there's no one I can relate to anymore. I've lost most of my unaided hearing, and all I've gained is a load of sympathy that I don't want. I just want my friends to act normal again, you know?" She risks a glance around the circle before Jonathon can interrupt, searching for someone who shows a sign of relating to her words, a sign of even listening to her. The only change in expression comes from Ryn: a scowl replaces his nonchalant grin. She turns in his direction and aims her next words at him as she's filled with a sudden spurt of confidence.

"Sometimes, I feel as if I'm going crazy," Asher begins, and her hand drifts up to clutch at her necklace for emotional support. "I'm just so…I don't know, desperate? Yeah, I'm desperate for someone to show me something other than sympathy. I want someone to care about me as a person rather than their idea of an invalid, as if my hearing might miraculously come back one day and they just have to wait it out. My own mum treats me like I'm broken. My dad's trying his best, but he's still struggling. My friends don't care anymore, because sometimes I can't even pretend that I'm listening to them. No one understands."

There's a flurry of movement as Ryn surges to his feet. His knuckles are white around his cane. "There's a chemical formula for love. I…don't remember what it is anymore, but it exists. For dopamine and serotonin and oxytocin," he says, and Asher finds it no easier to decipher his words than she did during her chemistry lessons. She's painfully aware that this must be the only thing Ryn has ever said voluntarily in this room, the only thing he's ever said since Jonathon picked on him a few minutes earlier. "You can manufacture it easily in a lab, but an overdose can cause paranoia and insanity."

Jonathon steps in as Asher parts her lips for a response, waving for her to sit down. She breaks her stare away from Ryn to assess the room's reaction. Still indifferent. "Ryn, I think we've heard enough from you today. I'm glad you want to share with the group again, but I think it's time for someone else to speak."

Before he agrees, Ryn turns back to Asher, as if he remembers where he last heard Asher's voice. She sits up straighter as if she's trying to show him that he's listening, not like he can tell.

"Sometimes," he says, his mouth barely moving, grip loosening on his cane, "having nothing is better than having something."

"There's a girl," Ryn announces to his father as soon as they're both in the car, seatbelts secured, radio playing the Top 40 on low. He's slightly breathless from rushing back ahead of his assistant to his father's usual parking space, desperate to speak to someone who cares. The older man's breath hitches in surprise.

"What's her name?" he asks. As other members of the group trickle out of the doors, Ryn imagines his father watching them intently, wondering which one has captured his son's attention. He can't provide any other identifying features, so finding Asher must be left to the imagination.

"Asher." The name tumbles out of Ryn's mouth before he can stop it. He knows his father is going to try to find her online, and he hopes that her social media is private. "She's so *different* from everyone else."

He can hear the smile tugging at the corners of his father's mouth. Ever since the post-surgery doctor's appointment, Ryn hasn't visibly expressed any emotions other than various metaphorical shades of blue. "What do you mean by that?"

Every session, Ryn listens with the blind hope that someone will be like him, that someone will understand what it's like to have a disability change the course of their life. In every session so far, everyone has had all of their senses intact. Until today, the first time in the past six months. The memory of the brief encounter plays back in his head like a movie score, then a kaleidoscope of information as he tries to imagine a face for the voice that spoke the only words that have mattered to him for a long time.

"I feel like there's no one I can relate to anymore. I've lost most of my unaided hearing and all I've gained is a load of sympathy that I don't want. I just want my friends to act normal again, you know?"

"I think...You know what? I think she could be just like me."

THREE

When Asher was a child, she had an imaginary friend. Well, less a friend and more someone to talk to. Not a friend, but a conduit for the stories she invented to entertain herself, not quite a person or an animal or an emotional support fictional character come to life, but rather a presence that hovered at the edge of her shadow, a something that would listen to her every word. She felt so misunderstood as a child that she would whisper in the dark to her something, about how she wanted the gap between her front teeth to close, and what she thought was going to happen next in her newest favourite book, and the fantasies she had about the expanse of experiences that she might still one day call her life. She named that something a friend, nothing more, nothing less.

But when she grew up a year or two, whispering in the dark wasn't what her mother would describe as the behaviour of a 'normal' little girl, so she turned to whispering in the pages of a journal instead, writing in abstract thoughts and song lyrics rather than concrete concepts, the closest thing this particular little girl could get to inventing her own code.

Now, the lyrics Asher scrawls across a fresh page of her notebook are bordered with a variety of doodled arrows, each one reminding her of something her grandmother used to say, back when she would adorn her hair with wooden beads and the summer afternoons without school were endless.

"You can only shoot an arrow by pulling it backwards, Ash. When you feel like you're being pulled back by your problems, you're about to be flung into something great, something beautiful."

Although her grandmother's inspirational speeches usually ended up in rambles about an all-girls archery club from her youth, the words stuck in Asher's mind all these years later and she prints the memory into the margins, trying to use the words of someone else to explain herself.

"He's so different from my friends," she murmurs, the words coming out more stable than they do any other time she speaks. There's a forced false confidence because she doesn't really have friends anymore, evidenced by the number of photo frames across her bedroom surfaces that are turned around to hide the faces beaming back at her, but the meaning is all the same.

Another song lyric comes to mind, and she scribbles it into a small gap at the bottom of the page, writing the date in the top corner before flipping over to the next, finally ready to write down her thoughts.

> It sounds crazy, but I think I've finally found someone who makes me feel less alone. I don't know his last name or even how to spell his first name, but I do know that he makes me feel <u>understood</u>.

The last word in the line is underlined twice with a small flower doodled above it.

> He said that having nothing can be better than having something when I was talking about feeling alone. I guess he means that being alone and unloved is better than experiencing the bad things that can come when you share your life with someone.
>
> I think he must be alone, too. And God, I miss having someone to share my life with.

She takes one last look at her page of lyrics before snapping the notebook shut and wedging it deep into her floral pillowcase where her mother will never find it.

Ryn sits with a guitar across his knees, trying to replicate the chords he can hear in the song echoing mournfully through his earphones. He swears as he plays the wrong one and skips back to the start of the song, plucking the strings along to the parts that he's already deciphered, building up his confidence in the easy way.

He's homeschooled, which really means he's *self-schooled* and spends more time teaching himself the guitar than doing homework—his father is supposed to be his educator, when he's not working full-time at a job Ryn cannot remember and doing single-parent things, but Ryn no longer has the patience for textbooks or study guides, only painting and pining and playlist curation, and thankfully the government doesn't enforce the national curriculum.

And, most of the time, it's okay. Or rather, it used to be okay. He's not sure when exactly 'homeschooling' had started to feel like 'house arrest,' just that it had.

He fumbles another chord, and this is when he wishes he paid more attention to his father's tutoring when they were both a few years younger, regretting that he didn't put in the effort until he could play songs by ear rather than a description of the sheet music.

He smashes a hand against the neck of the guitar, the strings warbling beneath his palm.

"If you break my guitar, you're paying for it." Ryn's

father walks into the room with the scent of clean laundry following him. Ryn hears one of his drawers open. "Where are you going wrong?"

Ryn rushes through the verse of the song, then points out the part in the chorus that makes him slam on the strings when his fingers slip and the sound that comes out is choked beyond recognition. And he can feel his heart rate spike with frustration that he can't get it right on his own, and a sweaty sheen sticks to his skin, and his breathing quickens with the embarrassment of asking for help, and—

And then he's overwhelmed with a familiar blue haze.

It's taken him the entire afternoon to realise why he cares so much about mastering this particular song.

Sometimes, Ryn wakes in the night with a hole in his chest and his mother's voice whispering around him, her voice from when she still lived at home, not the one he hears crackling through a telephone. The lyrics of her lullabies might be lost to time, but the ghost of the melodies never seemed to fade. He grew older and started to recognise where she picked up the songs from the radio, then he learned how to sing himself to sleep.

And he learns all the songs to recapture that feeling as if he can pretend his mother is still in the room kneeling at his bedside, as if he is easier to love so she doesn't want to leave, as if she's not part of the reason why he regularly attends the group therapy sessions she recommended to him.

And he's been on the brink of numb for so long that

he can't remember the last time he felt anything other than his perpetual blue haze and the heaviness of his grief, because it doesn't come in waves anymore, just a flood that fills his room and closes over his head.

And he can feel his father sit beside him on the bed, and he can hear him talking, but Ryn's not listening anymore. He's drowning, just for a moment, in the blueness.

And he—

"Ryn? Are you listening?"

Ryn jolts back to reality so hard that he can feel the mattress shake beneath him. "Yeah, sorry, I'm listening."

"It's just a load of C, A, and B for the chorus. There's an E minor at the end." He hears the bed frame creak as his father leans in to rearrange the placement of his fingers on the strings, guiding him to the chords he already knows how to play. He fights the urge to pull away.

"Thanks," Ryn mutters. A few years ago—hell, even a few months ago—he might've appreciated the hands-on help. Now, it feels as if people try to step in before giving him the chance to struggle through to a solution. And it's more than just audibly providing a solution: they feel the need to physically correct him, too. He's not fond of skin contact, most casual touching, breaching his personal space, and all that. He doesn't remember the last time he was greeted with an unexpected hug and didn't wince.

"Are you going to tell me more about the girl?" his father asks when he's finished the guitar lesson, returning to the laundry instead, sighing as the clean clothes already in Ryn's drawers are crumpled in ways he cannot even begin to fathom. Maybe the request for a wardrobe was serious.

Ryn sighs too. What more can he say about a thirty-second interaction? But he does have something to say about his father's dig for information and the teasing emphasis he puts on 'girl.' "Do you want to be any more subtle?"

"Well, I saw that coming."

"Really? I must've missed it."

"It's been four years and you're still making jokes." His father's laugh sounds forced. As usual, Ryn chooses not to overthink this. "Anyway, the girl."

Ryn sighs again. "Her name is Asher. She talked a bit about feeling alone. I think she's deaf, or some kind of hard of hearing. Seeing her again would be quite useful."

He imagines his father rolling his eyes as he heads toward the door. "It's a good thing that appearance isn't the thing you're looking for, right?"

It's a good thing that he isn't looking for anything, evidenced by one specific pride flag pin painted in sunset colours that lives on his denim jacket.

Ryn's eyebrows raise as the door closes, and he returns to strumming the guitar, a small smile appearing when his tune finally resembles the version screeching through his earphones, a miniature victory. He thinks of Asher as he plays, trying to piece together the small amount of information he has about her.

"I feel like there's no one I can relate to anymore. I've lost

most of my unaided hearing, and all I've gained is a load of sympathy that I don't want. I just want my friends to act normal again, you know?"

To Asher, Ryn is only a stranger, not even at the stage of being considered an acquaintance, he thinks, but he resolves to make her realise that she doesn't have to feel that way anymore.

He'll be the one to make her feel less alone.

FOUR

Three days later, Ryn sits on a bench in the park opposite the secondary school. Sitting beside him is Luke, a lanky, barely seventeen-year-old with a crooked grin and hair bright enough that it sometimes reflects light into Ryn's eyes. Ryn has known the boy ever since his family moved into the house across the street a few years earlier, and Luke has known Ryn from afar for a lot longer than that.

"So, what's your plan?" Luke asks, crinkling what sounds like a crisp packet.

Ryn holds out a hand, and something crunchy and salt-smelling is placed in his palm. He puts it in his mouth and winces. Salt and vinegar. "What do you mean?"

"We're sitting outside a girl's school waiting for her to come out."

"It's also your school," Ryn reminds him as if it makes the circumstances any less strange. He licks the salt residue from his fingers and fidgets with a loose thread on his jumper sleeve. "Shouldn't you be in there right now? Mock exams must start soon."

"Mine started last week. I've declared myself free of revision sessions to celebrate." Luke's voice drifts away then back as Ryn assumes he's finding a bin to throw away the crisp packet. "Anyway, back to Asher. We're here for her specifically. I think most people count this as stalking. What are we waiting for?"

Ryn turns over his lack of plan to befriend Asher in his mind. "I...haven't decided yet."

"She'll be coming out any minute." Luke's phone screen flashes on. "She spends most of last period with the guidance counsellor, and they usually finish a few minutes after the bell."

The bell signalling the end of the school day blares at three o'clock, sending eight hundred teenagers screeching through the corridors, shoving each other into the walls and the younger students. In all honesty, Luke's revision session was three hours ago, so his afternoon was freed up to act as a lookout for his friend, providing all the additional details about the girl trapped in his mind.

"How do you know this? About Asher?" Ryn asks, adjusting how his sunglasses sit on his nose. There is not a cloud in the sky and the light reflecting off puddles leftover from the morning showers brightens his remaining vision beyond use.

Luke's smile is evident in his voice. "About her schedule? Everyone here knows something about Asher.

I'm probably the least qualified person to be your spy."

"What else do you know about her?"

Luke's information pours out as if he's been holding it in all day. "She's sixteen or seventeen, depending on when her birthday is. I saw her in the exam hall during winter mocks, so we're definitely in the same year, but she's artsy, so we're not in the same place often. She got a lot of shit when she came here because her dad's Black and she looks more like him than her mum, and this town is still so white that *that's* what people find most interesting about her. The headteacher gave her a special tutor for all of her lessons like she's dumb, not deaf."

"What does she look like?" Ryn asks for the sake of having something to say.

Luke goes quiet as he thinks. "Other than being biracial? I'm not sure. She hides behind this bright pink hair that matches her hearing aids and doesn't look up enough for anyone to see her face."

With a sigh, Ryn sinks deeper into the bench, slipping in one of his earphones as he leaves his friend to hang over the back and keep a watchful eye on the school building.

"Asher, your teachers and I have been understanding about your difficulties with coursework and attendance to this point, but your grades this term have fallen far below what you were predicted. This has become unacceptable.

You have the potential to do well, but you are throwing it out the window."

Asher contemplates the politest way of telling her guidance counsellor—"*Ms Bourne, but please, call her Shelby*"—to kindly throw herself out of the hypothetical window. When she can't summon the words, she clenches her jaw until her teeth ache and tries to look at any object in the room where the woman and her hands—signing her thoughts word-for-word as she says them—won't be in her peripheral vision.

She sighs. Her breaths are shaky as she exhales. She screws her eyes shut and nods, the movement slow and forced and practiced, Ms. Bourne's voice still present but in a distant, underwater type of way. Asher knows her grades have fallen, but she doesn't have the energy to care about them anymore. She can almost remember how she felt when she chose the subjects, immersing herself in English and the arts despite being the former poster child for 'Women in STEM,' picking passion over practicality, but now even her passion is mediocre.

One of her therapists from her early teens said this would be a symptom of her hearing loss—not the poor grades, but the sadness, a significant change in her life that her brain can only cope with by plummeting her into numbness. The therapist started talking about grief and clinical depression and brain waves until Asher latched onto the phrase 'theta waves' and went home to research it herself, and that's how she learned that grieving people's waking brains seem to still be in a state of deep unconsciousness and, really, she's just sleepwalking through life.

But at least she's trying.

At least she thinks she is.

So, she opens her eyes, fixes them on Ms. Bourne's mouth so she can put all her effort into lip-reading rather than overthinking, and says, "I'll try harder. I just need a little more time, and I'll do better. I promise."

It takes a fraction of a heartbeat for her to realise that that was the wrong answer,

Ms Bourne sighs loud enough that Asher can hear it clearly and rubs at the bridge of her nose between her fingertips. "Asher, you are sitting your summer mock exams. These grades will go on your university applications at the end of this calendar year. You have run out of time."

And that is when Asher decides it is the perfect time for her to end the conversation, the door slamming shut behind her to disguise the sound of her tears as she flees the building.

"Hey, Ryn, I think I see her. She's early."

Ryn winds his earphones around his wrist and slips them into his jacket pocket. "Really? What's she doing?"

Luke's voice shifts to somewhere behind Ryn, as if he's draping himself across the back of the bench for a clearer view. "She's running." Ryn hears muttered profanities as Luke leans too far and collapses onto the ground. "I think she's coming over here."

"Well, is she?" Ryn adjusts his sunglasses again to fight off the puddle glare, squinting at the sunlight. He really needs to invest in a darker pair.

The first response is a groan, muffled against astroturf. The second is more legible. "Ryn, I'm face down on the ground, and I think my face is bleeding. It's wet down here. *I'm* wet. From the fucking rain, though, not my blood. I'm blaming it on you. Why don't you look for yourself?"

Ryn's laugh is forced. "Slight problem there."

Asher sits on a swing with her chin resting in one hand and her phone in the other. After an afternoon of an overwhelming amount of sound, she tucks her nonfunctional hearing aids into her pocket and blocks out what little she can hear with her earphones, the quiet calming her. She twirls the earphone wire around her finger as she scrolls through her playlist, aimlessly swiping through the songs as she tries to find a subtle way of staring at the two boys across the park from her. One of the boys—tall and thin with fluorescent red hair that she immediately envies—lies on the ground with his eyes up at the sky while the other boy faces directly ahead, his sunglasses blocking her view of his gaze.

She squints at the boy through her hair, his form tinted pink. He looks familiar. He looks like the human embodiment of winter: icy blonde hair and translucent skin draped in shades of blue.

After a few minutes, the heads of neither boy shift in her direction. Asher raises a hand, waves slightly, and receives no response at all. She notices that the boy on the ground is talking, but she isn't close enough to read his lips. His face is dappled with something red that sends her stomach swimming from a distance. She wonders if they're talking about her, or if they said anything when she stormed through the park gate with mascara tears blackening her cheeks.

No, they wouldn't have. Well, the one with the sunglasses wouldn't have, she realises as she places his figure to a memory from only a few days earlier.

He's the boy from group therapy who reminded her of herself.

She wedges her phone in her back pocket and stands.

The boy on the ground's eyes flick in her direction. He peels himself off the asphalt into a sitting position as if he needs a better view of her tear-stained face.

She steps forward with the intention of walking over and confronting the boys about whatever she's imagining they're saying about her, but her courage fails. She tries to avoid the redhead's gaze as she leaves the park, but she fails that, too.

Ryn hears the gate swing shut, metal screeching against metal. "Did she leave?"

"Yeah, she looked upset." Luke pries himself off the ground, wheezing with the effort, his forehead dirtied and hair more dishevelled than usual. "I guess you'll have to see her another time."

Ryn resists the urge to hit his friend and sinks even further down into the bench, bolts pressing into his spine. "Did you at least see what she looks like?"

"Like a chubby, pink-haired Bambi," Luke replies.

The list of adjectives does nothing to form an image in Ryn's mind. "What is that supposed to be?"

"She looks like a cartoon character come to life."

Ryn groans. "I still don't know what that means."

FIVE

They do see each other again at five minutes past three in group therapy a few days later. Jonathon is in the middle of introducing an activity when Ryn arrives fifteen minutes late with a smile on his face.

"After what we discussed last week, I think it will be good for us to revisit the topic of fear in today's session, unless anyone has any objections," Jonathon says as Ryn feels around for an empty seat in the circle, and all he can think about is whether Asher is watching his fortnightly humiliation ritual. "Fear is natural at this stage in the program. You are experiencing all sorts of anxieties, worries, and concerns about what might happen next. An effective way of dealing with these fears is to acknowledge them. We're going to lay them on the table—literally—without anyone laughing or making fun of us. Having your fears out in the open almost immediately cuts them in half."

Ryn hears Jonathon's knees crunch as he bends down for the stack of scrap paper from beneath his chair. He passes it to someone else to pass around the group, each teenager taking a piece. "You're all going to complete one of these sentences on your piece of paper. *'In this group, I am most afraid that...'* or *'In this group, the worst thing that could happen to me would be...'* Fold it up and put it in the middle of the circle when you're done."

Ryn smirks, wishing he could see the looks of sheer terror on the faces of everyone in the circle, a room full of people who are afraid of being afraid. He wonders if writing his fears and sharing them is any better than writing them in his journal. He hopes that Jonathon won't get any angry parents phoning him later about upsetting their child.

He writes down his fear in under a minute and spends the remaining four engaging in his favourite pastime: eavesdropping. Some people seem to mistake his lack of eyesight for a similar lack in other senses when instead they are enhanced.

"I can't believe she's dressed like *that* again," says a feminine voice to Ryn's right, one he knows belongs to someone who Luke once described as a Tim Burton character come to life, leaving him wondering how *interestingly* someone must be dressed to catch their attention. "Sharpie all over her shoes last time, skirt that she's clearly made out of scraps today."

"It's quirky," another voice murmurs, and their tone is indecipherable.

"It's *embarrassing*," the first person corrects a little too loudly. Jonathon coughs pointedly until their voice returns to a whisper, although it's a stage whisper more than anything else. "I know she's not lived here for that long, and it's probably, like, normal that she hasn't got friends yet, but it's not surprising when she looks like *that*."

The second voice sharpens in a way that tells Ryn they already know the answer to their question. "Looks like that, or dresses like that?"

"Both. Neither. Whatever." The first voice scoffs. "You know what I mean. She's not making an effort to fit in with anyone else."

Jonathon coughs again, and both voices are silent. Ryn files away this anecdote to dissect at a later date.

When the terrified teenagers have put their fears on the page, Jonathon mixes them up and calls a random person forward, asking them to select a fear from the pile and read it aloud.

A girl who speaks without an ounce of fear in her voice is called forward first. "I'm afraid that no one will understand what I'm going through because mental illnesses aren't taken seriously."

Read by Asher with confidence, only because the fear isn't hers: "The worst thing that could happen to me is that therapy won't help, and my parents will still get a divorce because of me."

And, forced through tears and a shaking voice that Ryn almost recognises: "I am most afraid that my friends will find out I'm in therapy and I'm not okay, and they won't want to talk to me anymore."

The fears continue, each person breathing an audible sigh of relief when theirs is read and no one laughs or whispers to a friend or mutters something under their breath. Jonathon tries to make helpful comments and start discussions with the reader when he can, and Ryn knows that this is far above both his paygrade and his qualifications.

After fifteen minutes, there is one fear left in the circle, and Ryn is the one person in the group who hasn't stood up to read. He's spent the duration of the activity trying to match the fears to what he's remembered about each person until he knows who the remaining one belongs to.

"Do you want me to read this one out for you, Ryn?" Jonathon asks.

"No, I know what it says." Ryn's confidence falters for a moment, and so do his knees as he stands. "It's mine. I don't want to be alone. That's what I'm afraid of."

Jonathon hums as he contemplates his next words. "That's perfectly normal, Ryn. Having many friends, being social, connecting with people…They're all things that are socially encouraged. We shouldn't be ashamed of not fitting into these expectations."

"I'm not ashamed." Ryn rushes through the thoughts that circle through his brain. "I like doing things alone. I like playing the guitar alone. I like walking along the cliff path alone. I like going to the cinema and watching films that have the shitty out-of-sync audio narration alone. I like listening to music alone. But, sometimes, when I hear kids playing together outside the house next door, or old couples sitting together in cafés, or people who sound like people who used to be my friend talking on the other side of the room, I realise that even though I like being alone, I don't like being lonely."

Jonathon doesn't respond. It's so quiet that Ryn can hear people breathing either side of him and the clock ticking through dozens of seconds on the far wall. A full minute passes before he speaks again. "I think I'm more afraid of being lonely than alone."

There are only five minutes left in the session when Ryn manages to recover from his own confession. Jonathon—also still in an apparent state of shock—introduces the last activity, hoping to do something helpful in exchange for Ryn's newfound honesty.

"This activity is something that will be ongoing over the next few weeks, or as long as you all find it beneficial," Jonathon says, and Ryn can hear him shuffling the fear papers as he talks. "You're going to write a letter to someone here who you want to improve your relationship with. The letters can be written at home, and you can exchange them here, or you can go somewhere where you're both comfortable and write the letters in person, whatever works best for you. You can leave as soon as you've picked your partner."

Ryn sits there, wondering if he can find a way to sneak out before Jonathon chooses a partner for him. But he was late and had to sit in a different seat than usual and is so disorientated that he isn't convinced he can find his way to the door without help. He can't even hear the clock that ticks above it right now. All he can hear is people fussing around him, pairing up with people they're already familiar with, and it's starting to seem like Jonathon will have to choose for him.

Then he feels a warm hand rest on his shoulder, and he smells raspberry shampoo.

"Can I be your partner?" Asher asks almost as anxiously as he feels. "I think I'm too new for anyone here to want to get to know me better."

Ryn smiles up at her voice as if she's a saviour, head tilted back, eyes closed, like he was waiting for her all along. "Of course."

SIX

Asher and Ryn agree to exchange their first letters in person, meeting at his house the next day.

Asher arrives ten minutes early and stands on the pavement opposite the powder blue house. She rode her bike—Ryn lives on the other side of town, and she was worried about using an unfamiliar bus route and risking a panic attack on public transport. She notes how the windows are framed with gauzy curtains, and bushes of heat-shrivelled hydrangeas border the paved path. There's a wooden gate and a picket fence, both painted blinding white, although the colour is peeling off to reveal the brown beneath. It looks like the dollhouse she dreamed of having as a child.

There's a car she remembers from outside the group therapy building parked in the driveway, so Asher crosses the road and opens the gate, presuming that someone will have noticed her arrival and is about to answer the door. She leans her bike—brand new, like most of the things her mother has brought into their 'new life'—against the porch before knocking. A blue sticky note falls off the door.

I'm in town.
Ryn's home.
Leave packages
on the doorstep.
Let yourself in if
we're expecting you.
—Darren

Asher lets herself in.

The house is lived in, in a way that her mother's could never be, always destined to be a picture-perfect show home of framed family portraits shot in a studio and crisp white sofas she can't sit on. Here, the sofa is adorned in a mess of poorly crocheted blankets, and the photo frames are mismatched and flooded with memories of Christmases, birthdays, and random weekend trips that span two decades. It almost reminds her of her father's house: each surface littered with dying potted plants, and handwritten attempts at novel prologues, and numerous Nigerian cookbooks propped open to the same dish as he attempts to perfect his childhood favourites.

Here, it feels like home.

Asher kicks her shoes off by the front door.

She stops abruptly in the hallway where most of the photos decorate the walls, the kind only interesting to someone's parent: a small child dressed as a pirate, their dad kneeling to tie the eye patch; the same child older and asleep next to a fluffy dog that is bigger than them; a shot of the whole family, Mum, Dad, and a baby wrapped in white.

She turns to a group shot where the child who is clearly Ryn must be no older than ten years old, with thick-lensed glasses doubling the size of his eyes. He shares his mother's white-blond hair and pale freckly complexion, the opposite of his less blond, less pale father. Where the freckles and sallowness look slightly grubby on his mother, on Ryn it looks so unearthly that Asher wants to paint him in watercolours.

Asher lingers on a blurry phone photo of a trio of small fair-haired children, each one caked in mud and beaming at the person behind the camera, and she knows that they grew up being asked how their day was. She smiles back at them and swallows down the envy that she wasn't once just like them—her childhood was as pristine as her mother's white sofas, spent wearing shoes with no sign of wear and curly hair fried straight to blend in with her cousins.

She tears her gaze away from the photos and heads up the stairs instead.

Ryn's bedroom is an exercise in entropy and order, a contained kind of chaos. It's small and cramped, the walls close in a way that would have been claustrophobic if it weren't so familiar, and anything bigger would risk making him feel as if he was stranded in the open ocean. CDs and cassettes have long outgrown their shelves and are stacked in precarious piles around his bed, several open so stray light reflects off the discs, and lyric booklets abandoned despite their well-thumbed edges, some splayed across his bedsheets like a blanket of glossy paper. Some people favour a genre or an artist, but Ryn has little preference, so long as there are sound waves— he wants to hear everything the world has to offer.

His bedroom is dark, and it's been this way for months. The ceiling light is always off, and the curtains are half-closed. He used to tell himself that there was no reason for them to be open anymore, used to pretend that he was completely blind instead of ninety-four percent, as if complete vision loss was easier to cope with than watching what he had left dwindle month by month.

He's become accustomed to darkness. It's the one moment where he can take off his sunglasses without the fear of someone seeing the mass of scars that mar his face. Not like the scars or the surgery is a secret anymore, but it's easier for him to exist knowing his appearance is a lessened factor in people's opinions.

Closing his eyes used to help him think clearly as navigating solely by light and shadow and no depth perception was disorienting at first, and his muscle memory was less distracting than his new and unimproved vision. He would lay on his bed on summer nights, windows open to feel the breeze, the Bon Jovi greatest hits album playing softly through his earphones. He remembers how he felt calm in total blackness without the complications of trying to see in it.

Now that he's surrounded by permanent ninety-four percent darkness, it has become so much more than a memory. He has no choice but to embrace it.

Ryn is enjoying the darkness until he hears a tentative knock on the front door and footsteps on the stairs. He assumes it's just his father returning from work or wherever else he's been, but his father would yell to announce his presence rather than lingering on the landing outside his half-open door. He's about to panic until someone knocks again.

There's a self-conscious cough, a nervous clearing of the throat. "Ryn?"

It's a girl's voice, one that hasn't yet become familiar, but he doesn't feel the need to grab his phone and demand Siri to call the police. He fumbles for his sunglasses before he hears the door open fully. "Who's there?"

"It's Asher. From group therapy." Another cough. "The note on the door said..."

"I know what it says." He does know, but that doesn't

mean he remembered that he's the one expecting a visitor. "Come on in."

Although this is the first time they've spoken outside of the confines of the therapy room, Asher knows that Ryn will be her next best friend, even if he doesn't know it yet.

After she makes herself comfortable in his dimly lit bedroom, she examines the waif of a boy sat beside her, telling herself that her fixation on his face is solely because she needs to read his lips, nothing else. He's a rare sort of handsome, she thinks. He's not the usual obnoxious masculinity that she sees adorning magazines, and he's not the over-preened, over-mussed style that the boys in her class at school aspire to. He has high cheekbones and a refined brow that Asher, with her plump cheeks and wide nose like an impressionist portrait, would have killed for once upon a time.

There's a timidness to his demeanour now that she's in his domain. Every time his head dips away from her, she wishes he would look at her again, and she knows that there'll be a real reward in his smile if she can figure out how to coax it from him.

And she will. She'll spend the rest of her days trying to make him smile.

They huddle over Asher's phone, her sitting cross-legged on Ryn's desk, him curled up in his desk chair with his knees under his chin, abandoning their plan to exchange letters and exchanging favourite songs instead.

"Do you like this one?" Asher asks, playing the first few seconds of a song she fell in love with after seeing the lyrics quoted on a book page, but never remembered to listen to with her hearing aids in. She cranes her neck for a clearer view of Ryn's downturned face and awaits his response.

His face crinkles in mock disgust. "I'm not really a fan of banjos."

Neither is she, at least not when she has fresh batteries. She contemplates her next words. "Can you show me what it sounds like?"

She watches his expression shift, overanalysing each twitch of his cheek and crease of his brow as he contemplates her request. It's in that moment when she realises he might not remember what specific shapes or colours look like anymore, or if he still recognises the symbolism: red for anger, blue for sadness, all the watered-down emotions she learned in a primary school art lesson. His contemplation takes five seconds. It takes an eternity. It takes so many of her racing heartbeats that she thinks he's going to think she's crazy and turn her down. She begins to reach for her house keys in case she needs to make a quick escape.

But he doesn't think there is anything weird about her request. He's just wondering if he can find the right colour pen to match his interpretation of the song.

He decides that it's green.

He taps the pen on the edge of his desk, brushing

against Asher's knee, twirling the cap between his fingertips as he thinks. Then, he puts the nib to a page in the notebook she holds out for him, the ink sprawling wildly as he captures every high and low of the song, speeding up at the chorus, soaring across the bridge.

"What's your favourite song?" he asks as the final notes fade.

For a moment, Asher's tempted to lie. To invent a new version of herself that's so much better than reality, to invent a new life to accompany a specific soundtrack. But Ryn looks earnest and interested, and so she tells him the truth. And despite her worries, she doesn't *want* to lie. Whatever *this* is going to become between them—she doesn't want to do it as someone else. Maybe that's why she tells him a lot more than she means to. About long drives with her father where he played his favourite song on loop until they couldn't stand it anymore, and short ones with her mother where they would sit in silence, and the preceding childhood with parents who spoke to each other in two-word sentences.

Her father's favourite song became her favourite, and then his changed to something else, but hers stayed the same.

Ryn listens, nodding in all the right places and letting her finish her rambling explanation before fumbling around for his next pen colour.

This is the moment when Asher decides that he must know they're going to be best friends.

Asher plays the song and guides Ryn's pen—red,

this time—to an empty space on the page, snapping a photo of the previous line so she can replace the tune in her head with one that is closer to being correct until she gets round to replacing her batteries.

This continues for the next hour or two, long past the time Asher's mother wanted her back, and Ryn's father returns home and delivers them an arrangement of sliced fruit and sandwiches cut into triangles. Asher gets along surprisingly well with him; he knows basic sign language to fingerspell his name and ask how she is even when she explains that he knows more than she does, and he tells a few jokes that make her laugh and Ryn scowl. He seems to stare too much when he looks at her, almost as if he can't quite believe she's real, but she pretends to ignore it.

It's another hour later when Ryn unfurls himself from his chair and fumbles for his desk lamp, knocking off half-empty pill packets and unused Biros as he flicks the switch. The room is illuminated with a soft golden light.

"What was that for?" Asher asks, squinting at the sudden brightness.

Ryn shrugs. "I forgot you can see."

SEVEN

Ryn asks his father to type Asher's letter into his notes app, deciding that he'll go back to the cliff and listen to the monotone voice of Siri read out her words. They spent enough time together the previous afternoon that Ryn thinks he understands her voice well enough to imagine the emotion. The older man stays quiet as he types, and Ryn can't decide if it's a good or bad thing. He doesn't put much more thought into it.

Ryn's father tells him stories during their drive to the cliff.

"Do you remember when we first moved here?" his father asks, his fingers tapping a familiar rhythm across the steering wheel. Ryn hums the second part of the melody. "I thought we moved to a better town, a better school, a better job. I thought those things would make you and your mum happier, but the only thing you cared about was the sea."

Ryn nods, remembering when he first became fascinated with the water, a childhood spent with the ocean tugging at his feet. "We lived closer to the beach. I could see it from my bedroom window."

"Then your mum wanted to live somewhere other than the edge of nowhere, so we moved here, closer to town." Ryn imagines his father rolling his eyes at the decaying dollhouse they now live in. Neither of them like it. Neither of them has the motivation to move. After all, the location is decent. "Once, in the old house, I gave you my camera and you took hundreds of photos, all of the sea and the sky. You used three whole ink cartridges in the printer because you printed every single one of the photos and glued them on your walls with PVA."

"I ruined the wallpaper, but at least I made it blue."

They both laugh at the memory. The conversation quiets, and Ryn continues thinking about the ocean.

For as long as he can remember, the back of his mind has been painted with bottle green and aquamarine and everything in between, a swirling watercolour to match the waves. He remembers chasing the shoreline of a coarse sand beach until the salt stained his shoes, because it wasn't ever nice enough to walk on barefoot. He remembers finding a hidden path that led to the top of the cliff and laying down to peer over the edge, scaring his mother senseless when she looked up at him from below.

His father doesn't know, but that was another one of the reasons why his mother wanted to move house.

To cope with the loss of the ocean view and weekends spent in the water, Ryn turned to sketching it, then abstracts and fingerpainting as his vision faded. He knew it well enough to draw it forever. It wasn't quite the real thing; his early sketches remained in two-dimensional pencil and nothing more, not warranting colour both because Ryn's inspiration didn't seem to have left that house, and he couldn't remember the combination of colours to mix to make the perfect shade of sea green. And it's not like the art could capture the smell of salt in the air and the feel of sand scraping his skin.

His father's voice breaks his thoughts. "We're here, kid. Do you want me to walk up there with you?"

"No thanks." Ryn shakes his head and pats his pockets to confirm the presence of his phone and earphones, as well as the handwritten copy of the letter. "I think I should do this on my own."

Asher leaves home with the intention of reading Ryn's letter at school, far away from the prying eyes of her mother. But she never reads the letter. Not because she doesn't want to, or because she can't find the right time, but because she finds another crumpled piece of paper on the way to school, covered in dirt and words.

She leaves in the middle of her English Lit revision session—the themes of ambition in *Frankenstein* taking a backseat to a suddenly more important pursuit of knowledge of her own—and says that she has a migraine severe enough that she needs to go to the office, risking the wrath of her guidance counsellor as she runs to the toilets and locks herself in the end cubicle. The toilet seat is missing, so she awkwardly squats with her back against the wall for support and ignores the uncomfortable sticking sensation of her shoes against the floor.

The paper looks like a letter handwritten in green ink—*who writes in green ink?*—and it is smudged beyond recognition in places, as if the writer knew that someone would be invading their privacy, but Asher reads it anyway, or at least what she can make out of the smeared inky mess that had once been of importance to someone. The only legible paragraph is at the top of the reverse side and explains all that Asher wants to know.

It feels like I've been underwater for some time, like all the air is pushed out of my lungs. But I'm drowning. I'm trying to convince myself that I can still breathe like this even though I can't. I'm gasping for air and all it does is let more water in. I have to do this, J. I have to do this myself.

Soon. August 31st.

And I'll do it on my terms.

Asher knows nothing else, and this knowledge distresses her as she turns the paper to the other side over and over again. She doesn't know who the letter is from—the name at the bottom is also smudged away with what she hopes is tap water, or rain, although she can faintly smell something salty. She doesn't need to know who the writer is, perhaps she *shouldn't* know at all what they're writing about, but from the look of things, she really, *really* wants to.

Just like that, Asher forgets all about *Frankenstein* revision, and her eyes meet the crude Sharpie poetry scattered across the cubicle walls, and the familiarity of harsh words does nothing to soothe her panicked mind because the letter and her newfound responsibility to it will not be able to relax until the writer is found.

She decides that she is stupid, but not quite stupid enough to convince herself that she could just throw the letter away and everything will be okay because she now cares about this stranger, even though she may never know who they are. No one deserves to feel that way, and Asher knows that feeling all too well. She's been there herself, only a few years ago when she lost the bulk of her hearing and then her life kept throwing her a series of unfortunate events she can't bring herself to recount without a medical professional present. She knows she can't feel exactly what the letter writer feels, but she's been close.

This isn't about her, though. It's about the writer, and she doesn't know how to fix it.

She could hand the letter over to the school, to someone in a shirt and tie who would claim to make the whole situation disappear from her mind. But what would they do about it? What *could* they do? The writer won't confess and hand themselves in to the wellbeing counsellor, assuming they even go to her school; it is clear that they are far past that point by now.

And Asher is out of her depth, knee-deep in the water that the writer wrote so passionately about. She can't deal with this on her own, but she isn't heartless enough to leave it alone. She's the one who found the letter, so now it's her mystery to solve, and her only clues are the sprawling handwriting and the green ink.

She takes her phone out of the front pocket of her rucksack, shakily types in her passcode, and texts Ryn.

Ryn settles down on the bench at the top of the cliff, repositioning his sunglasses to dim the bright spot near the horizon where sunlight hits the sea. A song Asher loves wails through his earphones. He's about to listen to her letter when a text message notification cuts through the music. Then another. And another.

"You have three new messages from 'Asher Therapy,'" Siri informs him. "Open, or ignore?"

"Open."

"First new message: 'Ryn! I have something to tell you.'

Next new message: 'Is this the right phone number?' Next new message: 'I have to go back to revision but please reply soon! Grinning face emoji.' Would you like to listen again, reply, or ignore?"

"Ignore," Ryn replies instantly, and he pretends that it doesn't sting a little.

He has a letter to read.

EIGHT

As Ryn's father pulls the car into their driveway, his mind is stuck in the past, although both Asher's letter in his pocket and her messages in his phone notifications are trying to tug him back into the present.

When he was younger and lived near the shoreline, his biggest concern was if his mother would be home late that night. Now, his biggest concern is deciding if he wants her to come home at all.

It's one of the paintings in his bedroom that triggers his reminiscing, the one that rattles against the wall when he slams the door. He no longer remembers the details, but he feels the texture of dried oils beneath his fingertips as he trails a hand along the wall, and he knows it must be another painting of the waves.

Back then, his mind had been alive: a mess of every shade of blue and green and hue in between, and a heart that beat too fast from the excitement of simply existing. It had taken six months of pleading to convince his parents to let him buy oil paints. He made do with flaky acrylics and cheap watercolours, but he fancied himself a painter from the older eras—researching their materials' origins and ingredients, glorying in the thought of grinding pigments and mixing them into the oil himself. His paints eventually came, of course, in tubes, purchased with the money his father slipped to him so he could purchase one colour at a time until the evolution of hues across his canvases became a way to mark time.

The colours in his head faded to grey when they moved to the new house, and he spent many sleepless nights trying to paint all of his memories onto a canvas before they faded, too.

When he lost most of his sight, it wasn't just the excitement of the ocean that he lost: he also lost a piece of his heart. He lost the will to keep himself afloat in his metaphorical ocean of existence, and although his lungs ached from the loss, he couldn't drown in it, not quite yet anyway.

So, he started writing letters. Pages and pages of letters were frantically scrawled onto paper and printed onto his desk when he forgot to check for the edge of the page. Lines overlapped or dipped dramatically down the page, and the occasional letter was written on top of an old one rather than a fresh sheet of paper. To some people, it might've looked like the ramblings of a lunatic, but Ryn knew only how much space they took up in a box beneath his bed, so he didn't really care what anyone else thought.

And, when he was short on paper, he'd type his letters with the volume turned low on his text-to-speech software until the clock crossed midnight and the sky turned light, or he would huddle beneath his duvet and whisper his thoughts into his phone mic, letting his fears fade away with the darkness.

Sometimes, he thinks that his letters were what convinced his mother to take the temporary job in another town and never look back. He can't remember how his father explained her unending absence, but he remembers weeks passing with no clean dishes in the cupboards because they were piled up in the sink and takeaway containers in the overflowing bin and the sound of his father's tears not being drowned out by late-night game shows.

He's becoming trapped in the past, so he switches back to the present.

Asher's letter is still in Ryn's pocket. His father described it to him: looping handwriting in blue ink, crisp cream paper with narrow lines, doodles of flowers— carnations, he thinks—in the corners of the pages, a complete contrast to the letters he writes. The other noticeable difference is that her words are full of hope. Hope that she and Ryn can become friends, even if it's just to appease Jonathon. Hope that the group therapy will help rebuild her relationship with her mother. Hope that everything will work out in the end. And he's surprised by her honesty with someone who's as close as a stranger.

If Asher reads any of his personal letters, she will soon realise why they will never be able to be friends.

The first heat wave arrives early this year.

An increase in temperature leads to an increase in Asher's headaches that she pretends aren't just from hearing loss and stress-induced overstimulation, so she's lying on the floor of her bedroom in her dad's house with the curtains shut and the lights off, head buried beneath her bed in case a stray flicker of light finds its way in. Not for the first time, she wishes her dad was the kind of parent who stocked the bathroom cabinet with supermarket aisle painkillers rather than relying on herbs, gentle exercise, and positive thinking. Then, she might be able to swallow a pill instead of lying on the floor, writhing in discomfort nearly two hours after she first felt the pain blurring the edges of her vision and she ran out of the exam hall without explanation.

She's going to fail her exams, and that's clear, but it's okay. Everything is okay, really: she just has to keep lying to herself and eventually she'll convince herself that it will all be okay. (Her guidance counsellor has already phoned her mother and agreed to reschedule the exam.) (She's hiding at her dad's house to escape her mother's wrath.) (She's been spending an above-average amount of time here recently.) (But it's okay, really.)

She survives another half hour beneath the bed before she admits defeat and crawls out to beg her dad for a lift to the pharmacy. Squinting around her curtains, she sees a hint of movement in the back garden greenhouse that implies her dad's presence.

The garden is long and narrow, lined with neat flowerbeds and the grass overgrown in a way that should encourage pollinators. The afternoon drizzle leaves a spiderweb of dewdrops across her shoulders. She lets herself into the greenhouse and gravitates toward the herbs: rosemary, thyme, something lemony that she doesn't know the name of and her dad will struggle to kill. She skims her fingers across the leaves, breathing in the mix of fragrances, wondering if she can pick out one that Ryn might like the smell of. There are some vegetable seedlings and some tomato vines too; for one insane moment, Asher wonders if she can stay here, eat the herbs and salad leaves and prune the flowers, refuse to come out for a year or two until the nonsense with sixth form and impending university applications and her future as a whole has gone away—or been dealt with by someone else.

Her dad sits at the potting table, hunched over his most beloved sprouting hydrangea that looks worse for wear. Asher watches him and sees her black-brown eyes and her wide nose and the full curve of her lower lip reflected in his face. She knows her mother resents her because she looks so much more like him, dominant genes and all that, a dark-skinned, coarse-haired girl rather than the 'mini me' of her mother's dreams.

She gets her love for broken things from her dad too. Her mother counts every blemish as a tally for failure, but Asher counts hers as a sign that she is alive: a scar to commemorate the hot glue gun incident of three summers ago, a scratch on her arm from losing a fight with a relative's beloved potted rosebush, a series of perpetual bruises that scatter across her legs like constellations.

She's her father's daughter, whether or not she likes it.

"Hey, Ash," her dad says as soon as he notices the commotion in his greenhouse is more than a breeze or the neighbour's overfed and under-cautious cat. He notes her lack of hearing aids and turns his body to face her. "Feeling any better?"

Asher shakes her head, bringing in a new wave of pain, and slumps to the concrete ground at his feet. She tilts her head back to rest against the worn wooden leg of the potting table and closes her eyes. The soft light pinkens the back of her eyelids, and the distant fuzzy movement of rain pattering on the greenhouse roof sends light scattering across her vision. It soothes her like a lullaby.

There's a short uncomfortable silence where Asher can tell that her dad is trying to approach a difficult subject. She can also sense what that subject is going to be before he taps her shoulder until she opens her eyes and squints at the return of brightness.

He inhales deep enough for her to sense, more a

disturbance in the atmosphere than a sound. "I know you said you weren't quite ready to meet Janine yet, but she's asking about meeting you again." He plucks a slug-eaten leaf off the hydrangea in a way that Asher supposes she could interpret as nonchalant. "If you're up for it, we were thinking about us going out for a meal together—out of the house, just the three of us, or you could bring a friend if you want. I know you're meant to be at your mum's this weekend, but…"

Asher remains uninterested in meeting her dad's new girlfriend. Although her parents were never married and she was more relieved than anything else when their relationship came to an end, she's still not ready for any more changes in her life, not with the endless stream of boyfriends she has to meet at her mother's house.

"I can't tomorrow," she says, you know, like a liar. "I'm seeing…a friend."

"A friend?" Her dad raises an eyebrow, but he doesn't laugh like her mother would. That woman is all too aware of the ghost town that's taken root in Asher's phone. "Have a good day, Ash. I'm glad to see you getting out of the house a bit more."

And that's it. She doesn't even flinch at his acknowledgement of her barely-there social life.

Asher pushes herself to her feet and heads toward the door, trailing a hand through leaves and across the rim of terracotta pots on her way. She winces as the sunlight shining through the rain scatters black spots across her vision.

Before she can hunt down a rainbow, she remembers what she came here for.

"Oh, Dad, before I forget?" Asher hesitates in the doorway, picking at the leaves of a surprisingly healthy potted rosemary.

Her dad tears a browning bud off the hydrangea with surgical precision then looks up, eyes instantly soft with an emotion she can't identify. Confusion? Concern? Hope that she's changed her mind about meeting his girlfriend? Either way, it's unfamiliar, and Asher doesn't like that.

"Yes, Ash?"

She slips a sprig of rosemary into her pocket. "Can you give me a lift to the pharmacy?"

NINE

sher doesn't see a friend. Instead, she stumbles around the high street for the sake of getting out of the house and holding up the illusion that she has friends, but she makes it through two charity shops and one underpriced bakery before she realises that the mysterious letter has crept its way back into her brain. If she knew that this scrap of paper would bother her quite as much as it's ended up doing, she wouldn't have picked it up, but of course, as has already been established, Asher isn't known for her bright ideas. She's a self-diagnosed loser.

A world-class loser, and somewhat proud of it, which only adds to the idiocy, because Asher could have the record for being the world's biggest loser and she'd still be proud, as at least then she'd be winning at something.

She settles into the quietest corner of a café with a concerningly coffee-stained carpet. After a second thought, she moves her rucksack from where she dropped it at her feet and drapes it across the back of the chair beside her. Much better. She opens the countdown app on her phone and adds August 31st as an untitled upcoming event. There's a sense of comfort in it, seeing the date nestled in amongst the birthdays of friends she pretends she doesn't think about anymore but doesn't have the heart to remove—because then she'd have to admit she doesn't have friends anymore—and the closest thing she does have to friends are an anonymous letter writer and a boy she met in group therapy a handful of weeks ago whose surname she is yet to learn.

Asher closes the countdown app and observes the other customers in the café—not to look for more friends, just to be nosy. Immediately, she notices how she stands out: the handful of other teenagers travelling solo in the café have headphones pressed into their ears rather than hearing aids. She resists the urge to tuck them into her pocket and reach for her earphones instead. No one else is paying enough attention to her for her to feel the need to blend in.

But Asher's paying attention to everyone.

The most interesting girl she's ever seen sits a few tables away, an explosion of dyed hair and band merchandise and song lyrics scrawled across tawny skin. Asher watches with hearts in her eyes, as if the handmade pink and orange bead bracelet around her ankle is enough to signal both her romantic orientation and availability. She mirrors the girl's posture, shoulders straight and chin tilted up in the right amount of inquisitiveness and hands wrapped loosely around a coffee mug, like mirroring someone she finds attractive will make her become attractive to them.

Obviously, the girl doesn't notice her.

Asher looks away.

She slips her hand into her pocket and thumbs at the edges of the letter instead. It keeps her awake at night from the confines of her bedside table—always within reach—because she's developed this awful habit of reading it in excess, as if that will somehow make the words any different. She reaches for it as if it's a friend, the message of the letter equal parts comfort and concern, the writer speaking to a part of her that she had hoped was long buried.

But each reread brings that part closer to the surface.

She needs a distraction.

Instead of giving in and joining her father and his girlfriend for lunch, Asher takes a left turn off the high street and heads toward her mother's house, knowing it'll be empty for a few more hours. It is her weekend to stay there anyway. But, as she arrives, there's a sign that someone else has been there recently: there's a sky-blue sticky note attached to her bedroom window. There's a time and a set of numbers printed on it, and Asher smiles when she looks down and finds a single white daffodil taped to her windowsill. It's still an unnaturally warm day for the time of year, and the heat has shrivelled the petals and tinted them brown. It's the thought that counts.

Asher removes the items from her window and carries them inside to her bedroom, pinning the daffodil to the wall above her desk and pressing the sticky note to the corner of her laptop screen. She takes another look at the numbers: likely coordinates, latitude and longitude. She doesn't know anything about directions, so she sinks into her desk chair and searches online for a map that lets her search for coordinates rather than a street address. Her screen fills with a patchwork of green. The location is in the middle of the woods.

Her phone buzzes violently on her desk, and the movement startles her so much that she bites straight into her lip. She sucks on the wound as she jabs at her phone screen and scrolls through her new notifications.

RYN
Did you get my note?

RYN
I'm glad your room is on the
ground floor.

Asher laughs to herself and decides that asking how he got her address and the exact placement of her bedroom are questions to ask at another time. She reaches for the daffodil and trails her fingers across the paper-thin petals.

ASHER
did u get my texts??

RYN
Yes.

Asher doesn't push him for a real response.

ASHER
where are we going?
what are we doing??

RYN
Wear comfy shoes.

RYN
Don't be late.

The buzzing stops.

Asher double checks the coordinates, zooming in on the map as if she can identify the exact tree that marks their meeting spot (the blur of green looks like it could be a towering oak tree, but maybe that's just wishful thinking), then turns over the sticky note to read the time printed on the back: 13:58. She looks at the clock in the corner of her laptop screen. It's 13:27. She has to get going.

TEN

Armed with fresh batteries in her hearing aids and a threadbare rucksack containing only a Polaroid camera and a half-drunk bottle of water, Asher is on her way. The forest is on the other side of town and the walk to it reminds her of when she first moved here, when her mother decided to pack her up and leave her dad behind midway through the school year and dump them in an unfamiliar place with the promise of starting a new life.

Asher didn't want a new life. She wanted her old one fixed.

The fact that the town was in the middle of nowhere hadn't helped anything. It felt like most of their six-hour car drive was spent with them driving in circles watching the same pattern of farmland-woodland-hills-woodland glide past the windows like an old home movie.

There weren't any cars on the road as they approached the town; they'd passed a convoy of tractors in the other direction, but no one else. Fourteen-year-old Asher had become increasingly convinced that there was no town and the whole 'moving' thing was an elaborate plan to steal her away from her dad and her friends and her *future*, but then the car reached the top of another hill, and in the distance was the town.

It was small, even smaller than she'd expected from the decade-old photos she found online. They'd seen the whole of it from the hilltop, tucked amidst the rolling farmland and clusters of oak trees and the shimmer of the sea beyond it, surrounded by another stretch of forest adorning the cloud-choked horizon. There was a boxy church steeple with a bell, a high street called High Street, a corner shop, and, thank God, a brand name café. Everything was decorated in the late afternoon shadows when they arrived, and the people on the pavements turned their heads to gawk at the unfamiliar car driving past. And then that was it. That was the town. Asher could still see the church steeple from their new front porch.

The house wasn't any more exciting than the town. It was somehow impossibly quiet and insanely noisy at the same time, to the point where Asher wandered through the rooms without her hearing aids in just for her own controlled silence. The tree branches scratched at the windows like a horror film which was, okay, kind of cool if you thought about it like that, but painfully loud in the still rooms, her dad's absence speaking volumes. The house itself creaked and moaned without any wind or storms, like someone was creeping up the stairs in the middle of the night.

Asher claimed the downstairs bedroom so she wouldn't worry about the house collapsing beneath her in her sleep (as if it couldn't collapse on top of her instead) but she insisted to her mother that she chose the room for the empty space on the floor that could fit an inflatable mattress if her friends came to visit. Maybe their houses also shifted and sighed like that, but only in the eerie stillness of small towns could you actually hear it.

After all this time, she still wonders if the old house misses them and the gaggle of preteen girls who once drifted down its halls, leaning forward and peering down the street with its window eyes, waiting for her to walk through the front door. Maybe it rattles its cabinets sullenly at the new tenants, or slams doors shut throughout the day, or…

And then, apparently, she has become stuck in a daydream, since she's stopped walking in the middle of the road and a driver is slamming their car horn with such passion that she suddenly wishes she didn't replace her batteries. She smiles bashfully, tightens her grip on her rucksack strap, and quickens her pace.

It isn't much further until she reaches the overgrown illusion of a public footpath that leads to the forest.

The path's faint impression winds through the grass and the hedgerows that stitch together a patchwork of fields, and she follows it absently. The sounds of the town fade and are replaced with the hollow rustle of greenery and the thud of her feet stumbling into rabbit holes.

The late spring sun is warm enough now that her T-shirt is dampening with sweat, even though there's a lingering hint of a chill in the breeze. Crossing the border of the forest, though, is actually quite pleasant, and Asher fights the urge to collapse in the shade of an oak tree and watch wisps of cloud—cumulus, she thinks, but recently she's spent more time studying the classics than cloud formations—float across the sky through the trees. She must keep plodding onward and find Ryn. Head down, she trudges through leaf litter and hopes that she won't wander lost for all eternity.

There's something strange about the forest, something intangible, almost spooky. A place Asher's never visited before but similar to the one she encounters every night in her sleep. When she looks up, the trees stretch overhead, arching like the skeleton of her hometown cathedral's walls against the blue flesh of the sky. The leaves are all vibrant shades of green that she hasn't been able to name since childhood art lessons, and some of them curl at the edges, fluttering any way the wind blows. She stops to admire them, her dad's voice floating back from a distant memory. She can picture him pointing out different trees in their old garden: oak, chestnut, a scrawny apple that would never blossom. Now, all he has is a greenhouse of plants he's tried to rescue from the discount section of the garden centre. He still points out their names, though.

Distracted, Asher catches the toe of her finest walking boots (secondhand, the toes and soles more hole than material) on a protruding root and falls face first to the ground, her chin bumping up into her skull so her teeth crash painfully together and pierce her lip. Again. She prods the wound with a ragged fingernail, then licks away the blood. "Fuck," she says to the trees. She stumbles to her feet and adjusts her rucksack, mud-streaked from the fall. "Drinking my own blood."

"Kinky," the trees in front of her say back, and Asher jumps backwards, windmills her arms frantically, and barely saves herself from falling into an unfriendly-looking gorse bush. She makes an embarrassing teakettle-like noise, still flailing.

"Oh, shit," a person standing behind her on the path says, sounding alarmed and amused. They're almost soft-spoken enough to be mistaken as a susurration of the trees. "We didn't mean to scare you that badly."

Asher wheezes as she turns, trying and failing to catch her breath. Her heart is beating seven million miles per minute. She rests her hands on her knees and inhales deeply. "What the fuck—what is your—where did you even come from?"

Ryn's vibrant-haired friend stands on the path, undeterred by his feet sinking into the mud. Thorns, twigs, and other woodland paraphernalia stick out of his unruly hair, but if he's noticed, he doesn't seem to care. "So, uh…you okay, Asher?" he asks, rocking back on his heels. Asher shudders at the sound of his shoes peeling away from the ground. "Still breathing?"

Asher brushes hopelessly with a leaf—sycamore, she thinks—at a muddy stain on her jeans that she'll eventually insist appeared from nowhere. She hopes it'll soon disappear into nowhere, because it was hard enough for her to find secondhand jeans that came in her size, let alone ones that fit this well. At least her pulse is slowly normalising. Her heart probably isn't going to explode, but it had been a close thing. She casts an accusing look in the boy's direction.

Once again, the boy doesn't seem to notice, picking at a nail and staring at it intently. His thumbnails are painted bright orange to match his hair. "Aren't you wondering why Ryn wanted to meet you here?"

Asher still rubs at the stain. Now that she isn't dying of premature heart failure, it's dawning on her that meeting a near stranger in the woods probably wasn't one of her brightest ideas. "Of course I'm wondering. What does he want?"

She turns to where she heard the first voice in the trees and sees Ryn thwacking at the undergrowth with his cane. If it's a fight, he's losing. A fake tattoo made from what she assumes is Sharpie and hairspray curls down the inside of his arm and up into his rolled sleeves, and Asher remembers a page in her old journal where she drew a similar design. Her mind drifts back to her dedicating hours to the doodle, painstakingly dotting the paper to make stars, joining them together with stems and leaves until it became a constellation made from flowers.

It feels like an invasion of privacy to see something so similar on someone else.

She grits her teeth as Ryn exits the undergrowth and the redhead enters it, a hand on an elbow nudging Ryn in the right direction before his friend departs.

"After our last group therapy session, I made a plan," Ryn announces. "But we'll talk about that later. We should walk for a while. I know all the shortcuts and shit. We should go and see the ruins, yeah?" Ryn's sunglasses are tucked into his shirt pocket, and while Asher struggles to look at his missing eye, she has no problem focusing on the remaining one: dark like coffee grinds, and it matches his wild, caffeinated laugh. The kind of laugh that people get addicted to, willing to do anything to hear it again. Asher can see herself becoming one of those people, you know, if meeting a stranger in the woods doesn't end badly for her.

"Sure, I guess," she says, giving up on the stain on her jeans and tending to the one on her rucksack. "Why the ruins?"

Ryn runs a hand through his hair, sending a leaf fluttering to the ground. "I'd like to have a dramatic background for my upcoming monologue." He pauses as if he recognises the absurdity of his statement, then laughs dryly. "Also, I've heard they look pretty cool, and they're more exciting than just standing by some trees."

So Asher and Ryn walk together, his hand tucked into the crook of her elbow as they stumble over tree roots, feet sinking into patches of undergrowth softened from the rain a few nights before. They walk in an uneasy silence, and Asher's shortness of breath is now from the uncertainty of what's coming next. There's nothing more terrifying to a teenage girl with an overactive imagination than waiting for an unknown conversation. The letter that now might as well be surgically attached to her comes back in flashes, and her heartbeat moves to her throat when she remembers how Ryn hasn't acknowledged any of her messages.

Her thoughts are disrupted by Ryn dragging her through a patch of leaves, which looks beautiful and innocent and serene on the surface, wavy-edged green oaks and yellowing downy birches, but turns out to have cold water and mud and probably leeches lurking beneath. Ryn ignores Asher's yelping as water splashes through every available entrance to her boots and attempts to escape to higher ground, ploughing ahead with his cane until Asher's socks are soaked through to her skin.

At least it's easier for her to find new socks than jeans.

"What the fuck, let me go," Asher whines, trying to yank her arm free from Ryn's surprisingly stubborn grip. "Let go. This is disgusting."

Ryn scoffs. "You walked into a thorn bush just now. You clearly need a handler."

"I can walk by myself." Asher winces as her boots squelch with her next step. "But it's okay if you need to hold on. Even if you did drag me into a puddle."

"Oh, fuck," Ryn says, investigating the patch of muddy leaves behind them with his cane as if he didn't just walk straight through them. "I guess I did. Oops." He looks totally shameless, so Asher decides he must be a sadistic prick and reconsiders her want for friendship. But then Ryn starts giggling, this ridiculously high-pitched laugh that Asher pretends she doesn't find endearing at all. "I don't get to go out alone much anymore, so I guess the freedom gets to my head. I'll start paying better attention to where I'm walking, with you here. Since you're not meant for the outdoors and all, I mean."

Asher tries to glare at him, immediately ineffective, but then Ryn distracts her by complimenting something shiny he can see reflecting in the sun at her throat, and then Asher is busy fighting a blush and babbling about how her house might be haunted. Her necklace appeared out of nowhere after a particularly spooky night, after all, maybe an apology gift from the ghosts. Her voice fades away when she realises she has no idea where on earth they are going, actually. They'd left the trail after a sessile oak and were just threading their way through the trees. The temperature in the forest must drop a lot throughout the day, or maybe the weather is changing, because the afternoon-warm air has become downright chilly. Seasonally appropriate, at least.

"So, uh," Asher says after she rips herself free from another bush—after some reflection, she thinks the new holes in her T-shirt are sort of aesthetically pleasing, so she'll survive the damage. "You actually know where we're going, right? We're not lost and wandering in circles?"

She pretends that she hasn't noticed that, at some point in the past few minutes, she became their leader: he's tucked away his cane and is following her following his directions with more trust than she has ever spared for a stranger.

"I find your lack of faith disturbing," Ryn mutters, so low that Asher's hearing aids almost don't decipher it, and then wheezes. "By which I mean, yeah, I know where I'm going. We're almost there."

ELEVEN

Ten minutes later, Asher and Ryn stumble upon a dilapidated stone house, and Asher halts mid-sentence. There had been abandoned buildings in her old town, sure, and ruined warehouses with broken windows that she roamed through with her friends, but this is different. This is something else entirely.

The house is hardly identifiable: trees twisting throughout, the front wall a rotting pile of rubble, the chimney one bad thunderstorm away from collapse. Branches and cobwebs stretch across the door, and the room inside is encased in shadows. Ruins, *real* ruins, real enough that Asher's fingers itch for a camera so she can document their existence forever. How has she never been this deep into the woods before?

(Because she hasn't made any friends in this town to explore with, that's why.)

Ryn doesn't seem to think that the ruins are *that* cool, but he stands back and listens with a smile as Asher coos over the decay, soaking in the broken glass and bricks crumbled from climbing vines as if they are essential to her existence. She always thought that woodland was supposed to be quiet, something even hearing ears couldn't detect, but here there are a thousand tiny noises filling the spaces in their conversation: distant birds, something rustling through the undergrowth, the breeze in the trees. The woods are sparser here, and fallen green leaves blanket the ground in deep drifts that muffle their footsteps. And then she hears Ryn's voice.

"I think everyone has a secret attraction to ruins. Something about the fragility of human nature and how it reminds us of how frail our existence is." He pauses as he tugs uncomfortably at his neckline, and Asher thinks she sees a chest binder beneath his sweatshirt. She wonders how he's not dangerously close to overheating from so many layers. "Ruins are supposed to inspire contemplation as they give you the sense that much more is going on than meets the eye. Allegedly. I think I read that somewhere."

Asher raises an eyebrow, sinking down onto a tree stump blanketed with ivy. She drops her rucksack to the ground, digs around for her Polaroid camera, and prays that there's film left. "Is that why we came here? You wanted to contemplate?"

"The rotting leaf smell isn't exactly inspiring." Ryn shrugs. His expression grows vacant for a second, but then he throws himself to the ground near Asher's feet, hands folded behind his head and legs crossed at the ankles as if he doesn't have a care in the world. His cane falls beside him with surprising grace for an inanimate object. "I wanted to talk to you again outside of the therapy room. I want to offer you a trade."

Asher's heart rate doubles. Her vision starts to swim. The sweat beading on her hands isn't just from the air and her exertion. "What kind of trade?" she asks, and she becomes even more aware of her shortness of breath. *Not now, not now, not now,* she pleads as the sharp edges of panic lace into her voice.

As a distraction, she raises the Polaroid camera to her eye and takes a photo of the ground in front of her, sneaking Ryn's feet and the tip of his cane into the frame as if she needs some kind of physical evidence that she knows someone other than her parents. She tucks the photo into her pocket before she can watch it develop.

Ryn winces at the unexpected flash and the whirring of the film printing. He doesn't question it. "A life trade."

Asher feels as if she's stopped breathing for a moment. Maybe she won't be leaving the woods today.

Ryn must sense her crescendoing panic. He sits up, hands flailing. "No, no, not like that—I didn't bring you out here to kill you." His gaze is fixed on the ground, but the wild grin returns to his face. "Jonathon wants us to spend another six sessions doing these letters, so I want to give you six fortnights out of my life that would otherwise be quite mediocre, in exchange for making the next six fortnights of your life the best they can possibly be. Starting now."

Six fortnights. Three months. August 31st. She thinks of the event tucked into her countdown app. The letter in her pocket. Ninety-one days and a handful of hours away. As of tomorrow, it'll be a satisfying ninety days away, ignoring the hours. Then less and less until it's just *tomorrow*, then *today*. She has nothing to lose, and there's so much she could gain.

In a sadistic sort of way, she finds it comforting that Ryn will be with her when the countdown ends.

She regains her ability to breathe. Her head stops spinning. Her heartrate slows. The sweat on her skin is now just from the warmth and the walk. "When are we meeting?" she asks, pulling out her phone so she can note down any details.

"My house. Next week. Around two." With that, Ryn fumbles for his cane, pushes himself off the ground, then disappears into the trees. A glimpse of orange in the distance tells Asher that the friend from before has been keeping a respectful distance, but she still watches him go until the mud on his back fades into the leaves.

JUNE

TWELVE

For the first time in weeks, Ryn wakes up on his own. No alarm or father knocking on the door, just the morning sun hanging at the perfect angle to flood his room with light. He's tangled in hot damp sheets, and his consciousness is blurred by the lingering haze of a nightmare: the same one his father dragged him awake from the night before, and it'll probably come back tonight, too. Ryn tries to push the feeling out of his memory, but it stays put, front and centre.

He inhales deeply and begins the grounding techniques his former psychiatrist taught him, counting each breath like he once counted stars.

Five things he can see: the silhouette of a stuffed bear sitting on his windowsill. A darker part of the sky where the clouds creep across the sun. Flickers of light from his suncatcher dappling his bedsheets. The illuminated screen of his phone, lit up from an unanswered call, the glow washed away when the sun returns. A sunbeam reflecting off his mirror and directly into his eye.

Four things he can touch: the damp bedsheets wrapped tight enough around his torso that he is far too aware of what his body looks like. A hangnail that he can't figure out how to chew into submission. Pins decorating the denim jacket that he never remembers to remove from his bed (easy access). A scratch across the back of his hand from dragging Asher into a bush.

Three things he can hear: his phone vibrating on his bedside table. The kid across the street singing a nursery rhyme in the garden and screeching at its conclusion. A neighbour struggling to park in their driveway, and he struggles to hear if the tyres are grinding over concrete or gravel to determine which neighbour.

Two things he can smell: some kind of baked good in the oven downstairs, maybe a frozen pain au chocolat heating up, maybe a freshly baked one from premade dough if he's lucky. Salty moisture drying on his skin.

One thing he can taste: he licks the back of his hand experimentally—definitely sweat.

He exhales and answers his phone. The voice on the other end greets him by a name he hasn't used in years, then corrects itself with an exaggerated sigh. He doesn't need to ask to know who is speaking. "I forget that you keep changing your name. What is it now?"

"It's still 'Ryn,' Mum. Like your granddad. It's been that longer than it's been anything else."

"Well, it's not the name I gave you, so how am I supposed to keep up?" She clicks her tongue until she realises Ryn isn't going to humour her with a response. The nightmare aftershocks haven't crept out of his system enough for him to start a fight. "So how are you and your father doing? You haven't answered any of my texts recently."

Ryn knows the routine—a conversation of questions that they don't intend to answer, and a series of passive aggressive statements to fill in the gaps until they simply become aggressive—so he plays along once more. "You haven't sent anything that needs a response. Dad still misses you. Are you coming back any time soon?"

"You know what it's like for me." He doesn't know. She's never spoken about the specifics of her new life without him, no further mentions of the new job or a newer house or an update on the distant family members she might've reunited with in her absence. Maybe that's why she won't come home anymore: she doesn't want a life with him in it. "Why don't you visit me? It's my birthday soon. The big four-zero."

In the house, Ryn can hear his father begin to climb the stairs, then linger at the bottom as he hears voices and recognises the nuances of his son's tone. Ryn pries himself free from his bedsheets and slams his bedroom door shut in response. Subtle.

His mother huffs into the microphone. "I just said, I'm turning forty, you know. It's like you can't be bothered to remember your own mother."

He does know. He just can't bring himself to care. "Do you remember how many of my birthdays you've missed?"

A sharp inhale. "I can tell you right now that you've missed more of mine than I have of yours."

They're equal for missed birthdays, excluding the ones she had before Ryn was born but knowing her, she'll be counting them.

"Do you remember how old I am anymore? What I look like?" Ryn's thumb hovers over the 'end call' button, but he doesn't have the heart to press it, not when he doesn't know how long it'll be before he hears his mother's voice again, no matter how unpleasant the circumstances are. "I don't look like you anymore, not like you care. Why are you calling me, Mum? What do you want?"

The only response is the line going dead.

Asher's art portfolio needs more work than she can squeeze into her remaining few days before the deadline, but she insists she'll figure it out. Her work is always sloppier, clumsier than she would like. She rushes; she waits too long; the paint cracks; it smears. Her art teacher tells her, "*Patience, be patient. Worry when it looks perfect, because that means you've caught up with your own ambition and judgement. Dissatisfaction is the engine of creativity.*" Or so they say.

There's something abstract about her canvas at this stage, almost avant-garde if she squints a little into the shadows where it rests in the corner of her room, but it's no different from the rest of her work. It'll only take a few more hours of painting today, and then she'll soon be parading into her art classroom after her repeat of her first English Literature exam to dump her penultimate art piece onto her teacher's desk.

Then there'll only be one more painting—inevitably incomplete. Then an inauthentic heartfelt essay about that painting's hypothetical place in the art world standing between her and spending the rest of the summer metaphorically rotting on her furry rug.

Her bedroom is littered with abandoned canvases and cheap sketchbooks and loose watercolour pages, half-painted and eternally trapped in the moment of their creation. The smell of oils and acrylics draw her in, and she finds herself in envy of those moments when she first picked up the brush, her mind overflowing with an image that she simply needed to rip out of her head.

Strokes of paint on a stretched canvas could bring her to her knees if they really wanted to, and they are one of the only things that she won't allow herself to spiral over, else she'll be crying on the floor of every exhibit she visits. The beauty of art is the mystery—the unknown against the known, bursts of colour, myriads of shapes, composition with a heartbeat—and it undoes her in the way that she hopes to undo the mystery of her letter writer.

If only she could finish a painting.

In between layers of paint drying, Asher sits at her laptop with the letter stuck to her screen and searches every social media site she knows for a hint of who 'J' could be. She narrows down her search to the local area—only a few hundred J-adjacent names—and then finds herself coming back to the date on the letter: August 31st. A date, the significance to the writer unknown—if there's even any—but the importance to her is that it's the day before her eighteenth birthday.

She needs this story to have a happy ending for the selfish reason of not wanting to cry on her birthday this year.

She imagines she will, anyway.

But back to J.

She opens a new tab for the profile of each J name based in town and scours each page for any sign of August, ultimately ignoring that the date is more likely to be significant to the letter writer than the intended letter receiver. She does find a handful of notable mentions—birthdays and first dates and death anniversaries—but none specifically for the thirty-first. Not like she was expecting these strangers' lives to coincide with her self-invented mystery.

She closes the tabs.

There has to be another clue.

She unsticks the letter from her screen and examines it again. It's the same as on her last look: the green ink, the singular legible paragraph at the bottom of the page, the saltwater stains. The message is the same, no matter how many times she wishes it would change.

She looks a little closer.

The paper isn't evenly soaked, not like she would've expected from something submerged in water, just crinkled in small, thumbnail-sized patches, and that's when she realises that the saltwater is in fact tearstains.

The realisation changes nothing, but she pretends it's the key to unravelling the mystery. At least she can now remove the ocean from her list of clues.

Ryn sits on a swing in the park opposite the secondary school. Luke frantically swings back and forth beside him as if he'll be able to swing himself over the frame and upside down. A toddler patrolling the baby swings gurgles enviously.

"My mum phoned this morning," Ryn says to fill the quiet between them, then recounts the phone call in as little detail as he can manage. He lifts his feet off the ground and allows the swing to twist lazily from side to side.

"At least your dad's decent, I guess." Luke swings less vigorously now. "Not like it makes up for your mum, but it's something."

"I guess." Ryn leans his cheek against the cool metal chain and blows air through his lips. He dwells on whether or not he wants to tell Luke about the minutes before the phone call, chewing on the memory of his nightmare as if that will make it easier to digest. The sun shines straight into his eye, and he sees the silhouettes and hazy outlines of what he assumes to be people moving in front of him. A figure passes on the other side of the park fence. Luke stops swinging as if he recognises them.

It's been decided for him: he's not going to talk about it.

"Hey, Mr.. Caldwell." Ryn hears Luke detach himself from the swing and walk toward the figure. "How are you coping without me?"

Mr. Caldwell has the fortune—or misfortunate, depending on the year—of knowing Luke since he was six years old. He taught the basics to various sciences for primary school children, then fancied a change around the time Luke entered secondary school, and then got stuck as his form tutor for the following five years. And then became the form tutor for Luke's younger sister as soon as he started sixth form.

"Mr. Jenkins." Mr. Caldwell's blurry outline nods toward Luke. "Mr...I'm sorry, Ryn. I don't seem to remember your surname at the moment."

He also doesn't seem to remember that he's never met Ryn, just seen him lingering in Luke's shadow so often that surely he must've attended the school at some point. His reputation precedes him.

Ryn smiles politely from his swing. "Just 'Ryn' is fine."

Then he detaches himself from the conversation.

As Luke recounts a memory from ten years ago involving a girl Ryn has never met and a lot of supermarket crayons, Ryn lingers on his own memory from the morning—not the nightmare this time, but the aftermath: the sunbeam on his mirror, the scratch across his hand, a kid singing outside, croissants baking downstairs, sweat on his skin.

Sweat trickles down his spine.

God, it's hot.

Ryn dwells on the memory for a moment longer, then he considers texting something vaguely vulnerable to Asher.

He opens his texts to her—well, *from* her, as he barely summons the nerve to reply—and considers being the one to reach out first. He screws in his earphones and allows his screen reader to narrate his unread messages.

ASHER

going back to the woods today!!

ASHER

taking a few more photos before

art exam

ASHER

last minute inspiration, yknow

He whispers a message into his earphone microphone and hits 'send' before he can change his mind.

RYN

Do you want to hear about my
nightmares soon?

Asher trudges through the woods armed with a film camera, a Polaroid camera, and however many other varieties of camera her rucksack can hold, following the nonsensical winding path Ryn followed when he led her to the ruins. She snaps photos as she walks, feeling the familiar comfort of a button press and film whirring into place beneath her fingertips. She wonders if Ryn will be able to see the shadows of her images if she holds the developed film strips up to the light. Just in case, she takes photos of things she thinks he'll enjoy: branches creeping across the sky, ivy adorning the ruined stone, sunlight hitting a puddle. She gravitates toward high contrast and distinct shapes.

As she walks, her mind drifts toward her mysterious letter writer and whether they might've walked this path before, then remembers there's little use in speculating about fiction when she barely has any facts.

But she does have one clue left, after all: J.

And she still has no idea who J is, or who J could possibly be, but she has to try, she has to ask around, because at the very least they deserve to see the letter, and surely, *surely* they can do something from there, she hopes.

Because Asher can only assume that the use of the initial must be similar to the use of a nickname, and with the nature of its contents she reckons that J has to be pretty important to the letter writer, and therefore J will probably know which of the few people they are close to who could possibly feel like this.

Or perhaps just recognise their handwriting.

And that all sounds easy, but Asher can't find anyone plausible whose name starts with J, and she is pathetically shy and no longer has any friends outside of whatever Ryn might be, and she is about to become so late to another exam that she considers skipping it altogether, and regardless of the argument with her guidance counsellor that will follow, the idea seems all too appealing. It's only an art exam, after all.

Because she can't focus anymore; she can't think, not about anything besides this letter and whoever wrote it.

She leans against a fallen tree trunk as she pops open the back of her camera and removes the completed roll of film. It'll never get developed, as much as she pretends it will, and she'll show Ryn the photos—she treats all of her art mediums the same, starting a project but never finishing, littering her bedroom with dozens of half-painted landscapes and 'in progress' sketches, just like how she hoards unedited photos and attempts at novels in her hard drive. She tucks the film into a pocket of her rucksack and pulls out the letter instead, worn at the edges and creased from her persistent touching. She reads it again as if the words could've changed.

She just wishes she could make out the rest of it; still, she can't help feel like the less she knows the better, because despite all this, she's still invading someone's privacy, and it had probably taken a lot for the writer to consider expressing this to J even if they never intentionally sent it, and surely it would feel like a kick in the teeth for a random girl to pick it off the ground and read it.

But it was accidental; it was dropped, and it isn't Asher's fault that her curiosity got the better of her, it's no one's fault at all, and Asher repeats this to herself as she returns the letter to her pocket. Though it is her fault that this is the first project she feels the urge to complete.

And it is her fault that she feels the need to refer to a potential suicide intervention as a project.

And, in that very moment, August 31st seems to find itself permanently imprinted upon her mind without the help of her countdown app or upcoming birthday, because just like that, this day matters, this letter matters, J matters, and the letter writer she knows so little about matters all so much.

Because they sound so alone out there, stranded out at sea, and Asher wants to be there for them as much as she can be, and not just because this hits home, but because Asher likes to think that she is a nice person.

She hopes she is a nice person at the end of this.

THIRTEEN

Asher is not feeling like a very nice person a mere two days later during her English Literature exam retake. This is nothing like her art exam from the previous afternoon—four hours trapped inside a heavily air-conditioned art classroom, creating her final masterpiece out of fingerprints and an ungodly amount of yellow oil paint that won't be dry before her next session.

And it should have been a calming experience, truly, except the sounds of the air conditioning and too-dry brushstrokes and people *breathing* were so overwhelming that she took out her hearing aids and sat in stubborn silence until she could calm down enough to breathe herself.

And then the dried paint on her hands cracked as she bent her fingers and flaked onto her handwritten notes and, all of a sudden, she'd had enough.

Now, the air conditioning in the exam hall is nonexistent, and the colours creeping into the edges of her vision are enough to distract her from the beads of sweat crawling down her spine. Her only way to get through this is to cry silently onto her exam paper for the next half hour and hope that the assessor takes pity on her tear-smudged attempt to analyse *Frankenstein*.

She stops by the toilets before she leaves the building—with enough time left to escape before the commotion of the class bell, she hopes—and looks in the mirror for a while, gripping the edge of a soap-stained sink as she grips onto the edge of reality.

It's okay, she tells herself. She just needs to make it through the few hours she's dedicated to seeing Ryn until she can collapse on her bedroom floor and pull the curtains shut. Maybe, if she texts her dad in advance, he'll ask her mother if she can swap houses for the rest of the week and there will be paracetamol waiting on her bedside table.

But that's still hours away, so she glares at her reflection once more for luck, cleans the soap scum from beneath her nails, and heads back out into the corridor as the bell begins to ring.

Asher arrives at Ryn's house seven minutes after two. He's hovering on the doorstep as she leans her bike against the fence and, when she announces her presence, he beams.

"You came back!" Ryn whoops, and he sounds ecstatic. Asher smiles helplessly at him—*of course* she would come back—and wonders if they are at a point in their friendship where they can hug on occasion. She leans toward 'yes' and launches herself into what was supposed to be a regular hug, but she must be a little out of practice because it comes out a lot more intense. She lets go almost immediately when he tenses up, but he stays close, almost nose to nose so she can look down into his eye, and she can smell the scent of fresh baked goods lingering on his clothes, which makes her feel like a creep.

Ryn takes a step back and laughs awkwardly. "Fuck, I was afraid I'd weirded you out in the woods and you wouldn't come back."

"I think I'm required by the law of newfound friendship to come back." Asher chews on her lip. She wonders if it's her first day on earth because this is surely not how you embark on casual conversation with an acquaintance. "No matter how weird you are."

They bump shoulders as they step through the door, his four inches lower than hers, and Ryn leads her straight toward the stairs. "Seriously, I'm so fucking glad you came back. This is going to be awesome." He walks up the stairs with one hand trailing the bannister and the other brushing against the photo frames that adorn every exposed square inch of wall in the house. He stops at the top and looks up toward the ceiling, as if he's six years younger and still has to look up to see the photos.

Asher hovers a few steps behind him, simply

observing. She sees photos that must document every year of a small blond child's life and sees the familiarity between their curls and Ryn's curls, their dimpled smile and his one, and the artistry of felt tip pen doodles across arms evolving into Sharpie over time, and she doesn't have to ask if the child is him, although a little more blond than he is now. Maybe not the version of him that stands in front of her—she notices the difference in dress sense and the outline of his chest binder beneath his T-shirt—but an earlier version.

She wonders if sometimes he is grateful for his broken eyes, for they stop him from seeing the dozens of photos of a past version of himself with long hair and frilly dresses that smile down at him. But they also stop him from seeing that he eventually grew into his father's face, no matter how many haircuts and hormones helped him along.

The speculation doesn't belong to her.

"Do you have a secret hunch about how you will die?"

Ryn sprawls across his bedroom floor, bare feet resting on the edge of his mattress, as Asher curls up on his pile of pillows and consults what she can only interpret as a version of the New York Times' 'questions to fall in love' article. Ryn insists it's a six-month-old questionnaire from Jonathon about how to make friends.

Asher comments that she's impressed that Jonathon has survived at least six months working with teenagers.

Ryn contemplates the question. "I'll probably just walk into oncoming traffic or off a cliff or something like that. It's not a secret hunch, though, just a regular hunch."

"We agreed that we were going to answer these seriously," Asher groans. The paper rustles as if she's clenching her fists.

Ryn rolls onto his stomach and buries his face into the carpet. "The questions are stupid."

"Answer the stupid question. I used to make potions with puddle water and flowers and shit when I was younger and *drink* them, and I'm still convinced I caught some disease that won't manifest until later life and kill me then."

Ryn audibly gags at the thought and comes up with an answer to stop Asher from elaborating. "Fine. I'll probably live a long and healthy life and die from completely normal natural causes."

"Can you lift your head up? Your voice is too muffled for my ears."

He lifts his head. "Natural causes."

"Okay then." Asher hums as she selects the next question. "If you were to die this evening with no opportunity to communicate with anyone, what would you regret not having told someone?"

"What kind of questions are these?"

"I'm still pretty sure Jonathon's given you that

'questions to fall in love' article, but a spinoff version that is very death centric."

"Maybe he's given up on friends and is trying to get me a girlfriend instead."

Asher folds the paper into a hasty airplane and launches it at Ryn's chest. He crumples it into a ball and throws it back. It ricochets harmlessly off her knee. She unfolds it to look for one more question. "If you could change anything about the way you were raised, what would it be?"

"Is this really what you ask someone when you're trying to make them fall in love with you?"

This time, when Asher throws the paper, it bounces off the edge of Ryn's desk bin. She lets out a sound of such pent-up frustration that Ryn crawls up onto his bed next to her and leans in as close as he can tolerate, hair almost brushing her shoulder. "How was your exam this morning?"

"I'm pretty sure I'm stupid." Asher shudders at the memory. Ryn's cheek touches the bare skin of her bicep for a second. "I had extra time to revise and memorise all the good quotes, but I could still barely remember what I was supposed to be writing about, and I've read that damn book and all the practice questions so many times by now. I spent months writing essays about ambition and knowledge and nature versus nurture just for them to ask me about *isolation* out of all the themes. And I've had this fucking headache for *weeks* now and I just can't think straight."

The words tumble out of her in a way where Ryn doesn't feel the need to reply, just listen to her ramble. He leans in a little farther until his hair does brush her shoulder. Asher doesn't breathe. She doesn't want to startle him. His head lolls slowly to the side, pressing against her arm, and she can see his dark eye close.

"The one yesterday was barely better. The exam, I mean. It was just an art exam, and I had to write a few pages about something I painted an hour earlier, but the words just wouldn't come out, and then I got paint all over my notes."

And then she's the one to lean in so her head rests on top of Ryn's. They lie together in unquiet silence, music playing softly from Ryn's phone across the room, Asher whisper-singing the lyrics she's learned since her last visit into his hair. It's one of the songs he drew for her, sprawling green lines across the page. They both remember. Neither of them mentions it until the song changes.

"This one is usually yellow to me," Ryn says, squinting as if it'll help him hear better, as if Asher isn't also listening the best she can with the low volume. "Sharp lines. Big peaks and valleys. It's all summer and energy and *noise*."

Asher picks at her nails. "My final piece for my art portfolio is yellow. It's this horrific fingerpainted, oil paint thing, but at least I think I'll get some marks for experimenting with texture."

"Can you show me your paintings one day?" Ryn

asks with such sincerity that it makes her chest ache. The notion of a smile creases the corner of his mouth. He wonders if an onlooker could see the same reflected in Asher: the sense of a shackle being broken. A bond being built.

She wants to say no, but she can't think of a good enough excuse, so instead she says, "You'll have to meet my dad. I keep most of my art stuff at his house."

"That's fine," Ryn says. "You've met mine."

"But mine is a bit...*much* sometimes." He's not, but she still can't think of a logical reason why Ryn shouldn't come to her house.

He grins. "Still fine. My dad put me in group therapy six months ago so I could make friends, and he sits in his car outside the entire time so I can't make a run for it."

"But..." She trails off. No more excuses.

"Show me your paintings."

"Fine."

FOURTEEN

After Asher's exam season ends on a random Wednesday afternoon, she meets Ryn outside the school, and they walk together to her dad's house. His hand tucks neatly into the curve of one of her elbows, a cumbersome still-drying canvas that smudges against her clothes tucked beneath the other one. She guides him down the high street, takes a left just past what he remembers to be a dying café, and then they walk through winding unfamiliar side streets until Asher announces that they've arrived.

"I don't think Dad is home yet," Asher says, struggling with her house key in the lock. Ryn pries the canvas from her grasp. "Thank you. Wrong key. His car isn't here, but he's not working today, so I guess he's out with the girlfriend." Her grumble tells Ryn all he needs to know about the girlfriend.

Asher leads him down a hallway lit so dimly that the

light spots in his vision fade away, and she counts the stairs for him as he walks and tells him where each door is that lines the landing and what is behind them. Then he's lying on her rug with the paint flecks scratching his stomach, typing his next letter into his notes app as she fumbles through a stack of canvases beneath her bed and pretends that her slowness is her choosing her favourite one rather than her stalling from anxiety.

An extraordinary amount of intimacy lies in exchanging art. Not for critique and not for an exam grade. Just to look. To feel. To understand each other. Maybe, one day, Ryn will show Asher one of his paintings or a scrap of a memory captured in one of his photographs.

Instead, he chooses a song from his playlist as a self-indulgent compromise.

The first painting Asher hands him is a distant cousin to the fingerprint monstrosity she described from her art exam. He can read this painting easier than he can read Braille, which isn't saying much as he's been resistant to learn, but the textures speak more to him than words do.

"I like it," Ryn says. "It feels expressive. My parents took me to an art gallery once and described all the paintings, and my favourite was this knockoff Van Gogh the curators were pretending was real, but I think it was beautiful no matter who painted it. Dad said you could see the emotion in the brushstrokes, almost as if the artist was capturing their mood in each layer."

Asher goes quiet. He hopes she's smiling, that he hasn't said too much and made her moment all about himself. She takes the painting from his hands. "Do you like Van Gogh?"

Ryn nods.

The next is an oil painting with a thick brushstroke texture that Ryn trails his fingers over like a kid with a comfort blanket. "Tell me about this one."

He feels the canvas tip slightly as Asher rests her hand on the edge. She clears her throat.

Her painting is a landscape, a night sky filled with swirling clouds, stars ablaze with their own luminescence, and a bright gibbous moon, waxing or waning—she doesn't remember the difference. Below the rolling hills of the horizon lies a small town with a tall church steeple reigning over the smaller buildings. On the left side of the canvas, there is a massive dark structure with no identifying features, magnificent when compared to the scale of the other objects. A metaphor for something, Ryn assumes when she provides no further explanation.

"It's inspired by the day I moved here." Asher says, and Ryn feels the canvas shift again as if she's fighting the urge to pull it back to herself. "You know, the view from the road that overlooks the town. You can see the entire thing trapped in the valley, and there's the sea twinkling in the distance."

Ryn hums as if he remembers anything from his journey along that road other than the sea. He runs his fingers over the canvas, dragging his nails across the thick swirls of paint that form the clouds, the smooth expanse that marks the dark structure. In the corner, there's four indents where Asher pressed her fingers into the paint as a signature. He rests his fingertips over her own, and for a second, he wonders again if they're the same. Just like each other.

His blue haze lifts momentarily.

"Can you describe yourself to me?" Ryn asks, rolling onto his back and tilting his head toward where he last heard her voice, then slightly to the left when he hears her inhale.

Asher stammers. "Describe myself? Well, my mum always says that I look just like my dad—"

"No, not your face." Ryn cuts her off, waving a hand in a way he doesn't intend to come across as dismissive but probably does. "My visual memory faded soon after most of my eyesight. I can't really picture things anymore. Tell me about *you*."

"I'm a terrible person to choose to be a friend," she begins after a minute of thought, and Ryn knows he's about to hear her most honest letter yet. "I don't think my mum likes me, because I look like my dad and not her and I act like him and not her, and I think our relationship broke down because implosive women seem to run in the family. We're not genetically meant to be friends."

She takes the painting from Ryn's hands but doesn't replace it with another. He drops his hands to his side and curls his fingers into her rug. Dried paint flecks scratch his palm. The song changes to something he would describe as moonstone blue with wild swooping brushstrokes and swirling shapes like his beloved knockoff Van Gogh painting.

Asher doesn't seem to know the song, so she continues her self-describing instead of singing along. "I don't delete my old friends' birthdays from my countdown app because then I'll have to admit that we don't speak anymore, and it's usually my fault, because I'm addicted to this kind of self-inflicted sadness my mum raised me on, and I can pretend that anyone but me is the problem.

"I pushed my friends away because I was too depressed to tell them how my hearing loss changed my life, and then they obviously weren't interested when I was ready. Which was a stupid thing for me to do in the first place because then I was so goddamn lonely, but also because I was the only non-white kid at that school and they were a barrier between me and getting bullied. And I can't blame them for not wanting to talk anymore, because I wasn't even a good friend when I had full hearing, and I didn't deserve any of my best friends in the end."

Ryn hears Asher flop down on the rug beside him. He twists onto his side and looks toward her, just in case she's looking back at him.

Asher sighs. "And, in summary, that was a lot of words to say that I can't describe myself without it eventually circling back around to how I look."

They sit in the silence between the song changes, and Ryn pretends that he hasn't noticed he scratched paint off one of her canvases with his thumbnail. She may not consider herself an artist, but she has no problem with painting her image in words.

He wants to push his luck and ask her to describe her bedroom, her house, the intricacies of her daily life that he'll one day get to know. He wants to look through the images she treasures in photo frames like he knows she's looked at his, to observe the arrangements of trinkets on her desk and the books lining her shelves, to trace the evidence of the friends that document a whole other part of her life.

"Do you believe in best friends?" Ryn asks as naively as if he's asking her if she believes in magic or fate or if it's going to rain tomorrow. But friendship is its own kind of magic. "Luke's my first and only best friend, I guess, if you believe in a hierarchy of friendships. Luke Jenkins. The redhead who came to the woods with me."

Asher inhales sharply as if his words have hurt her. She shifts the direction of the conversation. "I had my first best friend when I was five, or just about. She was as compelling and beautiful and interesting as someone that age could be. And all of those things about her just got stronger as we got older. I still haven't even grown into my face."

Ryn allows the conversation shift. "What was so special about her?"

"She was like a girl from a fairytale." Asher's voice softens, dreamlike. "She had these long fingernails that everyone complimented daily, and I was so envious of them. I still am. And the adults always mentioned how healthy they were, and it would become a joke that we'd roll our eyes at, as if her nails weren't real."

"Do you still talk to her?"

Her breathing quivers. "We haven't talked in years, but now I bite my nails down until they bleed just so I can't break one and think about hers."

Ryn hears her sit up, followed by the scrape of her grabbing something from her bedside table. A crinkle of some kind of foil packaging. The dull *click* of plastic slotting into place. Then a now familiar whirring sound, and he realises that Asher's changing the film in her Polaroid camera.

Asher presses the shutter and the dark slide ejects. "I keep most of my cameras next to my bed in case I look out the window and see something that might disappear quickly, like a double rainbow or a dog in one of those rain suits. The northern lights were visible from here the other night, but only through a camera, so I got to see them for a minute."

"Do you need to document everything?" Ryn thinks of his barren camera roll for a second—Luke once told him it was full of accidental screenshots and photos from inside his pockets—but he can't judge her love for documentation without remembering his obsessive tendencies toward particular bodies of water.

"Pocket-sized serotonin." Asher presses the shutter again.

Ryn jolts at the flash and the whirring sound and sticks his tongue out at her, then hears the crack of a Sharpie and smells the fumes as she scrawls the date beneath the photo.

"At least take a nice one," he mutters, pretending to be madder than he is. He's more flattered that she considers him worthy of documentation, as if he is also something that might disappear when she blinks.

Asher hums and counts down from three. The camera flashes again, and then she's pressing the exposed film and the Sharpie into his hands. "Sign your masterpiece."

Later, when Ryn has returned home and Asher's bedroom is coated in twilight, she tapes both Polaroids to her wall. Then the one of Ryn's feet in the forest. Then his sticky note message that she brought over from her mother's house, and the white daffodil, preserved as well as she can manage by pressing it beneath the cover of a recently read book. She adds the pages with the coloured lines, torn hastily from her notebook. Then the paper she looted from Jonathon's pile of scraps where Ryn confessed his fear, and she knows that she's wrong to have stolen it, but she's developed a tendency for taking things that don't belong to her.

Asher sinks down onto her furry rug to pick at the paint flecks and admire her tribute. Maybe it's silly, creating a shrine to her friendship as if it's a god, but maybe this friendship is the closest thing she has to something that feels holy. It feels like something worth honouring.

And maybe it's silly, because she's rarely chased this feeling before, this untamed joy before it goes up in flames, but building a shrine is a distraction from admitting that she cares, *really* cares about Ryn, whether or not he's going to let her.

FIFTEEN

Ryn collapses in to his father's bedroom at four in the morning, fingernails buried in his scalp, a stabbing pain in his skull feeling as if it's going to split his head in two. His knees press into the floorboards, the coldness spreading up his bare skin.

"Ryn?" his father says, torn between softness and ferocious concern, the words tumbling out somewhere in the middle.

Ryn stills at the sound of his voice. It's like he isn't sure where he is, as if he's erased the bleary moments between waking in pain and crawling out of his bed for help. He's suddenly overwhelmed by the embarrassment of wanting to ask. "Leave me alone."

"No." He hears his father switch on the bedside lamp. "You came to me, and you're clearly upset."

Ryn clasps his face with a kind of fierce desperation,

like he's trying to hold his features in place, to stop his skull from splitting apart. "Just fuck off."

"*No.*"

Usually, his father wouldn't fight back, never spar for spar, never dodge or parry Ryn's vicious words, but tonight he can see that something is wrong. He watches as his son begins to hyperventilate, gasps wracking his body as he tries to cling onto a breath.

Then he says something else, but it's so obscured by his wheezes that his father doesn't catch it.

"Can you say that again?" his father asks. He crouches beside Ryn, blanket in hand to wrap around his shoulders.

Slowly, silently, Ryn lowers his hands from his face, turning to the sound of his father's voice. His stomach heaves as he feels blood stick his fingers to his eyelids.

His eye is *gone*.

Not the left one—the one where the socket is surgically welded shut, bisected by a ragged gash from the bridge of his nose to the ridge of his temple. That scar is a faded purple, the wound now years old.

The functioning eye is gone.

When the pain lurched Ryn awake, his first instinct was to try and claw it out of him, fingernails scrabbling at his face as if they could somehow reach beneath his skin and pull it out, like the surgeon's scalpel removed his eye. He remembered pain jolting him awake at fourteen years old, then waking in a hospital bed a blurry amount of time later, sick from anaesthesia. It hurt then. It hurts now.

And, for once, he doesn't want to hurt anymore.

"Oh, God," his father whispers like a prayer, and bile stings the back of Ryn's tongue. He looks up, dizzy and disorientated, the feeling of waking from a nightmare but everything still feels *wrong*.

Ryn shakes uncontrollably. "I really did it then. Not a nightmare."

"Not a nightmare."

"I'm sorry." The blood left in his body thunders in his ears. "I'm so, *so* sorry."

Except he's not, not really. He's sorry that he won't be able to help his father clean the stains from the floorboards, but he's not sorry that he's turned his nightmares into reality once more.

"Does it hurt?" his father asks. There's a glow in the place his hands should be, and Ryn knows he's considering calling for an ambulance. Maybe the paramedics are familiar with him by now. Maybe he's just another screaming boy on a stretcher.

A frantic sob. "It feels like a knife." Ryn drags his bloodied fingers through his feathery hair, grabbing desperate fistfuls of it as if causing one pain can distract from the other.

"Were you awake when it started hurting?"

"The pain woke me up pretty quick." He shakes his frantically. It hurts more. "I thought it was a dream at first. It *has* to be a dream. It has to."

His father sighs. "Still not a dream."

Ryn covers his face once more. Maybe pretending that

it isn't real might actually make it a dream, just another nightmare he can wake up from and laugh about with Luke in the morning, a funny anecdote he can tell Asher as they leave group therapy arm in arm.

And, for a moment, he feels fourteen again, screaming in a hospital bed as infection burned its way through his optic nerve, a doctor screaming back that nothing was wrong, and *"Dear god, please stop scratching out your stitches."* What his father now refers to as 'the incident' was followed by antidepressants and house arrest and being pulled out of public school.

Ryn has played the memory over and over again enough to recognise that the aftermath of 'the incident' was to be the moment when his blue haze begun and never receded, and he became his father's patient rather than his son.

His father pries his hands away from his face.

There's a temporary glimpse of relief. His eye isn't gone—but he knew that when he saw the glow of the phone screen—his father shines a bright light at his face to inspect the damage further, and his vision blurs, shimmering like mist and silk and shadows. His eye is full of blood and tears and probably brewing a new infection, but it isn't gone, and that's almost enough for him.

As his father wraps the blanket tighter around his shoulders and prepares to bundle him to the Accident and Emergency waiting room, Ryn lets go, lets the pain and anguish and fear roll out of him in visceral wails. His tries to dig his fingernails into the floorboards as if he can somehow claw his way through them too. He presses his forehead to the wood, and his tears mingle with the blood. He's reminded that tears, being salty, hurt when they touched an open wound.

It's not the first time he's found himself in this position. He imagines it won't be the last.

Asher saunters into group therapy at three in the afternoon and forces herself to act as if Ryn's unexpected absence hasn't disoriented her day entirely. She sits in her usual seat and resists the urge to pull out her phone to ask Ryn where he is. They're not codependent, after all, just barely friends, she tells herself. She finds comfort in her old tricks of hiding behind her hair and glancing up at the clock.

Jonathon arrives a few moments after her, and his lateness is more intriguing, although it will remain unanswered. He stands in the centre of the circle and starts the session as if nothing is out of the ordinary. "Is there anyone here who would like to share with us today?"

As usual, no one answers. But, instead of picking on the least comfortable–looking person in the room, Jonathon chooses a smiling girl and smiles back as if he knows her. "It's nice to see you again after so long, no matter what the circumstances are. Would you mind reintroducing yourself to the group?"

The pretty girl Asher saw in the café steps into the circle. Her hair is different now, dyed a murky blue and haphazardly streaked with black, and cut short enough to barely brush her jawline, but her clothing is so distinctly *her*. Does the makeover look good? No. But is Asher pleased by the chaotic self-expression? You bet.

Today, the lyrics on her arm are scrawled in green ink, and Asher is suspicious to say the least. Her oversized black jacket tucked beneath her chair is blanketed with patches, her fishnet tights are ripped almost beyond function, and her bootlaces look more like the yarn Asher dabbles in for crochet than effective bootlaces.

And Ashers still thinks this is the prettiest girl she has ever seen, and it's someone who she's going to pretend won't make an appearance in her dreams tonight.

"Wow, there's a lot more familiar faces than I was expecting." The girl's smile somehow widens. Her accent is local, her mouth lengthening vowels and slowing the cadence, giving her away without Asher even having to hear her. She must've lived in this town for her entire life without Asher finding out. "And to those who are a little less familiar, my name is Jocelyn. I came here a year or two ago, then decided I was cured, then obviously realised that I'm not. So, now I'm here." She finishes with an unenthusiastic jazz hands gesture. The familiar faces laugh in solidarity. The unfamiliar ones do not.

Jonathon seems to be infected by her joy. He smiles more times per minute than Asher has seen in the past few weeks combined. "We're glad to have you back,

Jocelyn. Do you want to share what you hope to get out of these sessions?"

"I don't think I've worked that out yet." Doubt clouds Jocelyn's expression. Her hands trail down her green-inked arms. Just for a moment, but it's enough for Asher to tell that something is wrong. And, knowing herself, Asher has to find out what is wrong and force her way into finding a solution. "I think I just want to be happy again, I guess. To not feel like I'm drowning whenever I leave the house."

And there it is again. The drowning. The J name. A new suspect in Asher's invented mystery.

Jonathon's smile curls into a grimace. "Thank you, Jocelyn. Take a seat."

Jocelyn returns to her seat.

The rest of the session passes in a blur, an amalgamation of "Do you want to share?" and "How have the past two weeks been for you?" and "Can you elaborate on what they just said?" Asher's eyes are locked on the clock to avoid her pulling out her phone to tell Ryn about Jocelyn, and then she remembers she still hasn't told him about the letter or J or August 31st. And that feels too much for her to tell him over text, so she doesn't. She just sits there and counts down minutes instead of days.

After group therapy, Asher decides that she hasn't had enough of listening to people talk about their feelings, so she heads down the hall to the late afternoon group session. The letter with the green ink is stuck in her mind, and she suddenly remembers that the letter from Ryn lies unopened on her bedside table.

She arrives a few minutes before the session is due to start and finds Jonathon sitting at the edge of the circle. His face burns red as soon as he sees her.

"Why are you here?" Asher asks in a way which she hopes comes across as casually curious rather than downright nosy. She sits in this room's equivalent of her usual seat, leaving two empty chairs between her and Jonathon. She isn't sure if their relationship only exists in the other therapy room, or if they can act like acquaintances outside of the confines.

"I have my own issues, too, you know," Jonathon says. He scratches at his stubble. It looks like it's been there for a few more days than usual, and his eyes are noticeably bloodshot from up close. Asher decides not to comment. "Listening to Ryn's existential crisis week after week will do that to you."

Ryn wasn't there this week, Asher thinks. She smiles politely in response, arranges her skirt that is handmade from a dozen different skirts across her knees, and decides to end their interaction.

The seats around them soon fill up and the person leading the session is revealed to be a young woman—probably fresh out of university—overqualified and underexperienced, with glossy magazine hair that Asher envies and a billboard smile that she doesn't. The woman's radiant aura could make her a millionaire if she figures out a way to sell it in bottles.

She smiles at the beginning of each sentence, making eye contact with everyone in the circle so she's spinning like a ceiling fan. A sign language interpreter sits beside her, and three younger teens sitting across from Asher watch with wide eyes. Asher doesn't acknowledge him besides making a point of tucking her hair behind her ear and displaying her hearing aids as if having them is synonymous with not needing an interpreter. She doesn't take into consideration the fact that the interpreter would not have known she was attending the session and doesn't think to hunt out the other deaf person in the room. Strength in numbers, and all that.

"Welcome everyone." The woman beams to her captivated audience. "For those who don't know, my name is Gemma, and this is Daniel." She gestures to the interpreter. Asher makes a mental note of his sign name and pretends she doesn't notice the sting in her chest as she remembers her lack of one. "I see we have some new members in our community. Don't worry, I won't make you introduce yourselves. This is supposed to be a safe and welcoming place for everyone."

Asher breathes an audible sigh of relief, her mind turning back to each time she's felt as if she's embarrassed herself in the three sessions with Jonathon. She fights the urge to send a pointed look in his direction.

"Due to some requests from the end of last week's session, I've decided that we're going to wander further into the topic of death and mortality, if that's okay with you all. We're going to spend the first fifteen minutes of today's session writing a eulogy. Imagine that the version of yourself you're trying to grow from has died and what you're going to write is what will be read out at their funeral. You may leave the circle and begin writing whenever you're ready."

Asher's mind drifts back to the letter in her pocket. The one in green ink sounded like a eulogy, almost an apology for wanting to give up on life and leave J behind.

Instead of writing her own eulogy, Asher steps away from the group and sits on the floor against a radiator, cold metal pressing into her spine and using her paper to hide the glow of her phone screen. The carpet that is a decade older than her, worn nearly smooth, chafes her thighs as she crosses and uncrosses her legs. She sends a text or two to Ryn, telling him about things she hopes he will find funny.

ASHER
the woman leading afternoon therapy
is basically a cartoon character 😄

ASHER
jonathon is here. did u know he went
to therapy??? he's just like us!

Once again, there's no reply.

The fifteen minutes are up before Asher remembers that she's supposed to be putting her thoughts onto the page. A handful of people returned to the circle within the first few minutes, clutching their eulogies to their chest as if someone is going to take them away and reveal their darkest thoughts.

Gemma returns to the circle. "Is there anyone who would like to read their eulogy? You don't have to if you don't want to, or you could ask someone you trust to read it for you. I think it will be interesting for us to discuss our individual opinions with the group."

For the first time in her life, Asher raises her hand. Gemma smiles encouragingly and gestures for her to stand. Her shaky legs are noticeably absent. She clears her throat, tucks her blank piece of paper into her pocket, and replaces it with the salt-stained one, even though she's read it enough times that she doesn't need to see the green ink to recite it word for word. She takes a deep breath.

"'It feels like I've been underwater for some time, like all the air is pushed out of my lungs. But I'm drowning. I'm trying to convince myself that I can still breathe like this even though I can't. I'm gasping for air and all it does is let more water in. I have to do this. I have to do this myself. Soon. And I'll do it on my own terms.'"

She watches the interpreter as she speaks, and although her knowledge of BSL sentence structure is more fluent than her vocabulary, she can pick out specific words.

Underwater: palms held flat then rising over the head.
Air: fingers flapping beside the face.

Drown: a hand sliding down behind the other held still.

No one raises their hand to contribute when Asher is finished. She knows it's not a proper eulogy, and she knows someone will notice that she didn't write it during the session, but she's desperate for insight into what those words might reveal.

Gemma smiles again. This time, it doesn't reach the rest of her face. "Thank you for sharing. That was so brave of you. You can sit down now, if you'd like."

Asher sits. She wouldn't like to.

Jonathon stares at her with unblinking eyes as she tucks the letter back into the safety of her pocket. He doesn't say anything, but Asher can tell he knows something that he isn't willing to share.

He knows who wrote the letter.

And Asher thinks she might too.

SIXTEEN

A gentle glow from Asher's laptop screen washes over her desk, colours flickering in rapid motion, voices blaring through her speakers. The laptop whirs in self-defence of the growing heat, and there's an ache in the back of her head that promises rain. Her broken desk fan sits mockingly silent in the stifling air. Reclined in her chair, she spins around and watches her open window and the curtains for the slightest tremor.

Betrayal.

Beads of sweat collect near her hairline, and she distracts herself by scrolling through her phone where she's opened every publicly available social media profile that she can connect to Jocelyn. Each feed is swamped by friends, so many friends that Asher can't even fathom that many people without feeling breathless. There are birthdays and beach trips and a series of disposable camera photos taken on a boat, and Asher obsesses over the friends pictured in the waves. Their profiles are all tagged in the photos, so she taps on the links and scrolls and scrolls and scrolls, ranking them based on their suspected closeness to Jocelyn and their proximity to the month of August.

One thing that stands out to her is that she and Jocelyn share a birthday. She hopes that neither of them will cry during it this year.

"Asher?" Ryn asks faintly through her speaker. "Wait, did she leave?"

"It says she's still on the call," Luke says.

"Asher?" Ryn asks again.

Asher detaches her eyes from her phone. She adjusts her chair into an upright position and wipes the sweat from her face. "Yes, hello, sorry. I'm still here. I zoned out for a moment." She blinks to register what's happening in the game on her laptop screen, seeing Ryn and Luke's avatars crouching in front of hers. An echo of Ryn's screen reader narrates his movements through his microphone.

Spending her day playing computer games with two boys she barely knows wasn't part of her original plan, but she's got nothing better to do post–exam season than reluctantly pack her things to return to her mother's house and prepare to face that inevitable wrath.

"I wish I could see you right now," she says wistfully. The game's built-in transcription feature doesn't work, and her brain is so exhausted from processing sounds all day that she can't wait to take out her hearing aids and watch a sitcom rerun with the subtitles turned on.

Luke's webcam flickers to life, and his face and middle finger fills the corner of her screen. "I knew you couldn't wait to see me again."

He can't see Asher's face, but her scowl must be audible, because he says with a smile, "Don't pretend you're not excited to see me. I bet Ryn would be happy to see me, if he didn't already have to see me every day."

Ryn snickers. "It's true. Your face *does* get me excited."

"Now you're just trying to make me uncomfortable."

"Flustered, you mean," Asher interrupts. She thinks she's starting to grasp the nuances of Ryn and Luke's friendship, and how she might fit into it. They laugh and they joke, but they don't say anything serious when she's present.

Luke's webcam cuts to black. "Okay, no, I'm sick of you two." A message pops up in the game chat: *LUKE has left the game.* "Consider this a rage quit. We can play more another time."

Ryn sends a :(in their group chat, and Luke laughs as he disconnects from their call. Ryn's avatar walks across Asher's screen and stops to admire the scenery, narrated as *grass block grass block grass block oak wood oak leaves.* "So, what were we doing?"

Asher wipes more sweat from her forehead and looks longingly at the digital water on the edge of the screen. "I...I don't know. I zoned out for a bit. I think it's hotter in my room than it is outside." She walks her avatar into the water. Refreshing. Placebo effect, she hopes.

"Do you need to go out for a bit?" Ryn asks.

"I'm okay for now, I think." She turns around in the game. There's the illusion of a wooden construction amongst the distant trees: four walls arranged in a square and an alarmingly triangular attempt at a roof. "It looks like Luke was trying to build a house."

"I guess we should finish it for him."

They fall into a comfortable quietness for the next hour, Ryn's screen reader narrating his quest to mine virtual resources and Asher constructing a blocky masterpiece of a house. She smelts glass for the windows, and Ryn's avatar drops yellow flowers at her feet. They might be carnations, she decides, if she squints at the pixels for long enough and stretches her imagination, and they're a gift, so she plants them by their front door (*oak wood door*).

At some point, the wind picks up, and Asher worries that an incoming power cut will interrupt their evening plans. Her internet connection is struggling as it is. She peels herself out of her chair to close the window and cut out some of the noise, but the muggy air becomes suffocating. She returns to her desk and sighs into her microphone. "I think I'm going to log off now. It's windy all of a sudden, and I can't hear anymore."

"Oh. Okay." His voice is thick with disappointment, or maybe it's just his microphone crackling. "Enjoy your evening."

He leaves the call before she can say goodbye.

Asher spins in her chair to face her bed. The duvet has been kicked to the floor, pillows askew. New additions for her friendship shrine are littered across her mattress. She squints: it's only six in the evening, but the cloud cover plunges her bedroom into darkness.

She sighs and wishes for rain.

She remembers running barefoot through the streets as a child when a summer storm would roll through the valley, splashing in potholes and letting the raindrops frizz her hair. Those times were euphoric—a brief relief from smouldering, trees swaying in the wind, the threat of thunder and lightning taunting her headaches—but it feels so far away from her now. Especially now that the air is so thick she can barely breathe.

She turns off her laptop and reclines her chair. She's grown nearly accustomed to the dark when her phone vibrates, the notification lighting up her room.

A text from Ryn.

RYN
See you tomorrow question mark.

Asher looks at her empty rucksack abandoned on her carpet, the dirty clothes spilling out of her laundry basket, the haphazard pile of art supplies she carts between houses just in case inspiration strikes. Her parents live only a fifteen-minute walk away from each other, so she should be making the most of the relative peace and quiet of her dad's house. Packing can wait.

ASHER
why don't u come over? my dad's
home but he isn't that scary

RYN is typing...

An eternity of half-seconds pass between Asher's message and the response, Ryn's typing blinking on and off her screen as he writes and writes his reply, and Asher wonders what it is about her attempt at friendship that could cause so much inner turmoil. Maybe she's going about it the wrong way, coming on too strong. Maybe she's out of practice after all these years of self-inflicted isolation. Maybe he just doesn't want more of a connection than their mandatory letters.

But then, after what ends up being only a half-minute later:

RYN
Okay.

RYN
I will be there soon.

"What happened to your face?"

Ryn appears on Asher's doorstep as the clouds threaten to burst. She sees his father's car hovering down the street, and she waves when he catches her eye. He gives her a thumbs up, and his taillights disappear around the bend.

Ryn's face is covered in a cobweb of scabbing scratches, like he got into a fight with a one of the trees in the forest and lost. He scowls as if he wasn't expecting her to notice.

"It looks like you've been attacked by a bush or something." Then she smiles as if nothing is wrong, because something very clearly is, and he very clearly does not want to talk about it. "Come in before it starts raining."

She describes their journey down the hallway in more detail than she did for his previous visit—stairs to the left, living room to the right, kitchen covering the back half of the downstairs, small bathroom in the corner—and they weave their way precariously through her father's piles of junk and out the back door and through the garden, dodging cracks and crevices and plants that have grown over the edge of their pots. When they reach the greenhouse, Asher clicks on the light and lingers in the doorway, suddenly self-conscious that Ryn is once again in her home, and once again she didn't clean or tidy or even offer him a drink when he walked through the door.

There's some reassurance that he can't see the collection of things that she calls her own, but there's nothing she wants more than to know how he sees her life from his eyes, from the outside looking in.

It was in this space where Asher had reclaimed some scraps of her old self—her old laugh, the joy that came with tangling her hands in plant roots, the feeling of belonging that her mother wrenched away when she tried to separate daughter from father. Asher lugged in her dad's old record player and a handful of her favourite vinyl sourced from charity shops a few months after they were reunited, solely for the ambiance. It was soon joined by a corduroy beanbag she found for free in someone's garden, once covered in what she could only assume is love and hair from a dog she'll never meet, now covered in patches of embroidered flowers to cover the blemishes. Add a string of battery-powered fairy lights, and the atmosphere is almost pleasant.

Asher describes their surroundings as she strides over to the record player and sets the first record she sees on the turntable. She drops the needle, and the greenhouse fills with the sound of an eighties rock ballad.

Ryn sniffs the air. "It smells nice in here." He sniffs again, cautiously this time. "Well, actually, it smells like dirt. But it's homely dirt. Kind of herby."

Asher plonks herself onto the beanbag. Ryn tries to sit beside her but misjudges the distance and slips onto the floor. He stays there, leaning to one side until his head rests against the edge of her knee.

She slips her hand into her pocket and thumbs the worn edges of the tearstained letter until a small piece tears off, and it's then when she realises that she needs to talk about the page before it fades away entirely.

"I found a letter a few weeks ago." Her voice is muffled, and she coughs to clear her throat, but it comes out like a choke more than anything else. "I've been meaning to tell you, but the timing never seemed right."

"What kind of letter?" Ryn sits up straight. Her knee is suddenly cold.

There's no easy way for her to say it, so she just says it. "I think it's a suicide note."

She takes the letter out of her pocket and describes it to him—creamy lined paper, smudged green ink, recently identified tearstains—then reads out the words. Ryn sits in an undecipherable quiet until the song ends on the record player, and it instead becomes an inscrutable silence.

Asher stands to flip the record, dropping the needle midway through the first song. "I can't imagine feeling like that and having to feel it all alone."

She sits back down on the beanbag, and Ryn's head returns to resting against her knee, and she tentatively slips her fingers into his hair, winding the dandelion-fluff curls around her fingers like she winds her earphone wires. She wonders how many more weeks it will take for her to learn to map the galaxies of his faint freckles, how many more record spins it will take for their lives to become so intertwined that they spend each evening listening to music together, stretched out on the floor with his legs bent over hers.

She imagines it will only take the summer, assuming that Ryn shares the same all-consuming need for friendship. She suspects he might, they just have different ways of showing it.

The song changes.

Asher wonders if Ryn thinks of her every time a specific song plays, like how she thinks of him whenever she queues up a song that sounds like a sprawling green line. She wonders how he can stand to listen to music again if every melody becomes associated with a person, with a memory that may be too painful to bear.

This music sounds nothing like the songs Ryn drew for her, no memories attached yet. And because she hears it in the weird underwater type of way that her hearing aids allow, she doesn't even know what it truly sounds like. But it's different. It's alive. In some ways, it feels like this night.

It feels good to have told someone else about the tearstained letter, even if Ryn hasn't said anything in response yet.

Asher looks down at Ryn. At some point, he shifted to rest his chin on her knee, and he's looking up at her like she's all he's ever needed in this world, smiling softly like nothing has ever gone wrong or ever will. Asher's hand that isn't in his hair shakes in her lap. His hands flutter restlessly.

"Where do you feel stuff?" he asks, half-joking, half-sincere, as the B-side ends.

This time, Asher doesn't flip the record. "What do you mean?"

"Where do you feel your feelings?" He sits up straight and presses a hand to his stomach, slightly to one side, the spot above his liver where he feels the first spiders of his anxiety release their webs. His hand then slides up to his throat. "Sometimes, I feel them here. My anxiety is here."

He hears her sigh in understanding. Her fingers unwind from his hair, and it sounds like they're tapping across her skin instead. "It's in my knees. My anxiety, I mean. The second I feel nervous, my knees start shaking."

He nods, satisfied. "What about anger?"

She feels anger in her stomach; it burns right through his chest. He keeps joy in his fingertips, and she holds it in her palms. Sadness floods her skull while it sits stubbornly in his guts.

"Where do you feel love?" Asher asks eventually.

He thinks about it. To him, love is the salt from seawater drying on your arms and your favourite song playing through a crackling radio and the smell of petrichor after a midsummer drought. It's light blurring through a rain-soaked windowpane and fingers tracing your skin until your freckles turn into constellations.

It can't be contained to just one space.

"Everywhere." He reaches out and fumbles for her hand, accidentally slipping her hair tie off her wrist in the process, and presses her knuckles against his rib cage. "I feel it everywhere, like something is trying to explode out of me. It's making up everything that I am."

She intertwines their fingers and breathes a content sigh when he doesn't pull away. "Don't be silly. People are like…ninety-nine percent empty space."

He tightens his grip on her hand. "Everywhere," he repeats. "Where do you feel fear?"

They play this game until the clouds finally burst, and Asher tilts Ryn's face toward her so she can read his lips over the sound of rain pouring against the greenhouse roof, and Ryn realises that he is terrified of how these feelings might end. What if they change? What if this is just a temporary spark of friendship, not meant to last, rather than an eternal slow burn? What if her affection congeals in one place instead of radiating?

What he doesn't ask is the unspoken question he whispers in the darkness each night, when only the shadows can hear him: *Do you love me?* Because he thinks she might, in a completely platonic way, and, for the first time in his life, he might truly be wanted by someone, no strings attached.

He doesn't want to ask and risk not being wanted, so he changes the subject. "I have a neighbour who only comes outside when it rains."

His chin returns to her knee. Her hand returns to his hair. She twists a small section into a braid. "That's weird. Is he okay?"

"I think so. The people we bought the house from said he was, well…a bit odd. We thought it would just be a few noise complaints here and there that we could handle, but he was completely silent all day. It was like no one even lived there—you know, lights off, curtains closed, no one ever coming or going, those kinds of things. Until one day, maybe a month after we moved in, it rained. And his front door opened."

He feels Asher's knee shift beneath his chin as she

leans in, a captive audience. The beanbag crinkles in protest. "And then what happened?"

"He walked a few feet down the path and stood against his gate and just smiled up at the rain, arms out, like he'd been waiting for it. Like he was worshipping it. He was soaking wet and fully clothed, and he stayed out there for hours until it stopped. Then he went back inside and didn't come out until the next time it rained. And I don't think he ever misses it—I can hear his door opening at three in the morning."

"Have you ever asked him about it?"

"No. I don't know what I'd want to say." Ryn sighs. "He's the easiest neighbour we've ever had, but I don't even know his name. He'll be standing by his gate right now. I should probably also be by my gate right now."

There's a bright spot at the edge of his vision as Asher checks the time on her phone, and her remaining hand unwinds from his hair. "It's only nine o'clock. Do you have a curfew?"

"Not officially." The distaste is clear in his voice. "But my dad gets funny about me being out after dark because I have night blindness. I can sometimes see streetlights and car headlights if they're bright enough, but I have no depth perception on a good day, and my light-and-shadow perception doesn't really work in the dark. Dad doesn't think it's safe for me."

"I can walk you home some nights, if you want. If you want to stay for longer, that is."

He does want that, but he doesn't want her to walk

him home in the rain, and then to walk herself back home alone. It may not be safe for him, but the town being small doesn't make it safe for her. "It's fine. I'll text my dad to come get me."

Asher stands to unplug the record player and switch off the fairy lights. The greenhouse plunges into darkness, and the soundtrack is the storm swirling above their heads. They walk together through the darkened house and sit knee-to-knee on the front porch as they wait for Ryn's father's headlights to illuminate the street.

"I think we were supposed to swap letters today, but I haven't written one yet." Asher's tone is apologetic. "Exam season was kicking my ass."

Ryn tries not to think about her tearstained letter. "I finished writing mine the other night. I'll ask Luke to bring it around for you."

"I'll send him back with one for you."

The rain eases until it's a drizzle rather than a downpour. The bright spots of the streetlights become clearer, and Ryn tilts his head up to the rooftops and wishes he could see a sky full of stars one more time, or the aurora borealis Asher caught through her phone camera, even if she couldn't see it with her functioning eyes. For now, he'll stick to the streetlights and pretend they're stars instead.

"I still haven't met your dad," Ryn says after a moment, more an observation than an opinion.

Asher hums. "He shut himself in his room for a call just before you got here. It's been hours by now, so the girlfriend must've phoned, or he's gone to bed early. Work tomorrow, you know."

Then Ryn's father's headlights come into view before Asher can elaborate that, even though it seems like it, she really doesn't hate her dad's new girlfriend. She reaches out to squeeze Ryn's hand once as he pushes off her porch and slips into the passenger seat.

"She's waving at you," his father says as he buckles his seatbelt.

"She's waving at *you*," Ryn corrects. "Wave back."

They sit in silence all the way home, the radio silent, the rain on the car roof forming its own percussion. Ryn aims for a speedy escape the moment the car stops in their driveway, but his father leans over and tugs the door halfway shut, an all too familiar reminder of the day he met Asher, and says, "I'm glad you've got a friend, kid."

And the moment is so sincere that Ryn has to duck under his father's arm, clamber out of the car, and hold back tears until his bedroom door shuts behind him.

It's nice to have a friend. It really is.

SEVENTEEN

When your best friend of the past three years announces that they don't want to be alive anymore, there are a few ways that you can take the news. Some reactions are preferred to others, but most people just pick and choose between the predetermined acceptable options, depending on how they're feeling in the moment.

There's denial, saying that your best friend is just feeling down and there's no reason they could seriously want to die. People suffer from low moods all the time, and it's easy enough to deal with, surely. It's only one bad day. There won't always be another.

There's anger, claiming that suicide is an easy way out. Why on earth would they want to act like a coward when people suffer through worse every day?

There's bargaining, an eternal monologue of listing reasons why they shouldn't do it and what you're going to do to make the blue haze fade for them again.

There's depression, rambling on and on about how they're your best friend and you don't deserve for them to leave you alone. Because of course you'll be alone. How could they think you won't be?

When Ryn announces that he's been thinking of ending his life, his best friend of the past three years reacts in the fifth way, the most unexpected way: acceptance.

"How are you going to do it?" Luke asks, focusing on his friend's glassy eye and tearstained cheeks—still scabbed with scratches that he refuses to talk about— more than his own emotions. Ryn's sandy hair has lost its shine. There are creases framing the hem of his shirt and Luke presumes he must have slept in it the night before, if the nightmares hadn't kept him awake. The sun is almost setting, and he thinks it's likely that those nightmares will be returning within the next few hours.

Ryn shrugs. "I haven't thought about it that much." His breath catches in his throat, and he can't tell if it's from the nerves of finally putting his plan into words, or if Luke's inability to burn a wooden wick candle correctly is filling his lungs with sweet-smelling smoke, because confessing in his own bedroom would've made it feel too real.

"When are you going to do it?"

There's a pause. He knows this much. "By the end of the summer. Two months, I think."

Before Luke returns to school and sends off his university applications and sits his final exams and receives those acceptance letters and both of their lives become severed. It's so far away. It's too soon.

Another pause, this one flooded with unspoken questions that Luke is afraid to ask. He thinks he knows why his friend is doing this, why he's choosing to end his own life rather than fighting whatever he's going through. He thinks he understands. He wants to understand. Asking how he can help would be weird. Telling Ryn 'good luck' and leaving him alone would be unacceptable. Telling an adult might change their friendship forever. It might end their friendship forever. He's not sure if he has any other real friends right now.

Ryn doesn't take his friend's silence as a positive silence. "Are you…okay with this? Well, not *okay*. I'm just hoping you're not going to do anything to—"

Luke laughs, forcing Ryn into silence. The tears that stream down his face aren't from sadness. "Don't be stupid. I'm going to make sure you have the best damn two months of your life."

EIGHTEEN

sher likes the firsts of the month the same way that some people like New Year's. She likes Mondays too, the beginning of an untouched week, knowing that there's something she hasn't messed up yet. Because she will, and she does, and she's supposed to, and that's okay.

Now, the emergence of a new month resurrects Asher's fear that she's running out of time. She has sixty-one full days left, but she's no closer to discovering the identity of J or her mysterious letter writer. Her flimsy theory that J is Jocelyn and the writer is one of Jocelyn's friends is held together by desperation and wishful thinking.

Summer in this town isn't so much a season as a warning; by the middle of the morning, it's hot and humid enough to make Asher's hair frizz, and she's still not thought about anything other than the letter writer in hours. But it's not deep enough in the season that school holidays have begun for most children, so the streets outside are devoid of the constant background noise she depends on to fill the silence.

To kill the quiet, Asher takes out her sketchbook. For a moment, she wishes her oil paints weren't kept at her dad's house—her mother hates the stink of it, the oil, the turpentine. The way it stains Asher's fingers and her clothes and everything she touches, splatters of paint crawling up her forearms, decorating her face. There's nothing careful or pristine about her method of painting. She emerges streaked in umber and ochre, cobalt and cadmium.

So, she settles for pencil and paper.

Letting her hand glide over the page used to make her forget herself. Her father had been the first to notice it. One day, he was close to growing irritated by her restlessness and gave her one of his lightly-used notepads and a chewed blue Biro. She opened the notepad to the blankest page and drew great sprawling patterns. She never drew figures or landscapes back then; she just started in the corner and let her pen wander where it wanted to until she had filled pages with intricate interlocking patterns, things that looked like flowers and tree roots looping around each other until no empty space remained.

But today the blank page cannot hold her attention. Her mind will not leave the tearstained letter alone.

She sends a text to Ryn as if a virtual conversation can fill the void.

ASHER
stuck at my mums house 😔

ASHER
are u doing anything today?

As she waits for a response, she opens one of her long-abandoned text documents and works on a fantasy instead. She's been writing it on and off for years: a sweeping dreamscape that her dad once described as heart-warming and heartbreaking at the same time before she decided it was too personal to keep proudly showing him her progress, a patchwork of autobiography and folklore that makes her life easier to deal with.

She slips into a paragraph that's comfortable and fitting, just like her oldest grey-blue sweatshirt with holes in the shoulder seams that she refuses to throw out. Maybe the tearstained letter will be easier to understand if she turns it into a prophecy written on a scroll instead.

She threads sentences around her wrists and ties them together, and they replace the series of coloured string bracelets she once wore obsessively. And maybe, in this context, it does make more sense for the letter to be stained with saltwater rather than tears. Her fictional kingdom is built by the coast, after all.

She takes her prettiest thoughts and holds them up to the light, sending a stained glass window of colour around her room and across her cheeks, vibrant hues rather than constellations of freckles. Maybe, it'll be for the best if she cuts the letter from the plot entirely, if she can craft the writer into a side character with a guaranteed happy ending.

Her phone's notification sound brings her back to reality.

RYN
I'm going to the shop with Luke.

RYN
Come with us.

Then he sends a time and the name of the super-market, and that's how Asher finds herself crawling into a trolley half an hour later, hauling Ryn in with her and wrapping her arms around him like a seatbelt as Luke steers them through the crowded aisles, nonsensi-cally grabbing own-brand colas and discounted bakery goods as they go.

"Wait, we've gone past the crisps," Ryn says. He hangs over the side of their trolley and tries to grab at shelves to slow them down.

Luke pulls them to a stop, then drags them back a few feet. "How do you even know that?"

"I have no choice but to memorise the layout of every single shop in this town." He feels along the shelf until he finds what he's looking for. "Not seeing is exhausting."

This continues for the next few aisles, Ryn and Luke bickering back and forth about which snacks are filling their trolley and the ones that aren't, and Asher decides that it doesn't matter if she can't figure out how she fits into their friendship. Whatever *this* is? It's enough for her.

She's comfortable enough in their presence that she leans her head back and closes her eyes, the fluorescent supermarket lighting sparking fireworks behind her eyelids and Ryn's spine pressing against her knees more like a weighted blanket than a nuisance. Their argument washes over her like white noise.

She's so comfortable that when Luke takes a corner too fast and Ryn tries to grab at a passing shelf to stabilise them, she trusts one of them to stop their fall.

They don't.

The trolley tips, and Asher and Ryn and their hoard of snacks are sent sprawling across the supermarket floor.

"I'msorryI'msorryI'msosorry," Luke begins, a nervous stammer that breaks into laughter the moment he realises that Asher and Ryn are both relatively unharmed.

Asher stares up at the ceiling until she's convinced that the world isn't spinning around her and it's just her worst-case-scenario brain spiralling, then slowly she sits up, testing her limbs as if she fell from a much further distance and hit the ground with a much greater force. She reminds herself that her hearing loss is usual and not from a major head injury. She's fine, may be lightly bruised by tomorrow morning, but she'll be better as soon as she gets up off of the suspiciously-sticky floor.

An outstretched hand creeps into her vision, and

she reaches for it before realising that it doesn't belong to Luke.

Jocelyn pulls Asher to her feet, light limning around her head so the fluorescents give her a sickly white halo. Her hair is still black and blue, and her bootlaces are still falling apart, which means she's still the prettiest girl Asher has ever seen. Up close, she can decipher the song lyrics written across Jocelyn's bare arms, a temporary tribute to some noughties emo band Asher obsessively listened to a few years earlier. It did irreversible damage to her top one hundred most-played songs of all time.

Then Asher notices that Jocelyn's mouth has been moving, but she's been too busy staring to hear any words come out.

Jocelyn's eyes flick to Asher's hearing aids as if that was the problem. "I asked if you were okay."

"Oh. Yeah." Asher's hands tangle in the hemline of her T-shirt to hide their anxious fluttering. "I'm fine."

"I'm not," Ryn says from behind, and Asher turns to see him still sprawled on the floor, sunglasses missing, and Luke a laughing wreck beside him. She grabs his hands to pull him to his feet and notices that he's slipped her yellow hair tie from a few nights before around his wrist with an array of string bracelets that might have also once belonged to her.

Jocelyn frowns at Asher in a way she can't decipher. "I think we've met before."

"Oh yeah?" Telling a pretty girl that you know her from your shared therapy group doesn't seem like an effective pickup line, so Asher doesn't say it. She ignores the fact that half of her current friendship group met in that same therapy group.

"Yeah." Then there's a moment where Jocelyn must realise where they've met before, because her eyes rove over Asher's pink hair and her mouth makes a little 'o' shape for a second before she speaks, and she pretends that her surprise isn't so visible. *"Oh."*

Asher watches Jocelyn turn to Ryn and look him over as if she recognises him too, and this time her expression upon seeing the scratches and scar tissue across his face tells Asher that he's been noticed for different reasons. Jocelyn doesn't know him, but she's definitely known about him long before Asher did.

"Can someone help me find my sunglasses?" Ryn dips his head as if he's sensed the staring. "Jenkins, for fuck's sake, stop *laughing*."

Asher looks away from the boys and back to Jocelyn who is now holding back on her open staring. "We saw each other in therapy the other day. Ryn wasn't there when you were, but I think we're both regulars now. And the other guy is Luke, who is not in therapy as far as I know."

"Not yet," Luke confirms. He retrieves Ryn's sunglasses from beneath a shelf of tinned vegetables and wipes them clean with the hem of his T-shirt.

"Maybe we should see each other outside of therapy for a change of scenery," Jocelyn says, and it takes Asher more time than she's willing to admit realising that 1) Jocelyn is talking to her and not all of them as a group, and 2) Jocelyn might be asking her out.

Asher is so overcome by her burning red cheeks and suddenly thundering heartbeat and overall gay panic that her capacity to think straight has vanished. Her ability to be calm and collected is gone. All she can think of saying is, "Let's talk again after therapy, and I'll let you know about anything else."

Jocelyn only nods and turns away. As she disappears around the end of the aisle, Asher sinks to her knees and buries her head in her hands until she remembers that it's 2:15 and she's about ten years too old to be causing a scene in public.

"That was the single most awkward conversation I've ever had to witness," Luke says, tossing the scattered snacks back into the trolley, and then hauling Ryn in like a toddler having a tantrum. "But you somehow got a date out of it. I'm impressed."

"It's not a date," Asher mumbles into her hands. "At least, I don't think it is. It's just therapy. *Group* therapy. Ryn will probably be there."

"But it's still *something* with a girl that you've clearly had a crush on for some time, even if you've never spoken to her."

"How do you know that?"

Luke meets her gaze. "Your face gives everything away. You know that expression 'wear your heart on your sleeve'? Well, you wear your heart on your sleeves, your cheeks, your eyebrows, your mouth—"

He breaks off abruptly as Ryn leans over the edge

of the trolley and pulls him in. She's grateful for the distraction, because she's quickly being reminded of how there's nothing that makes her more uncomfortable in life than a boy talking about her mouth.

Ryn wraps his arms around Luke like she did to him and looks at the spot where he last heard her voice. "Asher, you're driving. Take us home."

NINETEEN

Ryn wonders how much longer he can sit smothered beneath his friends' laughter and pretend that he's not drowning. Because Luke knows, but he's acting like he doesn't, and Asher doesn't know, but she sure is on to something. He knows she found one of his letters. How fate managed to place it in her path, he can't even begin to think about, but it did, and he's learned enough about her by now to know that she's not the kind of person to let something go easily.

So, he sits between them on the nest of blankets they constructed on his bedroom floor and listens to them bicker over whether or not so-and-so stars in the film they're only half watching, and he tries to figure out how to explain that despite everything in his life seemingly going right for once, he still feels like it's breaking apart around him.

Maybe he'll feel better if he says something. If he says that Luke's arm draped around his shoulder makes him far too aware that he's wearing a chest binder, if he points out that the easy conversation around him reminds him that it's something he has to work for. If he asks them to describe what's happening on the screen because the film didn't come with audio description and he enjoys their voices more anyway, if Asher presents him with one more textured painting that captures how he feels so he doesn't have to talk about it in his own words.

Maybe, if he spends the entire night with them wrapped in blankets and laughter, he'll spill his guts as the sun comes up.

But he won't. He knows himself well enough by now to know that he won't, and he'll keep acting as if the growing discomfort in his chest is from wearing his binder for twelve hours straight rather than an unspoken confession. He'll linger in this moment for a while longer, resting his head on Asher's shoulder and pretending he isn't smelling her raspberry shampoo and the chemical scent of fresh hair dye, a smell that has remained on his bedsheets since the last time she visited.

"Do you really think she's in *that*?" he hears Luke ask distantly, as if he's a world away rather than a few inches. "She looks more like the girl in that TV show where the world ends."

"That doesn't narrow it down," Asher whines.

They keep arguing about films the other person hasn't seen, and Ryn keeps trying to hold his head above the water and hold on to the moment. Because he's now decided to squeeze a lifetime's worth of moments into a lot less since he's become so desperate to feel alive, yet so afraid of living, and more than anything he hopes that they'll stay friends with each other after he's gone.

The thought of their lives carrying on without him makes him swallow down bile.

Asher hums as she contemplates the television screen. "She looks like she could be daughter of this other actress. Bonnie something."

Ryn can feel Luke's frown. "I'm pretty sure I've seen her parents before, and they're definitely not in films."

"Not her biological daughter, just her screen one," Asher argues. "They just *look* alike."

"I think you're making fun of me now," Luke says, half joking. He grabs his water bottle, and a scrap of late afternoon sunlight reflects off the liquid inside, sending it shimmering across the ceiling. It crosses Ryn's bedroom like a tide coming in.

Ryn wishes they could stay in this moment forever, the future forsaken, the prophecy unfulfilled.

"I'm not making fun of you," Asher replies with a laugh.

"Ryn, she's making fun of me."

"She's not making fun of you, Jenkins."

Then there's a flash and a whir, and Ryn knows that Luke is the latest victim of Asher's Polaroid camera.

He closes his eyes, and the dancing bright spots from the water bottle go black.

He thinks the hardest part of all of this will be asking them to leave, now that he's allowed their lives to become so intertwined, how they come any time he calls, and they're rarely the first to leave. He's too lonely to be alone anymore, but he's going to have to accept that it'll be easier to go through with his plan if they don't speak anymore.

This self-inflicted fate is his decision. At any moment, he could rewrite the prophecy and remove the ending and bathe in his friends' affection forever. And he's almost brave enough to do it.

Almost.

Asher's sitting at the bottom of Ryn's stairs fighting with her shoelaces when his father walks through the front door. She notices his presence with enough time to look up and catch most of his sentence.

"—heading out? I'm sorry I missed you," he says, kicking his own shoes into the corner.

Asher tugs a shoelace into submission and shakes her head. "It was getting kind of stuffy up there so we're going to walk around the block for a bit. Enjoy the fresh air, touch some grass, all that."

He nods in approval, draping his corduroy jacket over the bannister and pausing to admire the family photos above Asher's head. She wonders if he does this often, if there's a specific photo he lingers on each time he looks, and then she remembers the frame from near the top of the stairs. "Are you okay with Ryn being trans?"

Asher knows there's a whole spectrum of reactions to coming out, demonstrated by her parents when she came out as a lesbian a year or two earlier. Getting kicked out is one extreme; being accepted wholeheartedly is the other. But in the middle, there's something else. The awkwardness, the refusals to acknowledge, the uncomfortable weirdness of becoming a problem her mother felt the need to turn away from. In the stories she's read online, some parents of trans kids seem obsessed with mourning the son or daughter they claim not to have anymore. Having feelings about it is fine, Asher thinks, just don't make your child's life that much harder.

Asher isn't good enough at reading facial expressions to work out what Ryn's father is thinking, so she assumes she's horribly wrong and the small child in the family photos isn't Ryn after all. "I mean, if he is trans, that is. Would you be fine if he was?"

Silence stretches between them, and Asher can feel every second that passes drag into oblivion, until Ryn's father sits beside her on the bottom stair and says, "So, he's told you?"

"Not really," she admits, and she breathes a sigh of relief that she was right and can avoid what could've been a conversation that ended badly. "Well, not at all. My dad says I'm observant."

"What gave it away?" he asks with a smile that Asher has to crane her neck to see.

She hums as she traipses through her memories. "The pins on his jacket. The chest binder. The photos upstairs of a kid who I don't think can be anyone else—not like I know your family that well—but the kid has Ryn's smile."

"Are *you* okay with him being trans?"

"It's none of my business." She hums again to waste a few seconds, because she realises this is something she hasn't really thought about, only accepted without any questions asked. She can't imagine a universe where the unconditional love her father fed her with as a child wouldn't be something she passed on to someone else. "I've only known him as this version of himself."

"Your parents raised you well."

Asher tugs at her necklace, the clasp scratching the back of her neck as a distraction from the ever-present ache in her chest that strengthens with any mention of her parents as a unit. "I'm not convinced they raised me that much, but my dad did teach me to be kind. To be gentle. I kind of raised myself between their arguments. Just me and the internet."

Ryn's father sighs in a way that feels more like an apology than anything she's ever received in words. "Then you did a wonderful job at becoming the person you are today, and I'm sorry that you had to do it yourself."

The ache in Asher's chest dulls just a little.

They sit together in companionable silence, until Asher conquers her shoelaces and the walls shaking from a slamming door upstairs suggests the incoming presence of two teenage boys.

"So, are you okay with Ryn being trans?" Asher asks again before company joins them.

"If it makes him happy, then that's enough of a reason for me to be okay with it." Ryn's father looks once more at the photos above Asher's head. She looks up too. It's a group photo: ten-year-old Ryn with thick-lensed glasses, a parent on either side. "I'd rather have a kid who wants to change every aspect of their identity on a daily basis than use their name in their eulogy."

Ryn rushes down the stairs, and Asher stands before she can become a trip hazard. Luke trails behind him with significantly less enthusiasm, a scowl marring his features. Asher means to ask him if everything is okay, but Ryn tracks her down through a floorboard creak or the sound of her breath or a shift in the air, because he grabs her wrist with perfect accuracy and pulls her alongside him.

Asher glances behind to wave goodbye to his father as she's dragged through the front door. He smiles at her, waves back, and then signs one of the few things she can recognise: *thank you.*

TWENTY

Sometimes, Asher wakes up, and she feels okay. A six out of ten, she'd describe to her therapist, neutral to positive, a little better than average. An eight when the sun is out. A four when her brain is so overwhelmed from hearing, then so underwhelmed from not that her head starts to ache. Always an even number. Never a full ten.

Today, she sits in the middle of her bedroom at her mother's house surrounded by most of the belongings she's accumulated since the move, and she decides she's feeling like a four out of ten.

She realises that she's spent her life thinking there's so much that she needs. Her favourite dress and battered trainers. The perfectly fitting jeans with the embroidered knees to cover the mud stains. Her phone and her books and her favourite songs. She needs her laptop stuffed full of unfinished photos and half-finished stories. She needs her journal and her dried flowers and the second-hand cameras her father gifts her each birthday that she insists on dragging between houses 'just in case.' The clean furry rug in this house to replace the paint splattered one in the other. The collage of album covers hanging above her bed. The dozens of dried-out colouring pens fallen under her desk.

Now, as Asher pulls cardboard boxes out from beneath her bed that are labelled 'keep,' 'donate,' and 'bin,' she wonders how much she truly needs.

Her surfaces—her desk and her windowsill and her bedside table and the scrap of space where her books don't reach the edge of the shelves—are littered with relics from a past summer, things she doesn't need but refuses to let go of. The gift shop trinkets and strips of photobooth photos and shells from a half-forgotten beach are more clutter than comfort at this point, but they hold the memory of one specific fragment of a perfect summer in a way that Asher can no longer remember on her own.

It was a summer of trying not to think too deeply, to get lost in time and barely keep track of the days and rarely care about the hours. A summer so bright and warm, the photographs burn brightly enough that Asher turns the frames around to face the walls, even if she once believed the heat would linger, there would be more days to lose to the sun, the ache in her chest when she looked at the pictures was invented indifference rather than a sign of homesickness.

In some ways, it became a summer of denial. Of her parents arguing in the kitchen, a 'for sale' sign in the front garden. A summer spent promising friends that she'd be back to visit regularly, promising that the potential distance wouldn't keep them apart for long. A summer of packing her life into boxes before 'for sale' turned to 'sold,' and her mother not telling her where they would be going, and then her father promising that he'd come and visit soon. A summer spent lying on the same fuzzy rug in a different house, hair fanned across the floor, sunshine on her face, and she and her friends wouldn't talk about their future or geography, and they no longer walked country lanes and cliff paths and coastlines in their worn-out shoes.

Asher turns around a frame to face her, and the photo is from a day she'd almost forgotten, three girls she hasn't spoken to in four years. They didn't go to the beach that day—tourists descended onto the sand from sunrise to sunset—so they rode the bus to a nearby village instead, laughing their way through the one bookshop and clothing boutique and independent café that was soon replaced by a name brand. They didn't talk about Asher's upcoming departure, because no date set in stone meant it wasn't worth talking about yet, and they made a rule to never talk about anything sad at all, not while the sun was still bright enough to burn their skin.

Once again, this summer is for pretending that the end isn't coming, Asher thinks as she removes some of the photos from their frames, leaving them face down on the floor beside her. She puts the empty frames into the box labelled 'keep.' The 'donate' and 'bin' remain painfully empty: everything that's ever come into her possession is too valuable for her to part with. Each expired train ticket and supermarket receipt and torn-off clothing tag. All the detached camera lenses and unfilled notebooks. Every photo frame, empty or filled. They're all a part of her.

Eventually, she decides that she won't donate or bin anything that isn't worth taking to her dad's house, she'll just leave it behind, because she knows what her mother is like, and the remains of her bedroom will remain untouched like a shrine until she comes back, or her mother admits defeat on pretending her dad doesn't exist and leaves town once more.

But there's a little less than two months until she can live with her dad full-time, and she wants to make that move as painless as possible, so she has to smuggle away as much of her life as she can manage into boxes without her mother noticing.

Asher thought she would've needed all of it, but she packs a rucksack with only her laptop and her cameras, and she decides that the rest isn't worth it anymore. She won't come back for any of it.

TWENTY-ONE

"Is there anyone here who would like to share with us today?"

It's ten minutes to two and Ryn wishes he were anywhere but here in the circle of chairs. For the first time, Asher is sitting by his side, and he's pretty sure Jocelyn is on her other side since he catches snippets of them whispering back and forth about something he doesn't care enough about to eavesdrop on. Something about exams being over and their endless summer and incoming results day. Something he pretends not to care about ever since his father pulled him out of school and he doesn't abide to those markers of a life next to normal anymore.

Someone across the circle must have a glass or a clear plastic bottle resting on their knees, because the sunlight sprays watery patterns across the ceiling like it did in his bedroom a few days earlier, and his thoughts are flooded by memories.

Six weeks after he lost his eye, Ryn snuck out of the house for the first time. To the beach, of course, camera in hand, and he sat where the waves met the shore and watched fading sunlight reflect off the water in silence for an hour, and he let his remaining eye fixate on a dark spot out at sea and the way each wave lapped over it. He zoomed in on the spot and observed through his camera lens, picking up details that he could no longer see with his fading vision.

He wanted a photo; he *needed* a photo. To have and to hold, to dig the crisp edges of glossy photographic paper into the soft parts of his palm and know that the pain represented something he loved.

He walked out into the sea for the photo, forgetting how strong and deep the water could get at high tide, and that was the first time that Ryn had nearly felt himself lost in the ocean, which was most certainly a feeling he wasn't accustomed to.

Ryn had never really experienced helplessness until that moment, and from that day on, he was treading water amidst a hurricane for the rest of his life. It didn't stop—it never stopped—and the small things stopped feeling so small, and his father couldn't know, and he stopped speaking as much, and he started hiding his letters better because his mother always found them.

But now at seventeen, he can't do this anymore, he can't keep himself afloat, and his lungs ache from the effort, but he can't *drown*, he has to do this to himself, he has to *end* this, and, by now, he thinks he has an idea as to how.

August 31st is the two hundred forty-third day of the year, and that's as meaningless to Ryn as what remains of his life, and he likes that, and it's as good a date as any: fifty-six days left to finally compose his last letters, explaining what it means to have your throat fill with water but never drown.

Asher taps his arm to get his attention, and he gasps as if she's pulled him to the surface. "You seem completely out of it today," she whispers as he composes himself.

He blinks himself back into the room and realises that he's spaced out for so long that Jonathon's questions and the surrounding chatter have long faded, and he can hear Asher's earrings jingle as she turns away from him to answer Jocelyn. He listens to them make plans together, and he hears it in the distant underwater way that Asher describes her hearing as, and he's propelled back to nearly drowning in the ocean, hearing someone yelling from the beach, and salt burning the back of his throat.

He doesn't remember what happened to the photo. He doesn't remember if he even managed to take it before the waves pulled him under. All he does remember is a stranger dragging him from the water and indecipherably talking to him until he could sit up straight and cough the water out of his lungs.

He remembers the stranger tucking his waterlogged camera into his hands with so much care that he thought it might've survived, and then him feigning disinterest in photography every moment afterwards so his father wouldn't catch on to the fact that he almost drowned.

And he remembers sneaking back into the house and locking himself in the bathroom before either parent returned from work and noticed he was gone. He washed the salt out of his clothes in the shower, then buried the remains of the camera in a shoebox beneath his bed.

Asher's hand lands on his arm again. Instead of tapping him, she's rubbing circles with her thumb into his skin. Scraping sounds surround him, telling him that the circle of chairs is being cleared away, marking the official end of the session. "We're going now. Me and you, not me and Jocelyn. We can wait until everyone else has left if you want. Jonathon is looking at us funny, but that's nothing new. I saw him in another therapy session at some point, and I think it's been weird ever since. Okay, everyone is gone now. Including Jonathon. I hope he hasn't locked us in."

Ryn soon realises that her narration is her way of easing him through what she has clearly noticed is a panic attack.

She presses against his back to convince him to stand then tucks his hand into the crook of her elbow, steering him through the remaining chairs in the circle and toward the door. All he can do is take deep breath after deep breath and try to match her pace.

Asher kicks the door shut behind them. "Hallway time. The room where I saw Jonathon is just down there to the right somewhere. It's really dark in here today—I think the lights' sensor doesn't realise we're here—so let's get outside fast. Maybe we could go for a walk if you're feeling up to it?"

"Not today," Ryn says, and he realises it's the only thing he's said in an hour. If Jonathon tried to speak to him again, an angel must've swooped in and saved him. "Tomorrow. I'll be better tomorrow."

"Okay. We'll go tomorrow." She pats the back of his hand encouragingly. His grip tightens on her elbow. "Today, we're just going to get you home."

Asher arrives home after her detour to Ryn's front door to find the curtains closed and lights switched off. She doesn't think anything of it at first: one side of her family has been so plagued with migraines that her house is found in darkness more often than it's not. But this is her mother's house, not her neurologically-afflicted father's, so now she assumes that something is wrong.

She finds her mother in her bedroom sprawled across wine-stained bedsheets, half-empty glass still in hand, empty bottle on her bedside table. She's lying so still that Asher kneels next to the bed and watches for the rise and fall of her chest. It moves, but barely, slow enough Asher can convince herself it's part of her imagination. As she reaches out to check for a pulse, her mother's eyes snap open.

"What are you doing?" she demands, going from unconscious to fully alert within a heartbeat, no hint of a slur in her words.

"Checking that you're alive," Asher stammers as if she's embarrassed. "Is everything okay?"

Her mother ignores the question. "Of course I'm alive. Don't be stupid."

They sit together in uncomfortable silence for long enough that Asher stops keeping track, mother lounging on her stained bed, daughter kneeling in the splash of wine on the wood laminate floor, until her mother speaks again. "Do you have a boyfriend yet? Your dad says you've been spending a lot of time with this boy recently."

"He's just a friend." Asher sighs at her father's betrayal. She and her mother seem to have a version of this conversation every six weeks, and the ending never changes. "I'm still into girls."

"I had a lot of girl friends when I was your age, but I ended up with a man."

"And I don't have a lot of girl friends, yet I'm still a lesbian."

Her mother scoffs. "No friends. No boyfriends. There must be something wrong with you."

Maybe there is. Maybe there's a diagnosis for her sobbing in bed because she can't figure out how to hold onto a friendship, and a prescription for her feeling as if she's wasting her teenage years trying to mould herself into someone she can never be, and a specialist for her pretending so hard to become a version of herself she can barely recognise that she's a shell of her former self.

Maybe there's a treatment for why she doesn't feel at home in her skin.

Maybe it's just the way she was made.

"Asher." Her mother crawls to the edge of the bed and grips her wrist with both hands in a way that Asher can almost interpret as motherly concern, if only the grip wasn't tight enough to leave a bruise. "Answer me."

Asher waves, eyes filling with tears as the grip tightens, fingernails digging into her skin. Her mother sees but doesn't soften. "I'm talking to you, and I expect you to answer me."

Asher has to get out. She has to do it before she falls apart, before the ugly little thing inside of her that resents her mother can escape. If her mother sees her break, she will never be left alone again. So, Asher speaks from the thin, angry place that barely conceals her hurt. "You're being ridiculous."

Her mother winces as if she's the one being hurt. "Excuse me?"

"And really insensitive. God, Mum, *of course* something is wrong with me. There's never been a time when something *hasn't* been wrong."

"That's not fair." Her mother's face is stricken. "That's not what I'm saying, and you know it."

"I'm going out. Please, just leave me alone."

Her mother laughs angrily. "I'm your mother, it doesn't work like that. *Hey.* Don't you make that face at me when I'm talking to you."

Asher rounds on her. "For fuck's sake, Mum, just *leave it.*"

Shock wipes her mother's face clean. Before she can

recover, Asher wrenches her arm free and rushes from the room, kicking up the rug behind her.

Outside, on the pavement, Asher comes apart. She ducks beneath the neighbour's hedge, shoves her face into her hands, and makes a sound that causes a horrible feeling in her throat she didn't know she was capable of, a scraping of confusion and guilt and sadness.

The ugly little thing inside of her rises like a wave. A horrible comprehension that is too vast, too frightening. She cringes from it, taking refuge in excuses: she's being paranoid. She's tired. She's sad and scared and *going through a lot.*

There's four weeks left until a list of grades in an envelope decides her academic fate, and fifty-six more days until she's run out of time to find J and save their letter writer, and fifty-five days until her eighteenth birthday and a court can allow her to live with her father full-time. She's going through a lot, but she only has to hold on for another two months until her life might start to make sense again.

Her hand slips into her pocket by instinct and she thumbs the edges of the tearstained letter. Still there. *Always* there. Still her greatest sadness.

If she can't figure out how to live her life for herself, then she'll just live it to save her writer.

TWENTY-TWO

"**D**o you think we need to write the letters anymore?"

Ryn lies with his head in Asher's lap, winding his earphone wire around his wrist like a friendship bracelet while she reads out loud from a book of fairy stories her grandmother once read to her. They debated the pros and cons of visiting the ruins again until Ryn decided the recent rain would've left the path even more waterlogged than before, so they caved to the horrors of small-town public transportation and headed to the beach instead. They climbed the cliff path together—the shoreline's closeness to the waves would be too loud for Asher to hear anything other than the water—and collapsed into the browning grass at the top.

Asher hums as she turns the page. "It's not like Jonathon wants proof that they exist or anything. He only wants to see people become friends, and I think we're friends at this point."

"I feel like he'd know somehow if we stopped writing them." He tries to make a joke to distract from the fact that Asher admitting that they're friends has sent his pulse skyrocketing. "He's got a sense for it."

"Then we'll write our July letters and hope he decides to end the activity soon."

Ryn nods in agreement. He closes his eyes against the glare of the sun and lets Asher's voice describing the book's illustrations soothe him to the brink of sleep. He clings on to the distant sound of waves as the constant soundtrack to his memories, inhaling the salty air until it burns his throat so he can remember the way that it tastes.

This time, he won't be gone for long enough to forget.

Asher reads to the end of a story, then Ryn hears her tuck a bookmark into the pages. One of her hands winds into his hair. "The letter I found is taking up so many of my thoughts that I don't think I can think about anything else anymore. I wish I knew how to stop them from feeling alone like that. The writer, I mean."

"Would that be your superpower?" Ryn asks, just to stop her from talking more about the letter. Just to stop himself from thinking about drowning.

There's a soft, wet sound, like Asher's chewing on her lip. "Would what be my superpower?"

"Stopping people feeling alone. Helping them. *Healing* them."

"I think I'd like to heal people," she agrees tentatively.

"Which people?"

"Everyone. *Anyone*," she corrects. "I'm not fussy. If I can stop someone from hurting, I want to do it."

Ryn laughs, mostly to himself. "That seems like a lot of responsibility that is going to make you more anxious than you already are."

She scoffs, but he doesn't think she's insulted by the words, just insulted that he's noticed. "What makes you think I'm anxious?"

He reaches up and pulls her hand out of his hair, brushing a finger against the chewed skin around her nails. The delicate latticework of her bones twitches beneath his touch. "Your nails scratch my scalp so they must be bitten down as far as they can go. And I hear you pick at the skin. And I think you clench your teeth a lot—something about the sound of you swallowing changes when you do it, and you seem to do it whenever you're stressed. Or anxious. Which is often. And—"

"You're observant."

"I listen. If I can tell, anyone with eyes should've figured out you're hiding something a long time ago." And then he asks, just to hear her answer: "Would you heal me?"

There's a quiet as she contemplates. Her hands return to his hair, twisting small sections together. "What about you needs healing?"

Her question is so sincere that Ryn almost sheds a tear. "I haven't decided yet." The half-healed skin beneath the scabs he scratched away from the edge of his eye stings as his face twitches into the semblance of a smile. "I'll let you know."

Asher traces a circle against his scalp, and then he feels her shift to sit up straighter as if she's trying to look over the edge of the cliff. She whistles the same melody as the wind and describes his beloved view to him.

The sea is calmer today than the sounds let on, and when the wind blows over the water, it ripples as far as the horizon, painting the surface with an effect like a brushstroke on canvas, Van Gogh textures before her eyes. Ryn thinks she's going to tell him more about the scenery, but then she says, "You never told me about your nightmare."

He remembers sending the message. He didn't think that she would remember receiving it. He can't wrap this side of himself up in a pretty little metaphor to make it more appealing to deal with, so he relies on his honesty.

"I fall asleep, and I start to sink," he begins, clawing a hand through the dead grass. "It begins with me standing in the tide pools at the beach near my old house, and there's a thickness to the air that feels like mist wrapping around my ankles and holding me in place. There's a seagull on a rock nearby, and I hear it pecking against some kind of shell or oyster or something, and each tap is a second closer to me drowning."

It's here when he wonders why he's telling her this, something he holds so sacred that he's only told one other person before. But he knows that there are some people you meet, and it already feels as if you've loved them for the entirety of your life, and he has to accept that

Asher is one of them, no matter how many unknowns still remain in their friendship. She is a permanent part of his life now, whether or not he wants it.

He swallows down his pride. "The tide comes in unnaturally fast, and I call for help, but no one comes. No one ever comes. The seagull keeps tapping, and the waves wash over my face, and I gasp, inhaling the ocean. I wake up soaked in so much sweat that it's like I've just been dragged out of the water."

"How do you know where you are? In the dream—*nightmare*—I mean," Asher asks as she weaves a section of his hair into a braid.

"It feels…familiar." He returns to the memory for a moment longer. "Like I've been there before. The smells and the sounds and the shadows that I can see are all the same."

And that's it. There's no danger in confession, no threat of rejection to press like a blade against his throat, another word and he could choke. Asher hums an acknowledgement, then she uses Ryn's head to prop up her book of fairy stories and continues reading from where she left off. His insecurities don't have to devour him anymore.

"How did I live for so long without knowing you?" he whispers to himself, quiet enough that he knows her hearing aids won't distinguish his voice from the wind. "How did I live without you?"

And then he thinks the obvious follow-up question: *Will you be able to live without me?*

TWENTY-THREE

Beneath the purple haze of the early morning sky, traffic lights flick from red to green. The high street is quiet and peppered with litter. The numbers on Asher's phone screen read 6:34.

She isn't sure how long she's been walking; it was dark when she stumbled out of the house, accidentally dropped her keys on the porch, and let the door lock itself behind her. Now, a hint of the sun slowly transforms the clouds—some kind of cirrus, she thinks—into faint pink streaks. More stray vehicles join her trek across the barren streets with each passing minute.

She'd been tossing and turning in the black molasses trap that is her bedroom for so long, overanalysing every photo and string of words and scrap of a clue that's trapped inside her search history, that she had to leave. She had to go. To go somewhere, anywhere, away from her laptop and online life and her ridiculous self-inflicted madness.

And now the town is so empty that she has to find thoughts to fill the silence before her imagination does instead, because she left both her earphones and her hearing aids behind, so all she can focus on truly is the silence.

Not for the first time, she wishes she had more friends.

Because she's told Ryn about the letter, and she's getting the vibe that he doesn't want to be involved in her little mystery, so she's officially run out of people in her life that she's comfortable sharing that kind of secret with. She's noticed how she hasn't texted anyone other than Ryn since the spring and wonders if the timestamps on her unread messages from the year before are the defining moment of when those old friendships drew to an end.

Asher walks aimlessly for the next hour or so until she's surely completed a circuit of the entire town, but once a location has settled on her shoulders, she knows it's inevitable.

She doesn't need her phone to map the way for her. She's overthought the location enough that the exact spot where she first found the letter has been committed to memory. It's near Ryn's house, at an intersection of streets where he would go right to go home, and she'd go left to her mother's house or straight on to her father's. It's a random spot on an insignificant residential street that's become oh-so-important to her.

She stands over the pothole that once held the letter and now holds the remnants of a puddle—dirt and water and no new scrap of paper. A weird- looking bug crawls out of a crack. She takes a photo of it to identify later.

And she once again remembers that she hasn't read Ryn's first letter. She's not even sure where it is anymore, if it's still buried in her rucksack from when she intended to read it and read the tearstained one instead, if she's stuck it to her bedroom wall as part of her shrine to him without opening the envelope.

She tears her gaze away from the former puddle and crosses the road, passing a few houses until she's stood by Ryn's gate. She looks up at the upstairs windows and tries to recall if his bedroom overlooks the street, remembering the room being streaked with sunlight, but no other context clues come to mind.

She pulls out her phone and sends a message to Ryn.

ASHER
are u awake?? sorry it's early

Asher looks up at the windows, as if the curtains will twitch open and Ryn will come out to meet her. They don't twitch open. He doesn't come out to meet her.

She sends another message.

ASHER
i'm near ur house
can i come over

'Near' is an understatement.

There's no reply. *Of course* there's no reply, it's barely eight in the morning, but she doesn't want to be alone right now, so she scrolls through her contacts list and looks for someone else to wake up.

Ryn's awake.

He's lying on his bedroom floor, dissecting, trying to pull out the remains of the scared child inside of him. Flat fragments of a past life consume every bad night, and this one is no different.

He awoke with the sunrise, soaked in sweat, arms coated with scratches as he tried to claw his way to the surface in his sleep. The scratches on his face have barely healed from when he tried to claw his eye out, and now he's mutilated himself again, soon to be more blood than body. He wonders how many more mornings out of his remaining fifty-three—or is it fifty-two now?— he'll wake with his hands wet and smelling like rust.

The drowning will end soon.

His grounding techniques can't save him now, no amount of counting light and shadows and salt on skin will pull him out of the depths of his blue haze.

He assumes that someone will have to pull his body out of the water in order to officially pronounce him dead, and he pities his father, who will be the one to identify his bloated corpse unless Ryn can make it clear in a letter beforehand that he will definitely not be alive by the time they look for him. For that reason, he'll make two sets of requests—one involving his body, and one involving a photograph.

The only photograph he'll take in recent memory.

Not of the ocean.

But of himself.

On his very last day.

And he'll smile.

Smile like he's oblivious.

Because he needs to control this down to the very last detail, and that most definitely includes what they have to remember him by.

They.

Just *they*.

Ryn feels like perhaps he doesn't care enough.

His phone vibrates with what he assumes is a text from Asher, but he doesn't check. He's told himself that he can't reply until he's found a way to pass whatever *this* is off as one of his blue moods, rapidly increasing in frequency. He'll see her tomorrow, and by then he'll have thought of a way to talk around the situation until she can fill in the blanks with whatever she finds most appropriate.

But he does answer his phone when it plays a ringtone that's designated to only one person.

"You're coming home this weekend," his mother says instead of a greeting.

"I'm already home," Ryn mutters, but he knows it means nothing to her. "What do you want?"

"It's your nanna's birthday on Saturday and we're having a party. The whole family will be there, so they are expecting you to be there too."

Ryn groans at the reminder that he has an extended family, and it's not even a family he particularly dislikes. They just have a very two-dimensional view of his disability and his gender and whatever's going on in his brain, and they don't take too kindly to being informed. They don't seem to grasp that he wasn't always a son/grandson/nephew, but he is now, and that one of his eyeballs is still in his head, although not functioning in a traditional way, because that doesn't match their view of blindness, and that he doesn't smile on command anymore.

"Are you listening to me? What did I just say to you?"

"Nanna's birthday." Ryn struggles to remember what she was saying before his thoughts took over. "Everyone's going. I get it."

His mother huffs at his tone. "You need to text me in the morning when you leave so I know you're actually coming. I'll tell your dad to drive you to stop you from being late. Dress presentably."

And then she ends the call.

So now he has Nanna's birthday to get through. And maybe two or three more therapy sessions, and surely a check-in with his doctor's recommended psychiatrist. And at least a month to spend trying to ease Asher and Luke out of his life. And time to take his photo, and to leave a note for his body—or ashes—to be returned to the ocean after it's been pulled out.

And, just like that, he has a plan.

By midday, the purple haze of the morning sky has cleared, a kind of cloud-free bright blue that rarely comes to this part of the country. The streets are still near empty; a car putters along the road and disappears around a bend, but other than that no one is out. Asher's sitting on her father's doorstep and can see an older lady across the street peering through the curtains at her and making cursory window cleaning gestures with a cloth as she stares, like that isn't totally creepy. Asher does a little finger wave at her, and the curtains swirl shut immediately.

A blue Toyota Yaris that looks dangerously close to falling apart idles to a stop outside of Asher's house, and she waves at the driver before climbing inside.

"Oh my God, Ash, your *makeup*," Jocelyn gasps as Asher sinks into her passenger seat.

Usually when going outside, Asher tries to look as much like herself as possible, but she is in a delicate mood and struggling to care about anything other than the tearstained letter and her unanswered text messages, so instead she tried to look like Jocelyn. She fights the urge to cover her face and smudge her already-smudged eyeliner even further.

"Is that an 'Oh my God, you look absolutely ridiculous'?" Asher asks, putting on her seatbelt. "Because that's an understandable reaction."

"No, I mean, I didn't know you were so…*goth* outside of therapy. But you're not actually a goth, are you?" She appears to be genuine.

Asher looks down at her secondhand sundress. It's yellow, faded from too many trips to the washing machine. She embroidered orange triangles along the hem last summer to cover up an unidentifiable stain that wouldn't come out, and the thread is looking a little worse for wear by now. She shrugs.

They drive out of town. Asher inspects Jocelyn's outfit out of the corner of her eye, committing it to memory: an unseasonably warm black and white plaid jacket, battered Converse that must've seen almost as many years as she has, distressed shorts, and ripped tights. Effortlessly cool, like the girl at the front row of some obscure indie concert. Unintentionally cool, in the way that Asher craves.

They wind through country lanes and reach the dual carriageway, and this is when Asher regrets sending the message to ask Jocelyn to hang out. With one hand, Jocelyn fumbles with the radio buttons, digs her phone out of her shorts pocket, and plugs it into the aux. Music blares from the car speakers. Asher is assaulted by a wall of noise. She tries to concentrate on the song until she can think of something worth saying, but the sounds twist in a very specific way, and she's suddenly struck with a nostalgia so vivid for a summer far away from this one that she can't form any words.

The song sounds like a memory from her hometown, from before her mother moved them to a dissimilar near-coastal town, one where the sea is always covered by the cloud-choked horizon. It's from the year of the eternal heat wave where she sweat off the song lyrics scrawled across the backs of her hands, and endless afternoons spent beneath red cliffs, and saturated sunrises captured on Polaroid film with her finger blurring the lens.

Asher thought the memories were trapped half a decade deep in her camera roll, never to be seen again, but now they're trapped in music instead; the song sounds like a version of herself that she can't return to anymore.

"Who's this?" she yells over the music to tear herself away from her thoughts. "The song that's playing."

She doesn't catch whatever Jocelyn says in response, but she pretends she does. She doesn't imagine asking her to repeat will make her any easier to hear, so all she does say is, "It's cool."

"It's my favourite album of theirs." Jocelyn pulls into the outside lane for reasons that Asher can't identify. Besides them, the road is almost as empty as the town was at sunrise. "What's your driving music?"

"I can't drive. I can't afford it, and I'm not even sure if I'm allowed to." Asher picks at her embroidered hemline as if it'll make the confession any easier to bear. She winds a loose thread around her finger and forces herself to think of the repair rather than all of the ways she and Jocelyn are different.

Jocelyn ignores the second half of the sentence. "Get a job. I worked forty hours a week last summer to save up for this thing." She pats her fuzzy steering wheel cover affectionately. "I'm the fifth kid so it's not like my parents could afford to get me one, and I *needed* a car. Seriously. Need to get out of town sometimes."

"Where did you work?"

"Spoons. Some of the customers are"—Asher thinks Jocelyn says 'rude as shit' here, but she can't confirm—"but the pay was okay."

"Fair enough."

Jocelyn turns the music up. Asher turns fully sideways in her seat and lip-reads Jocelyn's profile to the best of her ability. "Yeah, this band, they're almost the same age as us. I think that's why I like the music so much. Or I just feel like I've done nothing with my life."

"It sounds like you're in space," Asher muses, and not just because her hearing makes everything sound like she's on another planet. "Or some kind of city in the future where everything is dark blue and glowing, and everyone is floating around, and you're living on a spaceship."

Jocelyn looks at her, almost swerving back into the acceptable lane in the process. "You're a proper little storyteller."

Asher laughs, and she's not pretending this time. "I guess. Until I die."

The music suddenly increases in volume. Jocelyn shifts between gears and finally commits to moving out of the outside lane.

"I really like this," Asher half-lies, tapping the radio display.

"What?" Jocelyn says. The music is too loud.

Asher just laughs again and shakes her head. Jocelyn shoots her a confused grin. God, Asher barely knows her, but somehow here she is, having a vague hint of a good time. The dual carriageway stretches out before them, bright blue sky and endless white lines. It blurs past them like a time vortex.

An hour later, the dual carriageway fades into a minor city street, and Jocelyn peels off the road to find a car park. Asher pays for the ticket. Jocelyn walks through the streets with the familiarity of someone who visits often, so Asher trails behind her like a child, taking photos on her phone of graffiti that catches her eye. As they weave between buildings, Jocelyn talks about how this minor city hosts a university campus for a neighbouring major city, and how she and her friends sneak into the student union to attend open mic events.

"They make it look like a real club and everything, even if it's a daytime event," Jocelyn boasts, and Asher starts emotionally preparing for the most unpleasant few hours of her week. "It's dark and loud and full of people, and sometimes they don't bother checking your ID at the bar."

This afternoon, Jocelyn's ex-boyfriend is performing some original songs, and she seems proud that they're still friends, even if she invited a hoard of non-mutual friends for support. She tells Asher about him until they approach a squat concrete building emblazoned with a university logo, and a group of people that must be Jocelyn's extended friend group wave from inside the doors. Asher can hear the music pulsing from here.

She smiles weakly as a dozen different people introduce themselves over the music and pull her and Jocelyn toward their table. She's too overwhelmed to admit that she feels lost, or that she experiences this deep ache in her soul whenever she can hear so many sounds at once but they all sound as loud and indistinct as each other. It reminds her of a few years back, when learning to lip-read made her want to cry with frustration, and when other deaf kids chatted amongst themselves, she was too new at signing to follow. Suddenly, there seemed to be no conversations where she belonged, and that has barely changed over the years.

Then the room plummets into darkness as another singer takes the stage, and Asher loses any grasp she thought she had on the introductions. She sinks into her seat next to Jocelyn, watching as the other girl becomes lost in the music, and she allows the sounds to wash over herself as she fights against her racing heart.

It's a beautiful moment, Asher thinks, this girl in on the stage lit by a single spotlight, only her and her keyboard for accompaniment. Her fingers shake as she works her way through a lengthy instrumental piece and her eyes are locked on her hands rather than the audience. As she pauses at the end of her first piece, she takes a deep breath, and then she sings. Asher can't decipher the lyrics, but she knows that the girl's voice is one of the prettiest things she's ever heard.

She looks around at the strings of fairy lights and neon signs and a shimmering disco ball that illuminate the room, and she thinks, *Ryn would like this*, but she must've said it aloud during a quiet moment after the girl finished her final song, because Jocelyn looks at her as if she's interrupting something.

Asher tries to speak, tries to apologise for whatever mistake she's made, but then someone walks onto the stage, and the people around her burst into thunderous applause, so she can only assume that the next performer is Jocelyn's ex-boyfriend. Jocelyn leans her elbows on the table and rests her chin on her fists, watching him with an intensity that Asher can't understand. He's an average guy. Average height and average build and average shaggy brown hair. His clothes are unremarkable—blue jeans and black trainers and crisp white T-shirt—and, although his lyrics are more decipherable than the previous girl, they say nothing to Asher.

Jocelyn taps her shoulder and mouths, *What do you think?* during one of the songs, and Asher smiles a polite tight-lipped smile and mouths back, *It's great.* Jocelyn smiles as if she's won a contest.

The ex-boyfriend's performance seems to last twice as long as the girl with the keyboard's, and Asher is resisting the urge to intentionally interrupt something. She decides to text Ryn, phone beneath the table to disguise the light. She doubts he'll reply. Maybe he won't even read it. But she wants to talk to him all the same.

At the end of the performance, Asher glances over at Jocelyn and finds her in the same position as she was at the start, blinking slowly as if in deep thought. And then a tear drips down from the corner of her eye.

"That was sad," Jocelyn murmurs. "That was really sad."

Asher doesn't say anything.

"He's been writing these songs for months. He wrote one recently. Even after we broke up…he was calling out for me."

Jocelyn closes her eyes.

Asher sends another message to Ryn.

The next performer steps onto the stage, but Asher can't even pretend to pay attention anymore. Jocelyn snaps out of her trance to whisper to a nearby friend whose name Asher can't remember, and Asher decides to look up bus times. It'll take close to two hours and three bus changes to make it home, but she'll survive. It'll be better than being back in Jocelyn's car, the overwhelmingly loud music a welcome distraction to whatever tensions are now brewing between them. But then Jocelyn sees her phone screen, grabs Asher's wrist, and says, "I'm driving you home," with such enthusiasm that Asher can't say no.

They spend the car ride in silence, Jocelyn counting down exits on the dual carriageway, Asher counting down minutes until she can be alone.

TWENTY-FOUR

Asher concludes that her date—if you could even call it that—with Jocelyn went awfully. So awfully, in fact, that when Jocelyn dropped her off on her father's doorstep a few hours after they left, Asher went into her bedroom and didn't come out until the next morning, and by then Ryn had replied to her messages and decided to spend his day sprawled out on her floor.

She lies down beside him with her fairytale book tucked against her chest and presses her cheek into his shoulder. He jolts out of his all-encompassing spiral so fast it's like he's coming up for air. Asher pretends that his anxiety isn't visible as he takes in a quick breath. Another. *Keep it together.*

Asher can sense that a story won't be enough to fix this. She looks around her room for the next distraction: curled-up paint tubes in primary colours, loose sheets of lined paper she saves for writing letters, a tangle of cables that may or may not consist entirely of extinct phone chargers.

Her eyes drift back toward the yellow paint tube.

The hint of an idea starts to form.

She leaves Ryn on the floor and heads downstairs without a word. In the cupboard beneath the stairs, she rummages for the can of dandelion yellow paint her father once used to paint the exterior of the greenhouse. It reflected so much sunlight that she was blinded as soon as she set foot in the garden, so together they repainted it to be a sensible muted green. She successfully loots a pair of paint rollers, a handful of wide, flat brushes that have seen better days, and what she thinks is a tray for the paint, then carries her haul back upstairs..

Ryn's sitting cross-legged on the floor when she returns. "Where did you go?"

"I want to paint my walls," she announces as if that's an answer, arranging the supplies around him. She takes his hand and presses a paint roller into his palm. "No skill involved. Just cover the whole lot in colours."

He doesn't move, but his fingers curl around the roller handle. "I'm not an artist."

"Neither am I." She pours some of the paint into the tray and pushes it in Ryn's direction until it knocks against his knees. Paint sluices over the sides and onto the rug in yellow globs. She decides that the next step in her bedroom decoration will be a replacement that is washing machine friendly. "It's easy. You just get some paint and slap it on the wall."

In demonstration, she douses a brush in paint and fans the bristles along the skirting board. Colour drips down onto her floor like acid rain. Ryn fights a wince at the sound. "Van Gogh just rolled over in his grave."

Asher bites down on her smile. She swipes her brush into the shape of a heart. "Let's go. If I'm painting, you're painting."

He couldn't refuse her even if he wanted to. Scowling, he wets his roller and barely makes contact with the wall as he drags it along. A thin swath of yellow appears like a sunbeam. He tilts his head toward Asher for approval, and she makes a noise of content. "Are you happy with this?"

She beams at him, eyes bright, her cheeks already speckled with paint like pollen. "Ecstatic," she assures him, flicking her bristles so his cheeks are speckled too. He flicks her back and misses, but she laughs as if his aim was true.

"I used to want to be an artist when I grew up," Ryn says. His hand drops to his side, and paint drips onto his sock-clad feet. "I wanted to create a real masterpiece, contribute something to the art world that would make someone feel the same way about a painting that I did."

"What changed?" Asher asks.

Ryn sighs. He paints the wall as he talks, more confident this time. "I learned that the great artists aren't remembered because of one piece in particular; they're remembered because they kept on making, and making, and making."

"'Perseverance is greater than genius,'" Asher quotes. "That's something one of my art teachers used to say. I think she was implying that you can't have a body of work if you don't finish making anything, and I'm not known for finishing things."

Ryn nods. "And if one singular piece in those bodies of work stands out, it's only because human nature reduces everything to its simplest components. Most people think of Van Gogh and imagine the swirls and the stars and the blue rather than any of his other works."

Asher hums. She tries to nudge Ryn back toward his point. "So, what changed?"

"One day I woke up and I didn't want to make anything anymore."

They work in silence after that, Ryn covering most of the wall with his roller, Asher crouching at his feet to correct the paint-related crime she committed to the skirting board, then standing on her desk chair to catch the spots he can't reach. The heat-related crimes committed by Asher's stuffy bedroom leave their skin shiny with sweat and hair sticking to their foreheads. Her incoming migraine hasn't just been induced by the paint fumes. She excuses herself to change into a vest top and shorts in the bathroom. Ryn looks like he wishes he could peel his skin off.

"Do you want to change into anything less sweaty?" Asher asks him. "I might have some old T-shirts that'll fit you."

His hand rests on his chest, and he picks at the

neckline of his binder, and Asher realises that the issue is more than just the heat. "I'll survive," he says unconvincingly.

Asher pushes her window open wider as if it'll make a difference. The breeze remains stubbornly nonexistent.

They've nearly run out of paint by the time an abstract amount of two walls has been yellowed and Asher summons the courage to ask Ryn a question.

"Would medically transitioning help?" There's an awkward pause before she recognises that her question doesn't align with the trails of their previous conversation, and she remembers that she doesn't actually know if Ryn's gender journey is yet to contain medical intervention. "I mean, I've read that one of the hardest parts of being transgender is the body dysphoria, and I think I understand what that means now, and I was wondering if changing what your body looks like helps how you feel even if you can't see the changes."

He stops painting. Asher turns to him in time to see his jaw clench. She realises a moment too late that he hasn't come out to her, not yet. There's a moment where he seems defensive until he remembers that she's his friend and there's no malice in her question, not like there is when her mother comments on her stretch marks. He lifts and drops one shoulder in a shrug that's too casual. She recognises it. It's hiding behind carelessness because having feelings means coming undone.

"I thought transitioning in general would be easier," Ryn says slowly, still turning the question over in his mind. His roller falls into the paint tray. "I thought it would be easy. I thought that knowing that I am a boy would be easy because I don't have enough vision left to see how much I don't look how I want to."

You look just like your dad, Asher wants to tell him, but she isn't sure if it'll be a comfort. Her quiet encourages him to continue.

"When I was sure that my mum wasn't coming back, I got my hair cut how I wanted and started wearing the clothes that I liked and convinced my dad to entertain the idea of me going on puberty blockers, and I started to feel right for a while. But then the weather is too warm, and my binder starts chafing, and I'm all too aware that I can feel that something is wrong inside of me. I know that I'm not in the right body."

"Are the hormones and surgeries something you want?" Asher asks, and she makes a mental note to research what the surgeries entail. Hearing about them secondhand from the social media accounts of former friends of friends is the extent of her knowledge at the moment.

"Top surgery would at least mean I don't feel the need to wear a binder in this fucking heat."

Ryn collapses onto her rug, curling up in a sunbeam like a cat, and the light burns his hair golden like a halo. Asher doesn't tell him that he looks like an angel. Instead, she drops her brush alongside his roller in the paint tray and lies down beside him. She watches his profile until a cloud passes in front of the sun, and he doesn't look so much like an angel anymore, just a boy sprawled out on her bedroom floor.

She rolls onto her side toward him. "I know we see each other most days now, but you should definitely come over Saturday night. A neighbour down the street is having a barbecue and fireworks, and my dad is going, but I can sneak over and steal some food, and we can stay at home and watch, if you want."

"I'd like that." He hums her usual melody as he thinks. "I have to go to some family thing during the day, at least I think it's during the day, but I'll be there for food and fireworks."

And maybe Asher's being too pushy, maybe she's being the right amount to show that she cares, when she says, "And you can stay over tonight if you want. You seem sad, and I don't want you to be alone."

Ryn laughs. "You want to have a sleepover so you can check on me?"

She owns it. "Yes. You were sad when you got here, and you're still sad, so I clearly have more work to do."

"Fair enough," he says with a smile, then he crawls onto her bed and buries his face in her pillows. "Tell me how good the walls look."

Asher describes in detail the monstrosity of the paintwork surrounding the skirting board, and they spend the rest of the afternoon sat at either end of her bed, him playing her songs he thinks she'll like and her drawing him over and over again in the gaps of her sketchbook. After sunset, she makes him a bed of blankets on the floor, but he falls asleep on her shoulder watching a film she'll never remember, and she doesn't nudge him awake until sunrise.

Maybe this is what love is, Asher thinks as the sky starts to lighten.

Love doesn't come easily to her, she knows. To her, it's alien, nothing more than a plotline made up for one of her stories, painful and slightly out of reach after a childhood of flinching at the sound of a door. It's learning something new every day. To love and be loved. And each time she feels that she loves Ryn (a warmth blossoming in the pit of her stomach), she believes she's capable of it a little more.

Because maybe love isn't just what she's seen on a screen and disbelieved, scenes of climbing out of windows at night to steal kisses and learning the names of stars that suddenly become easier to touch after the sound of an 'I love you' and sometimes more. She thought she studied love enough that it wouldn't hurt her again one day, but now she feels unmoored by the speed at which she's lost sight of her preteen beliefs. She thought she knew better. But is it not better, giving in to the current and allowing herself to become swept away?

Because maybe love doesn't have to be anything more than your best friend by your side, with you holding your breath so they can sleep undisturbed with their head resting on your shoulder.

TWENTY-FIVE

Asher nudges Ryn awake at sunrise so she can regain some of the feeling in her arm, then falls back asleep until long after her father has left for work and Ryn has ventured downstairs to figure out breakfast, and she wakes to the smell of something burning.

"Ryn Middle Name Last Name," she says as she launches herself down the stairs and into the kitchen. "What are you doing to my— Wait, why don't I know your surname?"

"Last names are boring," Ryn says nonchalantly, and Asher's glad she took out her hearing aids during the night because she knows the fire alarm is screaming at them, and she can't remember how to make it stop.

He hands her a plate of blackened toast. She takes a seat at the kitchen table and rests her head on the cool surface. A stray crumb sticks to her forehead. "Okay. What's your middle name?"

"I...I don't know yet." He puts more bread in the toaster, and Asher pretends she doesn't notice his hands shaking. "My birth name doesn't come up much anymore unless Mum phones me, and I haven't even thought about picking a new middle name."

Asher takes a bite of the toast and quietly slides the plate away from her until she can find an appropriately subtle moment to take it out to the compost bin. "Choosing you a new middle name is second on our agenda for the day," she says, standing to open the fridge and survey its contents. Milk. Eggs. A reusable container brimming with an undetermined substance. Butter. All of the essentials. "First on the agenda is breakfast."

She changes the settings on the toaster to something less lethal, cracks a pair of eggs into a pan, and cooks until she constructs the illusion of an edible breakfast. They sit across from each other at the kitchen table and eat to the soundtrack of the fire alarm. Ryn's not wearing his sunglasses—thinking about it, Asher's not sure if he's worn them around her in weeks, and she warms with pride that he seems comfortable enough around her to reveal his scars—and she becomes aware of how much he looks at her.

"What's on your necklace?" He squints at her chest, and she resists the urge to adjust her neckline. "It looks shiny. My mum used to have a round charm on her necklace with her initial on it."

Asher tugs at the charm on her necklace and resents the initial for haunting her entire life. "It is a round one with an initial on it."

"But not your initial," he notes.

Asher swallows. "No."

"What is it?"

"It's a *J.*"

"Like J from your letter?"

"Like my dead best friend, J. Like Julia."

The silence between them would've been tolerable if the fire alarm didn't choose that moment to stop blaring. Then, cautiously, Ryn says, "I'm sorry." He picks at the crust of his toast. "Can you tell me about her?"

Asher sighs, her heart in her throat. "She died from— No, I don't want to tell you what she did. It's not who she was. It's like when someone talks about some random celebrity and just saying how they died, rather than a legacy that they built. She's so much more than that."

"You don't need to tell me about how she died," Ryn says gently as they steer into uncharted territory. "Tell me something happy about her."

"I wouldn't even know where to start." But she does. She's thought about telling Julia's story every day since it ended. "She died the summer before we both turned fourteen, so I blew out my candles alone and pretended she had never existed so I could go back to school and act like nothing was wrong, like I was the only one who had lost somebody. But I remember her every day. I see pieces of her in every person I meet. Her hugs felt like coming home, and I got jealous of anyone that made her smile brighter than I could, and I missed her even when she was right next to me. Her love was the only stable thing I had in my life for years, especially when my hearing started to go. And when she went, the rest of our friend group did too."

"It sounds like you might've been her one constant," Ryn comments as he shovels a forkful of scrambled eggs into his mouth, his previous attempt at breakfast forgotten. Asher takes a break in her story to watch his reaction to her cooking. He chews, swallows, then goes in for another bite. That's good enough for her.

She returns to remembering her first best friend. "She once wrote me a letter saying that I saved her life, that I *kept her alive* with my love and overall disregard for the worst parts in her, as if I was blind to them. She had a way of acting like we were the only people left on Earth who mattered, and she did it in a way where I almost believed her. But then she changed overnight, and she became elusive and unpredictable, and I didn't know how to love her anymore." And then, quietly, as if it's a confession: "I guess we found out what happens to someone's life when you're sick of saving it."

Asher twirls the necklace charm between her fingers. She can't believe she'd almost forgotten that moment from her past, those months of badness turning years of good sick with sadness. Though she had never gone out of her way to remember her resentment toward her best friend in those final months, she thought she had remembered enough to keep Julia as a full and complete and perfect person in her head.

But she *had* forgotten; she hadn't even known

something was missing until Ryn brought it back to her.

What other memories have gone astray? What other scars have healed over and vanished because she simply chose to not remember them anymore?

Ryn interrupts her thoughts. "It's not your responsibility to keep someone alive, no matter how much you love them," he says, finishing his toast. "You're supposed to be their friend, not their saviour, not anything else."

Asher sits in the heaviness between them, contemplating Ryn's words, agonising over her next. The lump in her throat grows larger, and she knows she's running out of time to confess before her throat closes entirely.

Julia was the other half of her soul, and she can't keep pretending that that part of her life never existed. Not anymore, when she sits across from a boy who shares Julia's freckles and her laugh and her gentle hands and understands Asher more than anyone else ever has. Well, almost everyone.

Because Julia hasn't been replaced, but her loss doesn't define Asher's life anymore.

"Maybe I was in love with her. Maybe I just loved her. I don't know if it matters," she whispers so softly she's not sure if the words are audible as the bravery leaves her body. "She's the main reason why I want to heal people, so I can help them when I couldn't bear to help her anymore. I want to change the world so I can feel like I'm doing something right for once."

"Is that why you say your necklace is haunted?" Ryn

asks with a tenderness in his voice that she hasn't heard before. "I mean, I think it's the same necklace."

Asher lets out a laugh so loud she hopes it conceals the fact that it is veering toward a sob. "It's definitely haunted. The house still keeps me up at night because it's just so fucking *creepy*, and it was worse when we first moved in because I didn't know it was creepy yet. And then I was so upset for weeks, as I didn't want to unpack out of spite and couldn't work out which box Julia's necklace was in, so I cried and cried and cried, but then I woke up the next morning and it was just sitting there on my windowsill, like she'd been listening."

But maybe the house wasn't always haunted, she's forced to admit. Maybe she brought the ghosts with her.

She doesn't realise she's crying until Ryn's hand slips into her own and his thumbnail scratches circles into her palm. "How can we change the world?"

She notices his use of 'we,' not 'you' or 'I.'

He continues. "We don't have to change it forever. Just for a night. Or an hour."

"Or a moment," she suggests.

"Or a moment," he agrees. "What's the probability of changing it forever?"

She pretends to do the math, squeezing his hand and audibly counting on his fingers in a way she knows will make him laugh. "Improbable."

"But not impossible."

"It's not impossible," Asher says reluctantly.

"So how should we do it?"

They form a plan over their cold eggs and toast, Asher still silently crying over her plate and Ryn still scratching circles into her palm. Her head drops to the table when a migraine creeps into the edges of her vision, and then Ryn roams through her house in an attempt to find a cabinet that houses painkillers until Asher reminds him of her dad's 'herbs and hopeful thinking' mindset. They talk about changing their prophecies until her dad returns home and hovers in the doorway for a few moments before either of them notices.

Later, Asher wonders if he saw himself and her mother in them, a refraction of a relic from his memories, a girl and boy sat across from each other at the kitchen table like a scene from the end of his relationship. A scene from the moment his life changed, acted out by his daughter and someone who might as well be her other half, illuminated by the still-open fridge door.

TWENTY-SIX

When Ryn enters his new psychiatrist's office the next afternoon, she makes him rate his emotions on a scale from one to ten. The routine is almost familiar to him by now, no matter who is conducting it: rank his anxious and depressive tendencies on a numbered scale, say he has no thoughts about harming himself, and convince the psychiatrist that his life may be tough but he has no desire to end it.

"What are some of your current coping mechanisms?" she asks when they've finished the cursory questions. "Is there anything you do that helps you feel happier during a spell of low mood?"

"I write a lot of letters," he says after a too-long pause, because he doesn't think that *"I spend all of my free time hanging out with my borderline codependent new best friend"* has the same ring to it.

The silence from his psychiatrist implies that she is pondering the logistics of a blind boy writing, so he says to get it over and done with, "I dictate them to my phone, and my phone writes it down for me. I can still handwrite stuff with guidelines to keep me on the page, and I can sign my name, even if I can't really remember what most of the letters look like anymore, but I can write."

"Ah," his psychiatrist says, and Ryn decides that this first appointment will be their last.

The rest of the appointment returns to the routine he's used to, making lists of coping mechanisms that do and don't work, and the negative thoughts that haunt him as he's falling asleep, and three things he's going to pretend to try before the next appointment that he thinks could trigger a crumb of serotonin. A routine that he's gone through so many times and is still waiting for its effects to show. Because the only therapy he's received a positive impact from so far seems to be Jonathon's fortnightly group, and that's purely because it eventually brought Asher into his life.

And now he needs to find a way to remove her from it before he runs out of time.

Because it's the last day of July, and he has thirty-one days left before his deadline.

He holds back tears as the psychiatrist talks through date and time options for their next appointment, and he noncommittally chooses the third one she suggests, noting that this is the kind of therapy where sessions are offered once every six weeks.

Suddenly, thirty-one days doesn't seem like enough time. Pain has its own rules. He doesn't get to choose what breaks him. There's no wrong way to feel, but he's facing the consequences of his own decisions.

Ryn thanks the psychiatrist and says goodbye as calmly and evenly as he can manage, then falls apart the moment she closes the door behind him. He slumps down into the plastic chair in the waiting room and cries himself into exhaustion as he hears people walk around him at arm's length, then adjusts his sunglasses to cover his bloodshot eye and blotchy cheeks and heads outside to face his father.

At the end of the day, appearances are all he has to keep him going.

"Can you show me some of your stories?"

Jocelyn is sprawled across Asher's bed—the bed at her mother's house, because something about her dad's seems too sacred for this early on in a friendship, and she's still trying to make a point to her mother that she has friends—and she's spent such a high percentage of the hour she's been there scrolling on her phone that Asher forgot that hanging out with your friends usually involves some kind of conversation.

"Huh?" Asher says, you know, like an intellectual. She spins in her desk chair to face Jocelyn and tries to decipher how serious the request is.

"Show me some of your stories," Jocelyn repeats as a command rather than a question. "You agreed in my car that you're a storyteller, and I want to read what you have to say."

Asher suppresses the full body cringe that comes with the reminder of being in Jocelyn's car and the events that came after. She can't think about it right now. "Um. Okay. I guess I can find something good."

She spins back toward her desk and begins the Sisyphean task of finding a piece of writing that shows off her talent as a writer yet says nothing about her as a person. There are expansive unfinished fantasies and subtle near-complete attempts at mysteries and an infinite number of documents that are titled with a keyboard slam and boast only the first paragraph of something she is yet to decide.

And then there's the tentative beginnings of a story that's definitely not loosely inspired by her and Ryn, titled 'Best Friend DRAFT 1' until the plot pulls itself together and she can think of something more suitable. It's vulnerable, sure, but it's a love letter to the complexities of their disabilities and the wrong ways to be okay and how new friendships change your world overnight, and it's just abstract enough in the emotions that maybe Jocelyn won't catch on to how autobiographical it is.

She double-clicks on 'Best Friend DRAFT 1,' turns her laptop screen around to face Jocelyn, and then wheels herself in her chair to the other side of her bedroom. To distract herself from overthinking every twitch of

Jocelyn's jaw and each blink of her eyes, Asher sends a message to Ryn.

ASHER
Jocelyn's reading my stories and i don't know what to do with myself 😳

Ryn's response is near immediate.

RYN
Can I read your stories?

ASHER
NO.

RYN
Why not? Jocelyn is reading them.

ASHER
i can't say no to pretty girls apparently

ASHER
and u know too much about me anyway

RYN
Crying face emoji.

RYN
Ignore that.

RYN
😟

RYN
Is she enjoying them so far?

Asher looks up and caves in to overanalysing Jocelyn's micro expressions. Relaxed eyebrows. Lips curved into the hint of a smile. No tension in her jaw. The one psychology class she took before changing to English Literature doesn't imply there are any bad thoughts behind Jocelyn's eyes.

ASHER

i think so. it does feel like she's reading my diary tho

RYN

I want to meet her but properly this time.

Asher reflects on their previous meetings. The first was in the supermarket, thrown across the floor post–trolley crash, and Jocelyn clearly knew who Ryn was before he was introduced. The second was in group therapy where he was sat in a trance the entire time and they didn't exchange a word. Maybe not the best first impressions, ignoring how Jocelyn already knew him, but she can help him out with a redo.

ASHER

i'll invite u both to my birthday party as a distraction from my relatives

Whether or not her birthday party will be a celebration is still up for debate, depending on if she can find out the identity of her mysterious letter writer, but she doesn't remind him about it. He clearly has enough going on right now, and he doesn't need the threat of a stranger's suicide to add to it.

Asher looks back to Jocelyn. She ignores Ryn's message saying that he'll save the date and watches Jocelyn reach the end of 'Best Friend DRAFT 1.' When she closes the document, Asher wheels herself back across the room.

"I found a letter recently," Asher says before Jocelyn has the chance to give her feedback, rummaging in her pocket for the letter, "and I was wondering if you could take a look at it and tell me if anything seems familiar."

Jocelyn takes the letter—now more scrap than paper—and reads the words, faded to near nonexistence by Asher's touch. She reaches the end, takes a deep breath, and then reads it again, her lips forming the shape of the words as she processes their meaning. When she reaches the end again, she tucks the letter into Asher's outstretched hand and folds her fingers closed around it.

"It's so sad," Jocelyn says slowly. "Where did you find it?"

Asher retells the story, her walk to school disrupted on a random street and her hiding in a toilet cubicle to read it. Jocelyn asks the right questions, and she adds supportive comments in the right places, and Asher can't tell if she's blinded by her crush or just the addition of genuine concern to her life.

"So, what are we going to do about it?" Jocelyn asks.

For the second time in two days, Asher notices the use of 'we,' not 'you' or 'I.'

"I've been trying to track down J on social media with obviously no luck," Asher explains, conveniently missing out the fact that Jocelyn's friends were her primary suspects. "I'm not sure what else to do without having to report it to someone. I don't think getting the police involved would end well for anyone."

"You're right," Jocelyn agrees. She hums to herself then opens her notes app, furiously typing what Asher interprets as a list from her upside-down perspective. "And you're sure that you want to find this person instead of, like, pretending you never found the letter and forgetting about it?"

"I want to find them," Asher confirms. Her grip tightens on the letter. She *needs* to find them.

"And you'll be able to live with yourself if you can't figure out the mystery and their identity is revealed on the six o'clock news?"

"I can live with myself." She sighs. "Sometimes, I'm not sure if finding J is the right solution. It would rely on them living locally, and the letter not being a one-off occurrence from a friend, and for them to know how to save a life."

"So, we're going to find the letter writer," Jocelyn says as if it's obvious.

Asher frowns. "How are we supposed to do that?"

"We have a lot of clues." Jocelyn turns her phone screen toward Asher and reveals her notes. "They live locally enough to drop a letter on the street. They're writing a letter to someone, so they're not a complete introvert. They have a weird fondness for green pens. The drowning metaphor is very prominent. That date in August might have sentimental value, but people in crisis are not really known for, like, having a logical decision-making process."

Asher mulls over the clues as if this is a fictional mystery and not her real life. "And you think this information is distinct enough that it could lead to the writer?"

"I know enough people who also know enough people that surely someone will have an idea of who this could be," Jocelyn says with enough confidence that implies the writer is not one of her friends, and Asher admires both the confidence and the connections. "It's a small town. And if I take a photo, someone might be able to recognise the handwriting."

She pries the letter back out of Asher's grasp and takes a photo to send to her friends who will send it to their friends. Asher leans back in her desk chair, and for the first time since she found the letter, she feels like this story might have a happy ending.

When Ryn gets home, his blue haze is suffocating.

He sits at his desk, a formality he rarely indulges in anymore. With pen not yet to paper and words circling above his head like vultures—never quite reaching him and serving a sole purpose of taunting him, as they refuse to be placed into sentences upon the page—he thinks about writing the last testament to the fate he's constructed for himself. He'll be forever trapped in a near-coastal town with his head in the clouds, and in every sleepless night, and in every word about him he's overheard, and in everything he's always thought and never told anyone.

He exhales a shaky breath.

He's never heard silence quite this loud.

He painstakingly chooses a song to play as loud as he can bear, the music tinny through his phone speaker, and then his restless hands consume his thoughts instead. He kneels beside his bed and fumbles beneath for the box that houses his waterlogged camera and the art supplies he hasn't touched in months, a series of plastic-wrapped canvas boards and brushes with bristles solidified from where they remained unwashed and tubes of paint in every shade of blue imaginable. Maybe he could paint the ocean once more. Maybe that'll soothe him.

He paints his room.

The walls. The furniture. The lampshades. He empties a tube of what he remembers to be cobalt blue acrylic into his palm and smears it across the closest surface until a dozen tubes are empty and everything around him is wet with paint. The fumes sting his nostrils.He smudges handprints across his windowpanes and covers the glass so his bedroom dips into darkness.

The song changes to something sad, something slow. He skips to the next one, leaving tacky fingerprints across his phone screen, and squeezes another tube into his palm. The cap on this one is so thick with a crust of excess paint that he knows it must be his beloved lapis lazuli, the exact shade of the ocean from his memories. What remains of the paint is pressed into his bedsheets and his drawers of clean clothing and the years of art he painstakingly crafted and put in a place of pride on his wall.

All of it is blue.

Everything is blue.

It doesn't feel like enough.

So, he tears down his paintings. His drawings. Photographs on printer paper that represent a decade's worth of love and obsession. He holds his bedsheets between his teeth and pull until they tear. He yanks on his curtains and rips the rod off the wall. He hurls his notebook against what should've been his door, but it's his mirror that shatters as the frame crashes to the ground.

Then, satisfied, he collapses onto his bedroom floor, half-dried paint sticking his fingers to the floorboards, stray specks of glass stabbing into the back of his head. In the quiet moments between the verses of the song, he notes footsteps approaching up the stairs.

His bedroom door slams open, and he hears his father swallow a gasp as he takes in the wreckage. Ryn sits in the middle of it, paint-splattered walls and torn bedsheets and shattered mirror glass in his knuckles dripping blood onto the floor, the imperfect picture of sanity.

His father steps forward, glass crunching beneath

his shoes, and Ryn is suddenly glad for his father's refusal to walk around in only socks. His music sputters to a stop. The crunching halts in front of him.

"I don't know how to hold you together anymore," his father says sadly, and then Ryn hears his bedroom door close, and he's left alone once more.

AUGUST

TWENTY-SEVEN

These days, they can hardly stand to be apart anymore, and not just because of their life trade. There's no reason for them to be separated for more than a nights sleep, and so they rarely are—Ryn only returns home to reassure his father that he is alive and well, and Asher only sees her mother for clothes she's left in the other house, and her backup supply of hearing aid batteries. When Asher leaves for pharmacy trips or snack runs, Ryn lets himself into the greenhouse and waits until she gets back. If Ryn is too full of blueness to leave, Asher brings him meals from the house on heart-shaped paper plates. On days when he is too miserable to eat or speak or to even sit upright, Asher drags him inside, and he rests his head on her lap while she reads aloud from the fairytale book. But even Asher can't make the sadness ebb completely. It won't, not on its own.

They can hardly stand to be apart anymore, so when Asher comes home from delivering raw meat for her neighbour's upcoming barbecue and sees Ryn sprawled across her bedroom floor with her pillow beneath his head, she doesn't assume that anything is wrong. He's set aside his sunglasses and laid on the nest of her blankets in his party clothes, watching her bedroom darken with the sunset through half-lidded eyes. Outside the window, at the outer edge of his vision, a lamppost flickers to life.

"You're earlier than I was expecting," she says, her voice bringing him back from the brink of uneasy sleep, and then she lies on the floor beside him. It's the first day of August and the sun is burning her cheeks, but it doesn't feel like summer to her anymore. She misses never-ending winters, frozen in longing for what she once had, instead of this summer, which seems to be ending suddenly and all at once.

Ryn rolls onto his side to face her, crumpling the collar of what must be his best shirt in the process—black and buttoned with a microscopic polka dot pattern. "One of Nanna's friends started getting a bit too transphobic, so I asked Dad to pick me up early. My mum hasn't stopped phoning me since."

As if on cue, his phone vibrates from his pocket. He doesn't answer it.

Asher fills the quiet. "I left some food downstairs for us. I'll stick it in the microwave for a bit, and then we should be able to see the fireworks from the kitchen window—I think it faces the right way. I'll turn off the big light, too."

She gets a head start down to the kitchen, and Ryn arrives as the microwave pings to completion, Asher's pillow in his arms as if it's an emotional support stuffed animal. It smells like cough drops and raspberry shampoo and a dusty trace of a drugstore perfume she rarely wears, deeply familiar and nothing like home. He sets aside his sunglasses and tucks himself beneath the kitchen table, his body folded around the chair legs.

Asher settles herself into the doorway of the small bathroom that adjoins the kitchen, the fluorescent light silhouetting her profile. She slides a paper plate of food toward him, and Ryn takes a bite: burgers with the buns soggy from grease and assorted other finger food, oddly reminiscent of what he ate at the birthday party only a few hours earlier, just significantly tastier. He makes a mental note to praise the cook.

"What's the occasion?" Ryn asks. "For the fireworks, I mean."

"The family celebrates anything and everything, so it could be nothing," Asher explains. "A friend of a friend of a cousin is having a birthday? Fireworks. Someone's colleague's kid passed an exam? Fireworks. Everything is a cause for them to celebrate."

A crack like thunder tears through the kitchen. Outside the window, at the outer edge of Ryn's vision, a firework sends a burst of light across the darkened room. Pulsating music drifts toward them from the house down the street—something Ryn barely recognises and already knows he doesn't like—but Asher hums along between bites of her burger. The vibrations fill Ryn's chest more prominently than his heartbeat.

"Can you see them?" Asher asks around a mouthful of food.

Ryn nods. "I can see the light, and sometimes I can make out the shape of the sparks."

"Do you have a favourite?"

"A favourite firework?" He stops to think. "Once, for Bonfire Night, me and Luke went out to watch them, and I remember this huge, glittering one, and the sparks lasted so long and fell so slowly that it was the longest I've been able to see a shape in forever. And then…"

Ryn tells Asher about his favourite things he's seen, and Asher listens as if his voice is her favourite song. Together in the dark with their bodies shaped around shadows, she feels more human than she has in a long time, and Asher is reminded of Julia more than ever.

One summer, they shared a tent in the woods behind Julia's house for weeks on end and stayed up late into the night, trading dreams and secrets and whatever else young girls held as treasures. Asher would sneak her hand out from her sleeping bag and Julia would find it, and they would let their fingers slide over each other, winding and unwinding.

That summer, they grew together in the way trees did—first alongside one another, and then twined together, their branches entangled. They learned about the phenomenon in one of Julia's grandfather's natural history books: inosculation, where the trunks of multiple trees grew so close together that they scraped each other's bark off and grew into one. That was them, Asher thought, only half-listening to Julia's secrets. That was them, with their roots so intricately knotted that neither of them could tell where one of them ended and the other began.

Asher remembers the feeling in the pit of her stomach as they lay together, an excruciating longing. It would be years and miles later when she'd finally realise what it meant—that maybe she had been more than a little in love with Julia, even if it was too late to act.

'Gay' was just a synonym for 'stupid' when she was growing up. 'Lesbian' was a punchline to a dirty joke said with a sneer. She'd been dipping into her teens when she accepted that other girls could be more than just friends if they felt the same way. And by then, even if Julia had once felt the same way, the past was in the past, and she was pretending that Julia was just another name in the graveyard of birthdays in her countdown app.

But Julia is still a person she loved, not just a memory, so Asher thinks of her fondly as she plays with the charm on her necklace. It's been four years, and the grief still comes in waves, pulling the memory of Julia closer and then further away. Asher thought she'd be better at navigating the waters by now.

Another firework booms to life, and Asher watches Ryn from across the room, his face alight with awe as a fiery orange illuminates the kitchen. He looks at the light the same way she used to look at her friends: first, with the tentative adoration of looking at something that doesn't belong to you, then with nothing but unconditional obsession.

"Do you love me?" she asks him when the light fades.

Ryn considers.

This time, there's no spiders in his stomach or pressure in his throat. This time, he doesn't look down: he turns his head toward her voice like a sunflower toward the sun.

"No," he says quietly, almost to himself, as if he knows she's been thinking about Julia. "I don't think I'll ever love anyone like that."

The following silence lasts for long enough that Ryn wonders if he's offended her, if he's broken some unspoken rule of their friendship about honesty that he's yet to learn. Then, another firework crackles, and she announces, "It's your favourite!", and she pulls him out from under the table and toward the window so he can watch the lingering sparks trail through the sky. And, in that moment, he knows what love is.

He slinks back beneath the kitchen table, and Asher sinks down against the bathroom doorframe, her silhouette almost identifiable to Ryn's vision. He looks at her wild, curling hair and the roundness of her cheeks and the glint of jewellery—a necklace alongside the *J* charm, and rings, so many rings catching the light—and he tries to commit her to memory.

"I don't have crushes," he says eventually, needing to finish his thoughts. "Luke tells me about his all the time, and I don't understand them. I can't. I don't want that kind of love. With anyone. If it happens, then it happens, I guess, but it hasn't so far, so I don't think that it ever will." His heart rate spikes. He's not sure why. "I've read that it's different for other people. But for me, it's…*this*."

"There's a word for that," Asher says, "if you like labels, that is."

"Asexual, I know." His hand drifts toward the spot on his chest where the blue and yellow pin would be if he was wearing his jacket. "Or aromantic, or both, which I think I am. That's what the pride flag on my pin is."

"You don't have to know if you don't want to. I didn't realise I was a lesbian until a few years ago, and that took months of me reading this document to understand how vast the spectrum is and that I could fit on it."

Suddenly, the bathroom light flickers off, and they're plunged into complete darkness. Asher gasps. Ryn squeezes his eyes shut. A mournful beeping echoes through the open window.

"I think Dad forgot to top up the electric again," Asher says with a forced calmness. Her phone screen flashes. "I'll let him know that the lights are off."

Ryn audibly shudders. "I know it's stupid, but I don't like the dark."

"Why not?"

"I think it's because I cling to the little that I can see so desperately that I feel completely helpless when it's taken away." Asher sees Ryn's dark outline detach from the surrounding darkness and crawl toward her.

His head falls into her lap, and he grasps at her skirt, rubbing the fabric between his fingers like a kid with a comfort blanket. Her hands curl into his hair as a reflex by now, and he breathes a sigh of contentment. "It's hard enough being partially sighted and having my vision decay each time I go to my ophthalmologist, and I don't want to be reminded that *this* might be all I can see one day."

She traces patterns against his skull until his breathing slows and his hand on her skirt grows still. She sits in her own quiet and watches the last of the fireworks illuminate the kitchen. Her father sends a message to let her know he'll sort out the electric in the morning, and there are portable power banks all over the house, and he won't be home for the rest of the night, so she settles down for another few hours of listening to Ryn breathe.

By the time the lights flicker back on, hours have passed and he's still asleep in her lap, arms folded loosely around his waist. This kind of stillness is so foreign to his body that Asher decides sleep looks unnatural on him. Awake, he's all edges, from the aristocratic line of his nose to the stark eerie contrast between blond eyelashes and dark brown iris. It's only when he is sleeping that Asher can tell how much of his appearance is a performance.

She lets him sleep until the cold shadow of the sunrise crawls through the half-light, and then she plays with his hair until he creeps into consciousness.

"I fell asleep again," he says nonchalantly as he wakes, rubbing the sleep from his face.

"I'll start keeping you a permanent bed here." Asher tries to shuffle into a more comfortable sitting position from beneath the surprising weight of Ryn's head. He either doesn't notice, or he doesn't care about her fidgeting. "I'll build you a little fort under the table."

"I'd like that." He smiles up at her, then squints around the illuminated room. "Is your dad back? The lights are on."

Asher shrugs. "I'm not sure. Our electric thing is outside, so he might've topped it up without coming in."

"I guess I'll never meet him," Ryn says with a sadness that she can't decide if it's forced.

"One day, if you actually want to," she reassures him. "If not, you can avoid him forever."

"I think he's avoiding *me*."

"Don't be silly. He loves you."

"Have you told him about me?"

"I've told him *everything* about you."

"*Oh.*"

Their conversation meanders toward what Asher thinks she can construct for breakfast out of what remains in the fridge after they devoured the eggs the other morning and Ryn's half-formed plan to live beneath her kitchen table forever. She tells him he can stay as long as he needs, and she can tell—from the desperate relief in his face, from the way his fingers unclench from the fabric of her skirt and raise to touch her knee in an awkward, fleeting thanks—that he believes her.

TWENTY-EIGHT

"What is happiness to you?"

A few mutters erupt from around the circle of chairs, and Ryn can tell that, for the first time ever, Jonathon has many willing victims. The older man invites them to jump into the conversation whenever they feel ready, so Ryn settles in for a nice long forty-five minutes of listening to other people talk about their feelings.

"Rain makes me really happy," says a girl whose voice Ryn doesn't recognise. Her tone is caustic and careless, the way his always gets when he's pretending not to be scared.

"And what is it about the rain that makes you happy?" Jonathon prompts.

The girl sighs dreamily. "I don't know. I love when the cars slow down, and people hide in bus stops with strangers, and when they run home with plastic bags on their heads, and when groups share the same umbrella.

It's just a moment where time slows down."

"That's a really nice thought, Katie. Does anyone else have any thoughts on what Katie has shared?"

Another overenthusiastic teenager's chair scrapes the floor as they stand to speak, and Ryn redirects his attention to counting the second hand ticking around the clock. Two people speak within the next sixty ticks, and Jonathon sounds like he might consider transitioning to a new topic until Asher's shadow shifts beside Ryn, and he realises that she's standing.

"To me, happiness is standing in the woodland around my childhood hometown," she begins. "I went back a few months ago for the first time in a decade, and I didn't remember the trees being so tall and *old*. I never appreciated them before. And happiness is finding a place in this town that reminds me of there, just with new friends that make *here* feel like home instead."

"That's a really interesting thought, Asher," Jonathon says, and Ryn thinks he actually might be sincere. "Could you talk more about new friends and the feeling of home?"

Asher clears her throat as if she wasn't intending to continue. "When I first moved here, I thought happiness was confined to everything that happened in my past, but now I know it's spending time with people who love you and give you room to grow and learn. I don't have to be perfect or cling on to recreating my old life and forcing people to play the roles of my old friends. Happiness is about changing your mind. It's changing what happiness is."

The final sentence triggers Jonathon's urge to pivot to a new conversation topic—something about uncertainty, or indecisiveness, Ryn thinks he says—so Asher returns to her seat, and Ryn scoots his chair a little closer to hers so they can whisper comments to each other more effectively.

"Why's Jonathon being so nice today?" Ryn murmurs. He finds some relief in the fact that Asher is whispering to him rather than Jocelyn this session, unless it's just his lack of panic attack that's keeping her attention.

"I don't know," Asher says. "Maybe he knows something we don't."

He chews the inside of his cheek. *Don't be suspicious,* he thinks. *There's no way Jonathon can know about the letter.* But what he says is, "What makes you think that?"

"He looked at me while I was talking with this sort of sadness in his eyes, like he pities me or something." She hums. "It's probably just the lighting. It's shittier than usual in here today."

"Yeah. Just the lighting," Ryn agrees, then settles down to listen to more teenagers dissecting thoughts that he pretends don't relate to him.

"Can you believe he's my uncle?" Jocelyn says as she, Asher, and Ryn walk through the doors of the youth centre together, her own friends trailing along behind.

"He's your *what?*" Asher repeats.

"Who are we talking about?" Ryn asks.

"Yeah, we're related. Me and Jonathon," Jocelyn confirms. "My parents wanted me in therapy, but real therapy is expensive, and they also want to know what I'm thinking at all times, so putting me in my uncle's therapy sessions made them think that he'd definitely, like, snitch on me. But he doesn't, as far as I know, but now he does know far too much about me."

"Doesn't it make things awkward?" Asher asks, because what else are you supposed to ask when someone announces they're related to your therapist.

Jocelyn shakes her head. "Not awkward at all. He brainstorms his sessions with me all the time, like he values what I think. Like…what do I think he should do about"—she pitches her voice down—"'this boy who's so pessimistic all the time, always refuses to take part, so how can I relate to the kid?'"

"He *plans* these sessions?" Ryn says. The edge in his voice tells Asher that the idea of Jonathon planning something is not the part of Jocelyn's statement he truly has an issue with.

Asher gently elbows him to be quiet in what she was expecting to be his ribs, but she forgets their height difference and hits him squarely in the chest instead. She rests her hand on his shoulder as an apology. "That must be exhausting."

"Right? Yeah!" Jocelyn throws her hands in the air. "Because, like, I do know what he should do about it because I'm taking psychology as one of my A levels right now, but

I'm his patient, not his employee. Like, yeah, my mind has other things to prioritise right now. *Different* things."

Ryn inhales sharply to Asher's right, and she grabs his hand reassuringly, because what else are you supposed to do when you realise your counsellor doesn't know how to help you?

"I don't know how he does it," Jocelyn continues. "Imagine having to deal with *that* every day and then having to go home and act like everything is completely normal for you. Like, does my therapist need a therapist?"

"He does go to group therapy," Asher confirms, then winces as she realises she's revealed a secret that doesn't belong to her. Jocelyn cackles in response, and suddenly the miniature betrayal almost feels worth it.

As they walk, Asher's thoughts linger on seeing Jonathon unexpectedly in that group therapy session, and her certainty that he knew who wrote the tearstained letter after she read it aloud, as if he'd already read the words before. And now, she's still sure, but maybe both he and Jocelyn know a lot more than they're letting on.

Either way, Asher has a dread that feels like premonition.

"I think we should do something later, or maybe tomorrow. Whatever suits you," Jocelyn says, turning so she's only facing Asher, and then immediately stumbles over a dandelion-sprouting crevice in the pavement, so she doesn't notice Asher fighting her blush.

Ryn makes an expression that Asher can only describe as a taunting kind of jealousy. She elbows him again in case he doesn't realise what his face is doing, gentler this time, almost apologetically. "Tomorrow works. I have to pick up my exam results, but we can do something after."

"Oh, shit, I've got to get mine, too," Jocelyn says with an air of exasperation that makes her sound genuine. Asher can't imagine going a single day without thinking about the looming threat of a handful of grades in a brown envelope. "We should go together."

Asher is faced with the mortifying ordeal of Jocelyn possibly finding out she's failed her exams so intensely that she objects, "No, no, it's fine. I might go first thing in the morning before it gets busy. Get it over and done with, and all that."

The thought of waking up at seven in the morning seems to deter Jocelyn, so she says goodbye and departs with her trailing friends, leaving Asher and Ryn to journey back to his house. Ryn monologues about an album he can't decide if he likes that came out a few days earlier while Asher pretends she's not spiralling into an inescapable pit of anxiety about her future imminently being decided by three letters in an envelope.

They're veering their way onto Ryn's street and he's concluding his speech about the closing track on the album—which he does actually like, by the way—when he stops in his tracks, dragging Asher to a halt beside him.

"Do you actually like her? Like, *like*-like her?" Ryn asks with a sincerity that catches Asher off guard enough that she knows she can't joke her way around it.

"I think so," she says, knowing that he's talking about

Jocelyn, knowing that the reason their date went awfully is entirely her own fault. "She's nice, and she finds my stories interesting, and I think she likes me when I don't spend too much time talking about other people."

"Is that enough for you?"

Asher has not had enough headspace recently to consider what she wants in her life, just that she wants her letter writer to survive. "It is for now," she says noncommittally, and she'll reassess how she feels on September 1st.

Ryn nods. "That's fine."

"Do you not like her?"

"I barely know her." He hesitates. He knows that's not what Asher is asking. "There's something off about her. I don't care that she's only interested in befriending you rather than both of us as you both clearly have a lot more in common, but it feels like she's trying to keep us away from each other."

She hums again, a sound Ryn has started to associate with her tackling difficult subjects. "I'll talk to her about it if that helps. I think she just likes spending time together, even though she does seem to only see her other friends in therapy. I think she might have a lot going on at the moment."

"Don't talk to her about it," Ryn says quickly. "It might make things weirder. Just…bear that in mind. Please. For me."

"Of course. Not a word," Asher agrees, because she'd do anything for him, right?

TWENTY-NINE

Asher forgets about collecting her exam results until she's ignored three calls from her mother and refused to acknowledge a message asking what her grades are.

She arms herself with sunglasses and sound-cancelling headphones to prepare for the sensory experience of being crammed into a fluorescently-lit classroom with one hundred other sweating teenagers. She might accidentally brush against one of those sweating bodies, so she folds the jacket into her rucksack for extra skin coverage just in case.

She completes her walk to school in her personal best time, fuelled by the anxiety taking root beneath her kneecaps. The faster she walks, the less likely someone is to notice her shaking legs.

Her guidance counsellor homes in on her the moment she steps through the doors, and Asher's plan to grab her envelope and hide in the toilets breaks into smithereens.

She attempts to hide behind a knee-high potted fern that guards the classroom door. It doesn't work well.

"Oh, Asher, hi, I didn't see you there," Ms. Bourne says, then embarks on the usual nonsensical call-and-response about the weather. Asher's learned her lines by now: "It's so nice out today"; "Oh, yes. Of course, it'll get warmer later"; "Maybe the humidity will drop off by the evening"; etc., until either the day ends, or someone else joins in to restart the conversation, or someone breaks the finely-tuned social conventions to change the subject, which Asher does.

"You think I'm going to fail all my subjects, don't you?" Asher asks bluntly, which breaks the call-and-response script and leaves Ms. Bourne visibly confused.

"Fail?" She blinks at Asher as if she has no memory of anything they've discussed over the past few months. "I never thought that you might fail, Asher."

Asher gets the vibe that history is being rewritten in this moment. "That's not how it felt the last time we spoke."

"I didn't think you would reach your full potential unprompted, but I never thought that you would fail," Ms. Bourne says again, softly this time.

Asher tries to think of a response, but then a hoard of teenage boys—sweatier than expected—surge into the classroom and push her to the front of the queue, and her opportunity disappears. She gives her last name to an almost-familiar teaching assistant whose name she can't remember, heads down a row of tables to a box of envelopes labelled M–P, and gives her first name to another assistant who rifles through the box and retrieves her envelope.

It's the most nondescript envelope Asher's ever encountered, and she's encountered at least one for each year she's been in secondary school: cheap brown paper and only thick enough to contain the single sheet listing her grades. But she carries it out of the classroom and into a quiet alcove down the corridor as if it holds the key to changing her life.

It's just a piece of paper.

It's so much more than that.

She peels the envelope open with the edge of her thumbnail and curses herself when the paper tears as if an imperfect opening will be a reflection of the contents.

She feels her phone vibrate in her pocket with an incoming text message and switches it to silent, as if the envelope will hear the noise and see it as disrespect.

She wipes the sweat from her hands onto her dress before taking out the sheet of paper as if a single sticky fingerprint is enough to seal her fate for the worse.

Holding her breath, her eyes skim down the page for the single letters.

Statement of Results

Exam Results

Title	Grade
AS Art & Design (Fine Art)	B
AS English Literature	C

Asher's filled with such relief that she doesn't bother checking her third and final grade, just tucks the slip of paper back into the envelope and holds it against her chest. She's passed. She can move on to her second year of sixth form and repeat the coursework stress and threat of exams once more. If she passes again, she can do it all three times more at a university she's not sure she'll be accepted into and less sure she wants to attend. But her mother wants her to be the first grandchild to go to university, so she will be attending just to avoid the inevitable comments about how her lack of higher education will make her a failure to the family for the rest of her life.

Asher's not sure if she wants this fate.

But she's earned it, so she'll take it.

Ryn and Luke sit together on the swings, and neither of them mention that 1) they're too old for this, and 2) this seems to be the only place they see each other anymore without Asher's presence. Luke babbles overenthusiastically about the contents of his exam results envelope while Ryn studies his darkened phone screen, refusing to admit that his lack of envelope is a sore subject and waiting for a sign of life from Asher. It's unlike her to leave his messages marked as unread, let alone not reply for hour after hour.

He slips his phone into his pocket with a sigh.

Luke says something about sticking his results to the fridge like a parent proud of a kid's drawing. Three A's in subjects Ryn can't remember, and a guaranteed unconditional offer from his top university when he applies at the start of the next school year, and Ryn can't remember the name of the university either.

He squints at his best friend's silhouette in the sunlight and wonders if there is a definitive moment in time when they started to not know each other anymore.

He wonders how he would react if Luke made the same confession as him during that late night at the end of June, if he would've promised to make sure Luke would have the best time of his life during his remaining months, if Ryn would've kept that promise.

He thinks he would, at least. He wouldn't let his best friend find someone else to fill the void.

Ryn squints harder at Luke's silhouette and tries to recall what he knows about his best friend, and if they've crossed the threshold that makes them more than just regular friends, as if either of them have enough friends to choose each other as the best.

He knows Luke's last name but isn't sure if he knows the middle. Their houses across from each other on a shared street and the excitement of a boy his own age who didn't know his past moving in. Meeting a younger sister, although he can never remember what she's called or how much younger she is. He wonders if Luke also struggles to recall what should be the basic facts of his life. They must have shared interests, shared hobbies, shared dreams, something that ties them together as true friends rather than just tied together through proximity.

They must have something in common, he hopes, but nothing comes to mind.

Ryn looks at Luke, and a twitch in the shadows suggest that Luke looks back at him, and Ryn feels like they're not quite in the same place where they used to be. He looks away and glares at his hands instead, pinching at his knuckles to resist reaching for his phone and sending another unanswered message to the person who truly knows him best. Because the universe responds when you meet someone who operates on the same frequency as you, even if they don't respond straight away to your messages.

"I need to go," Ryn says slowly, uncertainly, because there's nothing he needs more in this moment than to monologue into his voice notes or write a scrawling letter or just talk through his feelings into his empty bedroom. Luke's swinging slows, and Ryn senses a change in the atmosphere between them.

"Can we wait another ten minutes?" There's a tone in Luke's voice that Ryn doesn't recognise, or maybe it's another thing he's failed to notice until now. "It's almost three, so my sister will be done with school in a bit, and we can all walk home together."

"It's fine. I need to be alone." Then Ryn stands from his swing before Luke can intervene, stumbles through the park gate like Asher did all those weeks ago, and wanders into town with his cane tracing the edge of the pavement. He wants to see Asher, but he isn't sure if she's at her mother's or her father's house today, and he's too disoriented after a few false turns to remember how to find the house he's been to. He walks until his cane hits a lamppost and he takes that as his cue to stop, leaning on it as he opens the map on his phone and searches for a familiar landmark, allowing the electronic voice to guide him there until he regains enough confidence to take himself home.

There's a dead mouse on the driveway, or at least there was twelve hours ago. Asher hasn't been outside recently enough to find out whether the neighbour's cat has come for it. The day has given itself over to muggy heat and a sweating sunset that bleeds purple across the sky, so Asher's in her bedroom with the fan on high and a moth struggling to escape through her open window as company. It's almost ten at night, the house is quiet enough that she doesn't feel the need to take out her hearing aids, and the only lights are the orange glow of the lamppost outside and her blue-white laptop screen.

For a moment, she's at peace.

And then she acknowledges her phone screen properly for the first time since picking up her exam results and sees a handful of unanswered text messages from Ryn. She's been ignoring them for reasons she can't discern, as well as the dozen missed calls from her mother. She accepts that she can't keep running until she's eighteen, no matter how hard she tries.

So, she runs to her mother's house instead.

Well, she speedwalks through the too-warm nighttime air with her results envelope tucked under one arm and embraces the relief that comes with the humidity slowly dropping off, and she's turning her key in the front door lock before she can change her mind. She finds her mother in a state that's starting to become familiar, the living room darkened, a glass of red wine balanced on her hip bone. But this time she's awake on the sofa, and she notices Asher the moment she steps through the door.

"Am I a bad mother?" she asks as Asher sinks onto the opposite sofa, her hands already thumbing nervously at the edges of the envelope.

Asher knows how she wants to reply: honestly. To remind her mother of which parent it was who held her hand during ENT appointments, and rubbed circles into her spine after night terrors, and taught her to treat a plant's life as valuably as her own. To remind her that dragging a child across the country and isolating her into choosing a new favourite parent is no way to win an imagined popularity contest.

But although her father did raise Asher to be honest, he also raised her to be kind, so what she says is, "I think you're trying your best," although what she means is, *I think you don't know how to be a parent,* because what she needs is a mother, not a hurricane.

And Asher knows she's said the wrong thing, because her mother's eyes narrow and the rain begins to fall.

She leans across the coffee table and grips Asher's face in her hands, tucking her index fingers behind Asher's ears like she did ten years ago when her young daughter was too overwhelmed by her fading hearing to remember how to listen. The motion presses Asher's hearing aids uncomfortably into her skull, but she feels too much like she's caught in a predator's jaws to pull herself free.

They watch each other as a second drags into an eternity, cold blue eyes glaring into warm brown, mother and daughter separated by a barely spoken feud of different interests and disability and dominant genetics.

"You may look like your father, but you'll always take after me," she says in a voice that's devoid of the softness from Asher's earliest memories. "You'll grow up and still be a lonely little girl in a lonely empty house, suffocating under the weight of your own sadness, and you'll remember how you left your own mother for that man, and you'll wish you did something different."

Asher concludes that the darkness and wine must've been her mother's response to another romantic relationship failing, and she pretends that she's indifferent to it, as if her mother's mourning is none of her business. She's not indifferent to it—she would describe herself as an empath if people hadn't warped the meaning of the word—but it's hard to care when her mother's fingernails digging into her skin might be drawing blood.

"I won't let you be lonely when you're older, not if you'll let me," Asher struggles to whisper through her gripped jaw, and her hearing aids are not quite in her ears enough to tell if her voice is loud enough to hear. "Because, in a few weeks' time, I'll legally no longer have to be your dependent, and I think it'll be good for us. You'll be able to have a life without a daughter, and I'll be able to fix all the parts of myself that you don't like without you watching. And, one day, when we're both healed, we can start over, but only if you want that."

Her mother drops Asher's face as if she's been burned. Asher takes her freedom as a chance to escape.

She tosses her results envelope onto the coffee table, the piece of paper sliding out. She doesn't wait for her mother to pick it up, just announces, "I passed, by the way," as she storms out of the door as fast as her shaking body will let her and slams it shut behind her. Her pace doesn't slow until she's back outside her father's house. She rushes past the dead mouse still on the driveway and pretends everything is fine until she locks herself in the bathroom and wipes off her sadness along with her makeup.

THIRTY

"**W**hy do you write so many stories?"

Jocelyn sits on Asher's bedroom floor with her back pressed against the bed and Asher's laptop balanced on her knees. Asher's too busy spiralling about what Jocelyn could be looking at on the screen and the fact that there is someone other than Ryn in her bedroom at her father's house to overthink her answer. "Writing things down, even if they're just a semi-fictionalised version of my life, makes me feel real, I think. Like seeing it in writing makes it official."

"Are there reasons why you don't feel real?" Jocelyn asks with an undetectable amount of sincerity. Her eyes leave the laptop screen and roam around the room instead, and Asher can't tell what stresses her out more between Jocelyn's electronics nosiness and what she might think of the bedroom. The haphazardly painted wall sticks out like another unfinished project rather than an intentional art choice, stray specks of yellow still spattering the skirting board and surrounding floor.

"There's a few reasons, I guess." Asher sorts through her thoughts and picks out the ones that she thinks will lead to the least concerning questions. "The big one is when people talk to me like they're talking through me, as if there's a past version of myself stuck in my head and they're trying to talk to her instead of me. My grandparents do it a lot and it always feels like they're talking to me as a child who was only twenty percent deaf, rather than present day me who is…significantly more deaf." She can't dwell on the memory for too long— she doesn't think that Jocelyn's and her relationship is deep enough for them to cry in front of each other. "And I know it's unfair to everyone else, but most of the time I feel like I'm trapped in a dream and they'll disappear when I wake up. And I feel so old lately yet simultaneously younger than yesterday. Like, yesterday I was seventy years old, and today my dad is dropping me off at school for the first time ever, and I'm scared that he's leaving me alone. And—"

Asher cuts herself off. She's rambling, and Jocelyn isn't watching her with the same wide-eyed awe that Ryn does when she finds her mouth moving faster than she can think.

She's on the verge of apologising when Jocelyn grabs the Polaroid camera from the bedside table and snaps a photo of herself, beaming into the lens, two fingers held up in a peace sign. She fumbles around for a Sharpie as the photo develops and signs her name across the bottom of the frame, adorning it with hearts and too-perfect stars. She blows on the ink until it dries, and Asher hopes that the awkward moment is gone for good.

But then she notices that Jocelyn chose a green Sharpie, and she dots her i's similar to the writer of the tearstained letter, and Asher has to dig her nails into her palms to stop herself from spiralling again.

A preference for green ink means nothing, Asher tries to tell herself. And loads of people have similar handwriting, especially when it comes down to how they write a single letter. And she can't even begin to count how many people in the area are sad and lonely and know people with J names. And—

"Do you know who wrote the letter?" Asher demands, and she regrets saying it the moment the words leave the mouth. "Did you write it?"

"The letter that I'm helping you find the writer of?" Jocelyn asks, and Asher wants to scream that asking a question isn't providing an answer, and Jocelyn is yet to provide any help other than promising that she will. "Jesus Christ, Asher, do you think I'm in therapy because I want to kill myself?"

Asher nods and wishes she never spoke. Jocelyn's eyes narrow in a way that reminds her of her mother, so Asher glares at the paint flecks embedded in her rug until she feels brave enough to speak.

"The clues lead to *you*," she insists, even though she

knows she's far from correct and is unwilling to admit it. Technically, she thinks the clues lead to one of Jocelyn's friends, but confessing that might take the conversation to a point of no return, and Asher's only just got used to saying she has two friends rather than one.

"The clues could lead to *anyone* if you're desperate enough," Jocelyn snaps. "I thought that was the whole point of us investigating, so we could find out who actually wrote it and you could be their saviour."

Asher doesn't mention that they haven't talked about the letter since that day—no texts, no phone calls about theories, no follow-up emails after Jocelyn sent the photo around her friend group—and she doesn't think that mentioning it will make anything better. So, she does what she does best and sinks into the silence until someone else takes control of the situation and she can return to counting down seconds until it's over.

Jocelyn clears her throat in what Asher interprets as her changing the subject, no negotiations. "I read some more of your stories earlier, the ones you emailed to me. Some of the more recent ones you seemed less, like, *embarrassed* about. I was trying to find the documents just now so I could see if you've written more."

Asher's had too much going on recently to remember exchanging email addresses with Jocelyn or agreeing to have her documents folder investigated, but she must have. "Really? What did you think?"

"They're really cool." Jocelyn pauses for thought, then stumbles over her words in a way that resembles Asher more than her. "They…They've got *something*. The stories aren't, like, classic literature or anything, but like, the characters and the worlds and the language just sort of hypnotise you. Yeah. They're good."

Asher smiles down at her lap. "Do you ship River and Lane?"

Writing fantasies about her and Jocelyn increased exponentially this month, which Asher feels awkward about, since it is her and Jocelyn, and they are people in real life and not just characters in her stories. She hadn't even been trying to make the relationship romantic, not at first, but then the words poured out of her fingertips faster than her brain could keep up, and then suddenly there were lingering touches and longing gazes and the hint of an *"I love you"* on fictional Asher's lips, immortalised in Palatino Linotype and double line spacing.

Jocelyn thinks about it for a second. "I don't know. The story isn't about that, is it? Like, if they get together, it'll be nice, but if they don't, it won't ruin anything or change anything. You don't write about traditional romance."

"That's exactly what I think," Asher lies, because while she doesn't really write about romance, all she does write about love and whether or not it is real. And it's started to bother her when things aren't real, despite her fondness for fiction and imaginary friends and magic in the mundane.

At some point, she'll take note of how much of her authentic self she's sacrificed just because a pretty girl has shown interest in her, but now is not the time for that.

Not when Jocelyn's giggling behind the camera as she turns the lens on Asher, spouting cooing sounds and compliments until Asher's cheeks burn red and she offers a hesitant smile. The flash sends spots across her vision, and maybe it's just her flickering eyesight that makes her think Jocelyn is leaning in, chin tilted up.

As it does in most states of panic, her mind starts to spiral. She begins to compile a list to compose herself and, if she had a pen and paper, it would look something like this:

<u>Reasons not to kiss Jocelyn:</u>
1. This sort of love—if you can even call it that—is out of Asher's depth. She's still all knives and chipped teeth after Julia's death, and everyone around her seems soft enough to crumble in the palm of her hand.
2. No one ever taught her how to love. Her sole teacher is fiction, and she has no firsthand experience.
3. No one has shown any sign of romantic interest in her since Julia. Since *ever*. She's sure she'll drown at the first sign of love.
4. This version of Jocelyn only exists in the museum of Asher's mind, and Asher's merely here to gaze, and all the signs around her scream 'do not touch.'
5. Jocelyn touches her like she's fragile—fingers

barely grazing skin, more looks than true touches—and if Asher breaks, she won't be able to put herself together again.

6. Asher's version of Jocelyn is all sunlight and sparks, and Asher cannot watch the life run out of another person's eyes.

7. Jocelyn's gaze is too gentle, and Asher will not be the one to tell her that not everything can be fixed with a smile.

8. Jocelyn is good. She is so good, and Asher cannot ruin one more good thing.

9. She will not watch Jocelyn collapse under the weight of her sadness. Jocelyn is too light, too breathless to be caught up in the dizziness of Asher's heart.

Dissatisfied, she tucks that list away in her mind and forces herself to think of a more forgiving one, a version that paints her in a better light.

Reasons to kiss Jocelyn:

1. Jocelyn likes Asher, and she's smiling on the bedroom floor with her eyes half-closed, and Asher's father taught her to never leave a good thing waiting.

Jocelyn's smile dies off when Asher's lips touch hers. They both keep their eyes open, blurry-close and unblinking, Jocelyn's wide and murky blue and startled.

One chaste peck in primary school hasn't given enough practice, so she keeps her mouth closed, lips pursed against the slight part of Jocelyn's surprised mouth.

Jocelyn puts her hands on Asher's arms and holds her there—doesn't push her away. Asher dares a brush of tongue against her lips, and she tastes like cherry lip balm and whatever fruit-flavoured liquid is in her water bottle.

"Asher."

Asher closes her eyes, but Jocelyn has stopped kissing her. Their foreheads press together. "I'm not into girls," Jocelyn says gently.

"You're not into boys either," Asher says with a lot more confidence than she deserves.

Jocelyn's shoulders shake with a quick, quiet laugh. "You're not wrong."

Sighing, Asher drops her head down to Jocelyn's shoulder, ignoring the strain on her neck from how notable their height difference is even when sitting on the floor. Jocelyn's arms wrap around her, and it feels like the kind of hug friends give each other.

Are they friends?

"I'm sorry I didn't ask before I did that." The emptiness of rejection mingles with shame because Asher knows better than to kiss people out of nowhere, not like she's tried before.

"It's okay." Jocelyn pulls away so she can look at Asher's face. "I mean, if you need to, like, practice or something, we can."

Asher's face burns red, and she can't even hide it because Jocelyn's looking into her eyes as if she's staring straight into Asher's soul. "That's not what I meant," she murmurs through her trembling lips. "I just thought—"

Asher's phone ringing cuts her off. She looks at the screen, sees Ryn's name, then hangs up and texts him before Jocelyn sees. She ignores the handful of messages from him that she's neglected to answer over the past few days.

ASHER
with jocelyn. will call later
unless emergency??

His reply is near instant.

RYN
No emergency. Just lonely.

RYN
Do you want to go to the beach
tomorrow? The weather is
supposed to be nice.

ASHER
beach tomorrow 😊

She swipes away his reply that suggests a time and a meeting place and returns to pretending that her unrequited crush on Jocelyn isn't consuming her whole. So, she turns on a song about living through an endless summer and hums along, and Jocelyn joins in when she recognises the chorus, and for a moment it feels like that they will just be friends. Just friends. It feels fine, because Asher knows that crushes don't have to be reciprocated, and an unreciprocated one doesn't have to end a friendship.

"We should hang out tomorrow," Jocelyn suggests as she's packing up her rucksack to leave.

"I can't," Asher says, firm but polite. Unapologetic. "I'm meeting up with Ryn."

Jocelyn scowls, and Asher makes a mental note to tell Ryn that he can somehow see more than she can. "But you spend so much time with him already. You're, like, joined at the hip or something."

"We just like each other, I guess." Asher's confidence fades. "I like spending time with him. If he doesn't feel the same, then I'll leave him alone for a while, but I'm pretty sure he does, and we haven't seen each other in days."

They wait in stubborn silence, Jocelyn hovering in the middle of the room, Asher cross-legged on the floor. The song changes to something about first loves that Asher hasn't heard in years and she turns it off before she can be reminded of the ending.

Jocelyn breaks the silence.

"Will you still like him if it turns out he wrote that letter?" Jocelyn says in a way that definitely doesn't feel indifferent. She throws her rucksack over her shoulder, and her footsteps recede down the stairs, and Asher's not sure if she's ever going to see her again.

THIRTY-THREE

'Beach tomorrow' becomes 'beach today,' and Asher and Ryn walk arm in arm where the waves meet the shore, kicking at the water and tripping on the sand. The morning mist is yet to burn away, and the distant sky is dark with the threat of an incoming storm. Asher is convinced she can smell the ozone in the air.Or petrichor, maybe, but she wasn't listening enough in school to say that she knows the difference.

"You can walk all the way out to those rocks when the tide is out." Ryn gestures to a spot on the horizon that he has memorised, and Asher can't see through the mist. "People go out there all the time and get stuck when the tide comes back in. I think someone tried to swim back and almost drowned a year or two ago."

He asks Siri for the local tide times and concludes that it's safe for them to scoot along the strip of sand that runs along the base of a cliff outcrop so they can claim a hidden part of the beach as their own. Asher takes off her shoes and ties them to her rucksack strap by the laces, then navigates the terrain as if she's never touched salt water before. Ryn walks with his left hand trailing along the cliff and his right stretched behind him so Asher can grab onto his fingertips, and she wonders if he enjoys being the one to lead her for once.

As they round the outcrop, Ryn counts steps beneath his breath until he hits both seventeen and a large smooth stone sticking out of the sand. Asher sits herself in the centre while he struggles with his damp shoes, and she lines her dry ones up next to each other at her side.

Ryn surveys the beach with his bare feet, stepping over small dunes and crab shells, his head twitching to one side as if he can hear something Asher's hearing aids can't detect. She pulls out her digital camera and watches him through the viewfinder, almost silhouetted against weak sunlight reflecting off the bottle-green sea. The light limns around him, causing his outline to glow, and once more he's the angel of a boy who was lying on her bedroom floor.

"Are you watching me?" Ryn asks, and Asher wonders how he can tell, if the light reflecting off her camera lens is a giveaway, if he can simply sense that he's being watched. She takes a photo in response. He beams at her, and she centres his face in the frame before she takes another.

After his beach inspection has concluded, Ryn plonks himself onto the sand and sinks his fingers into it like he's trying to anchor himself to the ground. "If the world was ending, you'd come over, right?"

"So, we're giving up on changing the world?" Asher laughs. "We can sit together while everything falls apart if you'd like. Stare up at the ceiling and all that."

She points her camera toward the horizon, zooming in on the spots where the sun has started to burn away the mist, looking for rocks in the distance. She thinks she might see them, a blurry grey clump or three semi-detached from the mist, and wonders if she'd survive if she tried to swim back from them. She assumes not.

"Did I ever tell you about the tree when I was younger?" Ryn asks. He's dug deep enough into the sand that water pools at the bottom.

Asher hums in a way that could be interpreted as 'no,' or rather 'not yet.'

He continues. "There was a window I used to look out of where one would wait for me."

"A tree would wait for you?" Asher's brow furrows, wondering if he's describing a scene from a fairytale or just a childhood memory warped from nostalgia.

"Yeah." He laughs as if he's realised the absurdity of what he's saying. "I thought it had these reddish-brown leaves for most of the year, and then an eye doctor said I was colour-blind, so it was probably just a regular green oak."

Asher realises that the world could be ending, and

she wouldn't notice, not while Ryn is laughing.

He stops digging in the sand and traces patterns into the surface instead, an elaborate tangle of swirls unravelling beneath his fingertips. He forgets about the tree and switches topic to something Jonathon once said in group therapy. Asher watches him talk and draw patterns and erase them with the palm of his hand over and over again until she can figure out what feels different about him.

He has a funny way of talking today, she notices, as if he's trying to fit his entire day's worth of thoughts into an hour: he keeps cutting himself off to explain things, theorise, and mention similar stories he's heard elsewhere. He's talking like he's running out of time, and Asher grabs his flailing hands and rubs her thumbs over the fine bones in his fingers.

"Slow down," she says softly, and she can barely hear her own voice. "We have all day, and the day after that, and the day after that. We have as long as it takes."

He lets out a strangled sound that is halfway between a sigh and a sob. "But what if we're running out of time? What if the world has ended, and we've just not noticed yet?"

"Ryn."

"What if everything has ended, and we're just stuck in some dreamland together, and there's nothing left worth living for anymore? Is there any point in surviving?"

"*Ryn,*" Asher says again, and stops there, but by 'Ryn' she means 'Me, too,' and she means 'You can't say that," and she means 'But if I want better for you then I have to want better for myself,' and she means 'If you deserve to exist without a purpose then I do too,' and she means 'Oh.'

"Do you not think about it?" he asks in the softest voice she's ever heard him use, soft enough that he almost fades out of her hearing aids. "Do you not wonder what will happen after you die?"

Time seems to stop for a moment, the air holding its breath. The waves still. The screeching seagulls fall quiet. A beach ball rolls across the sand of their hidden alcove without a child to chase it. For a heartbeat, the world stops turning.

"I want to live forever," Asher says eventually, as if her optimism can balance out his blue mood, as if she doesn't have a handful of days left to try and prevent a life from ending. She squeezes Ryn's hand like she is the only thing tethering him to the earth. "Honestly, I just want to know everything. I don't think I can handle the concept of not existing simply for the fact that things will continue to happen, and I might never know about them."

Asher thinks that this day will become the marker for the year, the second time in her life where she's thought about what will happen if she dies. In school, the year was the marker. All five years of primary school. The last year of secondary school. First year of sixth form. Then after, she imagines that university and jobs and houses will be the markers. A specific bedroom in student halls. Photos above a desk in an office cubicle. All of her stuff in her bedroom at her dad's house, rather than being split between two. But now that she's in the awkward transient summer between school years, she's not sure what the marker really is. Moments and memories, she assumes, but she knows that this day with Ryn will eventually become her way to identify the time.

Asher stares out at the spot where the sky meets the sea until Ryn's continuous fidgeting beside her catches her attention. She watches him rummage through his rucksack, placing various items from inside in an orderly line beside him on the sand. There's a spare pair of sunglasses and a half-empty water bottle and a stack of what Asher can only identify as envelopes, and he thumbs through them until he finds one in particular and reaches out for her hands.

"It's my letter for August, but save it until the month is officially over," he says, tucking an unlabelled envelope into Asher's hand and closing her fingers over it. "I'm sorry if you can't read my handwriting. I was going to type it up, but then I felt like it was more important for it to be handwritten."

Asher hums in agreement. She lets go of Ryn's hand long enough to slip the letter into her own rucksack, then intertwines their fingers. He rests his head on her knees as she describes the colours of the hazy horizon to him, watching the sun rise toward the precipice of the sky and the sea begin to creep up the beach toward their toes. They remember to walk around the edge of the cliff with minutes to spare before they're cut off entirely and traipse along the sand in wet shoes back to the bus stop.

Ryn falls asleep on Asher's shoulder on the way home. She nudges him awake as the bus slows toward the stop just down the street from his house.

"Hey, wake up," she whispers against his skull as he blinks his way back into consciousness. "It's your stop."

"Not yet," he decides, and they ride together for ten more minutes until Asher's stop where they both disembark and stand beneath the lamppost at the end of her street, not late enough in the day for the light to encase their skin with a golden glow. The wind blows warm and strong through their hair, buffeting against them with the strength of an incoming storm. Asher tilts her head back and sniffs at the air. Ah, yes, there it is: petrichor.

"See you tomorrow?" she says as she checks the time on her phone. The purpling sky and the missed call from her father tell her that it is later than expected, and although it's still daylight, it's probably for the best that she doesn't look at the exact time. "Actually, maybe not tomorrow if the rain starts soon. I'll see you the day after."

"The day after?" Ryn's face crumples slightly as if she's said something wrong.

"Or tomorrow afternoon. I'll bring my umbrella if I have to."

His expression doesn't change.

"It's fine." She squeezes his hand reassuringly as if she can tell telepathically what's worrying him. "I'll email you some of the photos I took today in case you or your dad want them for anything, and I'll find another song I like that you can draw for me, and I'll open up the most embarrassing story I've ever written for you to read. I'll see you soon, okay?"

He frowns but doesn't say anything. Asher lets go of his hand, and he unfolds his cane, hesitating for a few seconds longer before turning in the direction of home. Asher waits until he's rounded the street corner and she can't decipher his cane tapping anymore before she looks up at the darkening sky and sighs.

It's fine. Whatever it is, it'll be fine.

She'll see him tomorrow.

The dusk deepens. The stars emerge. The embers of the sun glow hot orange. There's a gathering weight in the air, like rain. Like a consequence, coming straight for her.

The ocean was one of Ryn's first memories.

He remembers excited shrieks becoming the soundtrack to running through waves, the ghost of a strong warm hand in his, the lullaby of his mother's once gentle voice. Sun cream, and empty jam jars full of saltwater, and crab hunting. Learning to spell his name by tracing the letters in the sand.

The ocean was one of his first memories, so he wants it to be one of his last.

The plan is made, and he sits on the edge of the bath with sand still stuck between his toes as he goes over it again and again in his head so he doesn't have to put it onto paper. His room is already littered with evidence, littered with things for people to find—a whole mystery to unravel, but only when it's all too late, because no one sees through him enough to actually look at the junk upon his desk or in his drawers, but that isn't their fault.

Because Ryn yearns for the sensation of water filling his lungs: a burning without a fire—something tragic, something magic in his own mind and horrific in others. He's well aware that he's beginning to romanticise, to even fall in love with the idea of his own death, because it's not that different from falling in love with the ocean, and at least that shade of blue is welcome.

He tilts his head back until his hair is drenched by the shower spray. The water hasn't warmed up yet.

Asher once asked him if not being able to see his body made it easier to accept, and he is reminded that the answer is a definite 'no' as he strips his salt-stained clothes and holds his hand under the showerhead. Still cold. He hates showers. In recent years, as his body has developed into something he no longer recognises, he's grown to hate bathing in general.

He once went through a month-long phase of sitting on the bath mat while the water was running, hoping that the sound would convince his father that he'd washed himself, even though he clearly hadn't. There's only so long his feathery hair can remain unwashed before the dry shampoo can't hide the visible grease, so he stopped faking showers and forced himself to pretend that the feeling of his body beneath his fingertips didn't make him want to vomit in the plughole. After that, his father agreed to pull him out of school, and Ryn sat in his bedroom with the curtains drawn for so long that no one questioned his changed appearance when he finally returned.

He steps into the bath and under the showerhead, scrubs as fast as he can, and gets out, swearing as he scrapes himself dry with a cardboard-textured towel. He's practically dressed—loose-fitting shorts and oversized sweatshirt to hide his lack of chest binder, as if he's going to see anyone else this evening who'll have the nerve to point it out—when his phone alerts him to a text message.

"You have one new message from 'Asher Orange Heart Emoji,'" Siri informs him. "Open, or ignore?"

"Open."

"New message: 'Birthday update! Just a garden party at Dad's, but we're allowed to decorate the greenhouse. Grinning face emoji.' Would you like to listen again, reply, or ignore?"

"Ignore," Ryn replies, and he curls up into a ball on the damp bath mat.

The plan is selfish. He knows it is. *He's* selfish, as much as he pretended he wasn't until this point. He's selfish because he's become so committed to a choice to stop him from backing out that he can't even delay it until after his best friend's birthday party. She'll turn eighteen, and he never will, and maybe one day she'll get everything she's dreamed of.

But he's going to wear the title of 'selfish' like a crown in these final days, as he clings to Asher's love like a lighthouse beacon guiding him home, as they spend most days together, but he's so alone, and in three days, she will be too. And that'll be one hell of a birthday party, fuck, one hell of a birthday present—a bitter twist to it all.

He's already apologised to her in his last letter. Maybe that'll be enough.

THIRTY-TWO

Two days pass without Asher hearing from Ryn, and it's sometime during those silent forty-eight hours that Asher begins to piece together that something must be wrong, and not just because she broke her promise to see him. She perches on her windowsill, although it's barely wide enough to fit her, and stares out her open window down the street as if she'll see Ryn waiting beneath a lamppost, but all she sees is her face reflected back in the glass. She looks tired, she thinks. Her breath fogs the windowpane, and she resents the rain because it's barely caused the temperature to drop. Another migraine hovers at the edge of her vision. She wipes away the thought along with the condensation.

She's not sure why it's suddenly so urgent that Ryn replies, but it's the eve of her eighteenth birthday and the day documented in the tearstained letter, and she knows she's run out of time, so maybe she doesn't want to watch the countdown end on her own.

Two days have passed since Ryn gave a one-word answer to her apology about the rain being too intense for her to visit, and she knows he isn't the best at replying to text messages, but he's never been quiet for this long before. She scrolls through every message she's sent in the past week and overanalyses her punctuation use just in case she's said something wrong. She doesn't think she has, but that won't stop her from pulling up Luke's contact and sending him a message.

ASHER
have u heard from ryn??

LUKE is typing...

Then he stops typing, and he starts again, and he stops and starts so many times over the next few minutes that Asher's impatience wins, and she decides to confront him with her first initiated phone call since she got her hearing aids.

"I don't know where he is," Luke says as a greeting after the penultimate ring, which tells Asher that he knows exactly where Ryn is.

"I was just calling to ask if you've seen him," she says cautiously, as if he's a wild animal ready to bolt. "Or heard from him. Any proof of life, really. I don't need to know exactly where he is or what he's doing or anything."

Luke's sigh crackles through the speaker. "He's fine. Don't worry about it."

"Did he say that?" Asher asks, her frown audible.

Luke pretends he doesn't hear it. "Say what?"

"Did he say that he's fine? That I shouldn't worry about him?"

"He hasn't said anything to me in a week."

Asher isn't sure about the correct way to respond to that, but Luke's distress is evident. "Are *you* fine?" she decides is the only acceptable response.

Luke lets out a sound that's halfway between a laugh and a sob. "He's ruining his life. You don't have to ruin yours too."

"What are you talking about?"

"He'd want you to be happy, even if he can't even try to be happy for himself," he continues without explanation. "At least one of you should have a good life, otherwise you're just a fucking Romeo and Juliet cliché, and that's just a waste."

"What do you mean?"

Luke ends the call. Asher calls him back, and he sends her to voicemail. She calls back again, and there's an electronic voice telling her something which she can only interpret as him blocking her phone number.

Asher concludes that the only logical next step is to continue trying to get through to him, because this clearly isn't the kind of situation where you can bring in an adult without upsetting someone.

She puts on her shoes and flips up her hood and

furiously speed-walks through the rain to Ryn and Luke's street as if she's intending to yell at them in person, but she hovers by Luke's gate until the anger leaves her body. It's not worth it, but she's here now, and she's not willing to waste a journey.

She turns around and watches Ryn's darkened bedroom across the street, the lack of car in the driveway, the front door that's free from a note. She turns to the right, squints through the rain, and notices that Ryn's neighbour's door is wide open, the windows open, and the curtains blowing in the wind, letting the storm into the house every way possible. The neighbour sits on the doorstep, a wiry, early-thirties man who looks as if he's never seen the sun before, head tilted up to the cloud-soaked sky like he's praying.

He looks peaceful.

She doesn't want to disturb him, to bother a stranger for her own convenience, but it's been raining for two days, and he only comes outside when it rains, so surely he must know if Ryn is inside the house. That's the logical thing to do, she tells herself as she unlatches the man's gate and walks up the gravel path toward him.

His gaze drops toward her as she stops at the bottom of his porch steps. He says nothing, only raises an eyebrow at the strange, soaking wet girl intruding on his property.

"Hello," Asher starts, suddenly uncertain. "I was hoping you could help me with something."

"Come up out of the rain."

The man shuffles to the right and gestures to the spot on the step next to him. Asher does, dripping all over his porch and her shoes squelching with each step. She sits beside him, puts down her hood so the wet fabric is no longer touching her hearing aids, and spreads the skirt of her dress around her in a desperate attempt for it to dry and not ruin her embroidered pockets. She pinches the bloated thread of a flower and watches the water squeeze out.

"I'm Asher," she offers

"You're here about the boy. About Ryn," the man says matter-of-factly, as if there's no doubt that the only reason a strange girl would approach a stranger man is because of a boy they both happen to know. She wonders if he's seen her coming and going from the house in the past, the only biracial girl in a ten-mile radius, a very recognisable face.

Asher nods. The rain is so loud on the porch roof that she has to read his lips to understand, and she thinks she detects a hint of a northern accent—his mouth forms vowels the same way that hers does. If the situation weren't so serious, she would be smiling. "I haven't heard from him in days, but I have heard that you only come outside when it rains…"

"And it's been raining for days," the man finishes. "You want to know if I saw him leave?"

Asher nods again. "I don't want to be alone right now, but I don't know where to find him, and I don't really have any other friends anymore."

The man squints up at the sky as he thinks, a hand stretching out to catch raindrops in his palm. "His dad left for work at eight, and Ryn left less than ten minutes later. No coat, no umbrella, nothing. Soaking wet within seconds. Stood under the bus shelter at the end of the road for a while, so I stopped watching."

"He's been gone for hours?" Asher tries not to let the defeat in her voice be evident and starts wondering where Ryn could've gone in this weather.

"Hours," the man agrees. He rubs the cool water across his brow. "He's been gone all day. Who knows where he is by now if he got on a bus." He reaches out to fill his palm again, then says, "His friend across the street left too, but in the past half hour. Went the opposite direction."

Like he knew she was coming, Asher thinks, and she's reassured that coming here was a good decision, even if she didn't get to yell at Luke in person.

"Are you going to look for him?" the man asks. "Ryn, not the other boy, the Jenkins' kid."

Asher sighs. "I don't know," she says, and she thinks she's being honest. "If he's not answering his phone, he probably wants to be alone right now."

The man nods, but his expression doesn't shift, and not for the first time, Asher suspects that another adult in her life knows a lot more than they're letting on. But, once again, she doesn't question it. She just thanks the man for his time and his dry porch, waves goodbye at the bottom of his steps, and flips up her soggy hood to walk home in the rain.

Back at her father's house, Asher kicks off her shoes and throws herself into her desk chair, spinning to face the shrine to her and Ryn's friendship. The tearstained letter is unexplainably pinned in the centre and, the more Asher looks at it, the more she thinks she's seen the handwriting somewhere before. The handwriting in the letter is huge and messy, slewing across the page. Her finger traces the loops of the y's, the dashes above the i's in place of dots, the lines that run into one another. It feels familiar, and not just because she looks at it every other waking moment. But it's nothing like the tiny, precise lettering Jocelyn used to label her Polaroid, no matter how many minor similarities there are.

But who else's handwriting does she recognise?

It's August 31st, so she knows she's obeying Ryn's request to open his newest letter at the end of the month as she tears through the envelope.

He's written it in a green Biro that must be most of the way to drying out based off the splotchiness of some of the words, and it turns out he was right: she can't read his handwriting.

Not this time around, at least.

She reaches up to the shrine and takes down the Polaroid that Ryn signed with his name.

There's definitely some resemblance in the blockiness of the letters.

She fumbles through the pile of paper on her desk and pulls out Ryn's first letter from the end of May, the one that has remained unintentionally unopened to this day, as if seeing the signs again is going to change the third time around. She soon finds out that the letter is typed and printed on plain white A4 paper, but his name is written blockily at the bottom in that distinct green ink.

And it's still the same handwriting as the tearstained letter.

For the second time that week, Asher feels as if the world has stopped turning.

"Fuck," she says, because there's nothing else to say.

She puts her shoes back on.

THIRTY-THREE

Asher calls Ryn seven more times on her way to the bus stop, hanging up before the automated message begins and forces herself to reach the end of the road before she calls again. No answer.

Maybe an hourly bus isn't the best mode of transport for what Asher now knows will be a rescue mission, she realises as she misses it by a minute, but she's almost more afraid of the irreparable damage done to her and Ryn's relationship if she tells someone than if she arrives too late. You would think that a coastal town would be slightly more adept at less-than-sporadic public transportation, but it's not really a coastal town, just a town surrounded by nothing, which happens to be in close proximity to a stretch of coastline which the local council hasn't worked up the courage to conquer in the name of tourism. Their money goes to other important things, like another antiques shop.

Asher waits at the bus stop for the next fifty-eight and a half minutes, catching her breath and overcomplicating everything Ryn has ever said to her, wondering how many signs she must've missed. She calls him one more time, just in case he answers. He doesn't.

She hesitates before she buys her ticket, paralysed between feeling frozen and feeling everything, because she doesn't actually know if Ryn will be at the beach when she arrives. And then she remembers that every second spent hesitating is another second spent letting August 31st slip away, so she gets a return ticket and commandeers the back row of seats so she can spiral in peace.

The journey takes too long, another almost hour winding through country lanes and what feels like infinite stops to let farm vehicles pass. Plenty of time for Asher to hold her breath and wonder if it's too late to overcompensate for everything she never said.

She's clinging to hope like a life jacket by the time she gets to the beach, wind whipping her hair against her cheeks, cold water spraying against her ankles and soaking through her sweatshirt as she searches the sand and the base of the cliff and glances out at the rocks Ryn pointed out in the distance. No signs of movement other than the waves, no boy-shaped shadows caught out at sea. She squints toward the horizon and ignores the fact that the sun is creeping down to it.

Then her eyes fall on the outcrop of cliff that they rounded a few days ago, and she remembers the stretch of sand that will be underwater now that the tide is coming in.

"I swear to God…," she begins, but the fight leaves her body as soon as it appears. She walks into the water, shoes on and hood down because she can't possibly get any wetter, and traipses along until the waves hit her knees and she can trail a hand along the base of the cliff. Okay. Breathe. It's a bit of water, even if it is significantly rougher than it is most days of the year. All she has to do is keep her head above water, walk to the end, and take a little look around the edge to see if Ryn is there, right? It's not that hard.

She finds him in the water, and suddenly it's all very hard.

There's no beach left around the edge of the cliff. The rocks are damp and slick with sea slime, carpeted with silt, sand, and washed-up flotsam. Ryn is at what was the base of the cliff during low tide, the water rising up to his neck, his chin tilted upwards as if he's trying to stay afloat. A wave rocks in, and it slams his body into the cliff with such force that his head snaps back and his face crumples in pain. Asher thinks she hears something crack, but that could just be the water working its way into her hearing aids. The water here is only waist-deep, so she tugs them out of her ears and tucks them into her bra. A wave slamming into her chest tells her that that was a bad decision.

For a moment, she thinks of wading over to him

and dragging him back to the sand by force. But the water around him is deeper than she can manage, and she knows she'll barely be able to keep herself afloat, let alone both of them without his cooperation.

All she can do is speak and hope that he is listening.

"Ryn. I'm not going to talk you down. Or talk you out, I guess," she begins uncertainly, because she's only needed to do something like this once before, and it didn't end the way anyone wanted. "I think that's what you want, for someone to prove to you that they care, but I'm not going to stop you."

He turns his face away from her so she can't tell if he's replying, and she can feel the wind ripping at her hair and assumes the force of the storm is swallowing down her voice, but she screams out for him until her lungs feel like giving out just in case. "I respect you enough to let you make your own decisions. I love you too much—and you know that—to decide for you how you should live your life."

A wave sweeps the sand out from beneath her, and she falls to her knees, head plummeting beneath the surface for a disorientating five seconds. She splutters as she comes up for air, the salt burning her throat, but at least it washes away the coppery taste forming on her lips. Whitewater pours into Ryn's mouth. Asher struggles through the waves toward him, the water deepening with each step.

"The only thing I'll ask if that you'll try one more time." The wind chill out here steals the words from her tongue. "One more time, please, because I'm so fucking selfish I can't imagine the thought of living a life without you."

The salt in her throat is joined by her tears. She staggers a few more steps until the water rises to her chest, and then within Ryn's reach, and she grabs at whatever part of him is closest beneath the surface—the cuff of his sweatshirt, she thinks—and it slips straight through her fingertips. She can't take another step without losing the little balance she has, and he won't step toward her until he's decided to change his mind, so all she can do is the only thing she can think of: she waits.

Ryn tilts his head toward the remaining bright spot in the sky and gasps for one more breath.

Five things he can see. An illuminated sky above him, daylight fading fast. Dark rainclouds choking out the glowing sun as it sinks toward the horizon. Water rippling—no, water *crashing*. Light ricocheting off waves. A dark outline of the rocks in the distance where he should've stranded himself to avoid getting caught.

Four things he can touch. The waves wrapping around his throat, touching him more than he's touching them, choking him. Asher grasping at his sweatshirt sleeve. Sand shifting beneath his feet, sinking him against the rock stabbing into his spine. His waterlogged clothes trying to drag him under the surface.

Three things he can hear. The full force of the ocean crashing against the cliff face. Asher's crying. Her pleading, a siren song of suffering.

Two things he can smell. A stale, sulphury stench that must belong to the seaweed. Raspberry shampoo beneath the brine.

One thing he can taste. Salt. From the waves crawling into his throat. From his tears dripping down his nose. From her tears falling onto his tongue.

He exhales and, just for a moment, the big things stop feeling so big.

Ryn lets Asher pull him out of the water.

September

THIRTY-FOUR

After Asher pulls Ryn out of the water, she drags him up the beach until they both collapse on the sand, coughing up water as the sun finally sets. Ryn's memory is immediately reduced to a fragmented version of events. The darkness of the water. The thick, briny taste of it. The way it burned down his throat when he gasped. He remembers the cold, and the rain, and he remembers Asher's hands eventually meeting his, impossibly strong.

They sit together on the sand for a while until the rain eases enough for Asher to wring the water from her clothes and drape her damp sweatshirt over Ryn's shaking shoulders. When he's calm enough to stand, she guides him away from the beach and hauls him down a street for what feels like hours with his arm slung around her shoulders until they collapse again, this time on the floor of a hospital waiting room. He coughs brine onto the linoleum as she struggles to explain what's going on to a nurse, and then he's the one to do the talking through his salt-strangled throat as her hearing aids are waterlogged and she's crying too much to lip-read. At some point, a stress-induced headache threatens to split his skull into two, and he resorts to clawing at his face, and then he's reminded that eyes are the organs with the highest concentration of nerve endings. He's in an amount of pain that can't be spoken, and a nurse covers his remaining eye with a patch to deter his scratching, and for the first time in his life he's totally blind.

After the clawing, Asher was clinging to his bedside, but through bad luck and worse timing, someone realised she wasn't family and escorted her back to the waiting room. She worried about leaving him, worried about what she described as frothy pink tears leaking out from beneath his eye patch, but she accepted her plastic chair fate. He couldn't bring himself to even whisper 'happy birthday' as her footsteps grew distant.

Now, he's alone, crying blood in a hospital bed.

"I've got you," a gentle voice says, gentler than he thinks he's worthy of. "Don't worry."

A soft hand holds his, soft like hand cream, with manicured nails touching his palm and skin wrinkled from age. The woman talks to him through the tears. Her name is Andrea. She has a wife named Grace. She lives near the train station, the one a few miles away from their near-coastal town, not the one near this remote hospital. Grace had a bad fall a week or two ago, but the X-rays seem to be coming back better than expected. Andrea says she has long, dark hair—dark from dying over the greys—and "more fine lines than you can imagine." She describes every chair in the room and every person moving throughout the ward and every bouquet of supermarket flowers. She talks about her adult children and her vegetable garden and her favourite memories from when she first moved to town.

A doctor comes in. Ryn is walked to another room. He clings to Andrea's hand, and she comes with him, following him. She doesn't let go. She talks the whole way: "More beds on your left, just a few more minutes maybe, to your right is the ugliest painting I have ever seen, you're doing great, darling, just a few more steps and we'll be in the ward."

In the quiet of the next room, she props up Ryn's pillows in his new bed and sends a text to Asher after he recites her phone number, telling her where he's gone. And Andrea still stays, just talking, her voice echoing strangely in the silence. Gently describing the room to him. And then someone she hasn't had the chance to identify speaks. A child, he thinks, from the sound of the voice.

"Why is he crying?" the child asks.

"He's lost his vision," Andrea says, and Ryn's thoughts are dragged back to a dissimilar hospital bed from four years earlier. "He can't see."

"Oh. That's scary," says the child.

The child tells Ryn that they're here because they

have something stuck up their nose, and Ryn's laugh isn't entirely forced. Their mother groans and tells Ryn about the child (they're six; they love the animated Barbie films and not eating their vegetables), about herself, about moving houses soon, even if she can't quite commit to moving to the countryside.

Eventually, Andrea says she's sorry, she has to leave now, she's got to check on her wife.

"Don't worry," says the mother. "I've got him." And then Ryn feels her hand press into his.

For hours, he's taken care of by strangers, each person talking about whatever comes to mind, not for any reward or reason, he hopes, just because he's scared and alone and in the hospital and more blind than usual and needs to be distracted. Not everyone needs to be told the story—they just perk up in moments of silence with, "They're playing *Grand Designs* reruns on the TV, do you like that kind of thing? Yeah, me too, but I lose interest when they keep going over their budgets—"

By the time Ryn's father arrives at the hospital, the room is buzzing, and the sun is rising. They talk to each other like old friends, laughing, joking about "If you don't like hospital food, wait until you get on an airplane," and "Can't believe I stayed up until sunrise, what a party animal I'm becoming." Ryn's holding the hands of someone called Taylor, who has a tattoo of a vintage fountain pen and spends their free time crocheting stuffed animals.

He never sees any of their faces. He can't keep track

of most of their names. But, as his father arrives and insists that he's moved into his own room, he thinks about them and their radiating kindness, and the way they all took a deep breath and did something gentle for him amongst his pain: "Let's be here together, let me help you, let's keep going, just one more time."

Asher sees Ryn's father walk into the waiting room eight hours after they arrived, and she's the one to tell him where to find his son. They don't exchange any other words, any excuse for his lateness, any reason for not noticing his missing son, just a pained look.

She's stolen a pen from the reception desk to draw across the back of her hand, and she alternates between inking designs and holding a paper cup of lukewarm water that someone pressed into her palm. She doesn't drink it, though; she thinks she's had enough of water for a few days.

At some point, a cleaner comes in to mop the salt water that's pooling around her feet and says something she doesn't catch. He hovers until her eyes rise to his, and says grudgingly, "You've got some talent there, sweetheart."

Asher looks down and sees that she's adorned her hand with flowers, the petals folding over her fingers, the ink bleeding just a little. She says thanks and cradles her cup with her flower hand, looking at the way the petals form rings and realising it's the first time she's drawn anything in months.

Eventually, she stands, unsticking her damp dress and sweaty thighs from the chair, and begins an every-five-minutes routine for the next two hours consisting of begging any passing person wearing scrubs if they can tell her anything about Ryn. When a doctor tells her, "Yes, he'll be okay; no, she can't see him yet," she finally stops pacing the waiting room and collapses back into her salt-stained chair.

Something in the air tells Asher that things are coming to an end. Not the world, exactly. Just the summer. There'll be other summers, but there'll never be one like this. Never again. She doesn't even think she wants it again, this summer that was so full of Ryn and loving him and prematurely mourning the loss of a person she didn't think she knew. She can't do it again, she realises as she curls up in her plastic chair, scratching at a spot on her arm where salt has dried on her skin. She can't keep putting her friends above herself, letting her life spiral obsessively around someone else, platonic or not. She doesn't have the strength to do it one more time.

THIRTY-FIVE

"**W**hen you told me you wanted to die, I didn't think you were being serious."

Unlike Ryn's father, Luke doesn't sit beside the hospital bed. His voice comes from the foot of it, and Ryn can only imagine Luke's folded arms and cold-eyed glare as he once again wonders if they're even friends anymore. But people who aren't friends wouldn't visit each other in a hospital room, right?

"Why would I joke about something like that?" Ryn asks without an ounce of the venom that he feels.

"*Everyone* jokes about mental health and killing themselves, and I thought you'd just laugh it off and we would forget about it, but you're not joking, and I don't want to forget," Luke says, and there's nothing Ryn wants more than for everyone to forget about the past two days , as if his actions have affected no one but himself. "So I want to offer you a trade."

"No more trades," Ryn says firmly.

Luke scoffs. "What do you mean?"

Ryn regrets saying anything, because revealing his trade with Asher feels too intimate, too personal, to talk about with his former best friend, but he has to say something. "Three months ago, I made a deal with Asher to give her the best few weeks of her life while we were writing those letters in therapy, and then I made no effort to change her life, and now she's spent her birthday in a hospital waiting room. So, no more trades. I'm not going to make a promise that I won't keep."

"That's selfish," Luke decides, and there is the venom that Ryn was missing. "That's so fucking selfish of you."

Ryn continues as if Luke hasn't said anything or else he'll never say anything again. "And I assume you're going to ask me to trade lives and promise to never do anything stupid again, and I personally think that's more selfish than anything I would ever ask from you."

An exasperated sigh. Rubber soles squeaking on the linoleum. A voice muttering a swear word as it rounds the corner.

Ryn is alone once more.

For the first time since Asher's parents separated, they're sat in the same room without arguing, which would be an otherwise exciting moment if they weren't sat together on the other side of the table from her in what they have decided is neutral territory: the brand name café on the high street.

"Can you tell us anything else about what happened the other day, Ash?" her father begins. She knows she's going to have to talk about it eventually, but she was hoping it would become one of those anecdotes she could talk about and laugh at a decade later, not a handful of days. "It's hard right now, worrying about what happened to you and Ryn. And then sitting here knowing that things might become so much harder for both of you if you keep it between yourselves."

He sniffles. Asher hopes that it's a sound she will never hear again.

"Stop making it sound like she has a choice," her mother snaps, and Asher would believe that the past two days haven't worried her if it weren't for her mother's makeup-free face and Asher's focus on lip-reading making her far too aware of the smell of wine on her mother's breath. "We're her parents. She should tell us everything."

An argument about parenting techniques ensues while Asher reads and doesn't reply to a text from Ryn asking if she's okay. Her phone didn't survive the water, but the SIM card miraculously did, so she's using her father's prehistoric mobile until she caves to embarrassment enough that she forgoes having a phone altogether.

She's not sure why she isn't responding to Ryn's messages, just that she's not quite sure what the right thing is to say to someone after they've almost died, and that she's drowning in the relief that he didn't die, and if

"Are we still friends?" is an acceptable thing to ask when you've ignored everything else they've said.

It's like someone else has woken up in Ryn's hospital bed, and she's not sure who it is. She wants to skip ahead one or two or a dozen years until all of *this* is over and she feels like she knows him again.

"I met Ryn at the beach," Asher says, just to stop her mother's voice from reaching a pitch her ears cannot tolerate.

"And what else happened? Why did you go to the beach in the rain?" her mother presses. She swirls a teaspoon in her coffee (decaf cappuccino, more almond milk than water, sugar-free caramel syrup) with over-practiced nonchalance. "Why did you go so late in the day that the buses might've stopped running?"

Asher clicks her phone screen on and off without a crumb of indifference. Ryn's sent another message. "We went in the water, which was a stupid idea because it was raining and cold and the waves were rough."

"And then what happened?" her mother asks again. "How did you end up at the hospital?"

"Just a precaution, I guess. Ryn swallowed a bit too much water and we weren't sure if it was safe." And then, as if it's important: "We walked."

Asher's father seems content to leave the conversation there, reaching for the jacket draped across the back of his chair, but her mother snaps loud enough for the other café customers to hear, "The boy is *still* in the hospital, and you're going to pretend that nothing is wrong?"

"I am well aware that something is wrong," her father says evenly in the voice he usually reserves for difficult customers at the garden centre. "I can also tell that whatever happened—accident or not, or whatever you've chosen to believe—might've been traumatic to our daughter, and she clearly doesn't want to talk about it at the moment, whether it's because both of us are here or because we're in public, but she'll talk when she's ready."

A stone-cold sobriety reaches her mother's eyes. "You don't know that."

Her father's expression saddens. "You might not know our daughter anymore, but I do."

"How dare—" Her mother doesn't finish her sentence, just pulls something pink from her handbag, slams it down beside her half-empty mug hard enough to send coffee drops spilling, and storms out of the café. Her father picks up the pink thing—a crumpled envelope— and inspects it before sliding it across the table to Asher.

Her name is scrawled across the front in her mother's usual careless handwriting. She's suddenly paralysed by the urge to not open it. She doesn't really even want to touch it, because she imagines that it'll contain the emotional equivalent of an atomic bomb, and she doesn't want to deal with that today. But maybe it'll be something nice. A birthday card. Maybe with a special message inside, maybe with nothing but a signature. Whatever it is, it's just something inside an envelope. It will be harmless.

Her dad is watching intently, so Asher opens the

envelope, pulls out a violently glittery birthday card, and opens it to see every inch of blank space written over. Another letter. She puts the card back into the envelope. Maybe she'll read it later, she tells herself, but she knows it'll remain crushed in her pocket until she forgets that it exists.

Ryn is discharged from the hospital that afternoon.

He hovers in the doorway of his bedroom as if it doesn't belong to him anymore, a tribute to the boy he was a month before. He crosses the threshold; lingering broken glass crunches beneath his trainers, his toes hit the empty mirror frame he's left on the floor, and his fingers trail the dried paint he hasn't cleaned from the surfaces. Any other evidence of his outburst—the blue-stained clothing and bedsheets and painted-over paintings—are long gone. The lifetime's worth of letters is gone from his desk, too—all of his emotions, no matter how messy they were, carved out onto a page but now taken away as if they're proof of a crime.

At least his father never saw the letter Asher found.

Ryn lies face down on his bed and thinks for too long about what's going to happen to him next, and then he shakes his pillow violently as if his thoughts will come tumbling out. He feels everything. He feels nothing. He just wants Asher to text him back.

Ryn expects it'll be another claustrophobic six

months before his father lets him leave his house unattended, so he resigns himself to sitting on the front porch when the confines of his bedroom grows too unbearable, chin resting on a crooked knee as he glares in the general direction of the picket fence at the front edge of the garden. He wonders if his father ever got round to repainting it over the summer like he planned.

He stares at the fence's shadow until he hears gravel crunching to his left, footsteps approaching the hedge between his house and the one next door, and then an unfamiliar voice says, "Your girl came looking for you."

"My girl?" he asks in feigned obliviousness, because he doesn't know anyone else other than Asher—let alone another girl—who would come looking for him, and he's sure as hell that it wouldn't have been his mother. He doesn't recognise the voice, but through an over-extensive process of elimination of the direction it's coming from and the people who know the comings and goings of his household, he concludes that it must belong to his weird neighbour, and he's suddenly ashamed that he still doesn't know the man's name.

"You know who I'm talking about," the man says. "Pink hair. Quirky dress. Wanted to check in on you because you wouldn't text her back."

"Now she won't text me back," Ryn mutters, and he thinks, *Has she always had pink hair?*

The man stifles a laugh. "It seems like she found you, whether or not you wanted her to."

And, despite everything, Ryn's still not sure if he

wanted to be found, but he was, so now he has to live with the consequences of his own decisions, whether or not he wants to. He has to live, because Asher wants him to.

Ryn buries his head in his hands. "I should've said something months ago."

"What do you mean?" his neighbour asks, and Ryn has a feeling he knows exactly what Ryn means.

His hand gestures meaninglessly in the air as he tries to summon the words. "She found a letter I wrote at the start of the summer that I hoped no one would ever read, not because I didn't want anyone to know what it said, but because I didn't want to get caught. But she found it, and she told me she read it and wanted to find who wrote it so she could help them, and I said nothing. I acted like I wanted nothing to do with it, and she's spent the past three months in a downward spiral trying to find the writer. And then—"

"Slow down. Breathe," his neighbour says, and then Ryn hears the crunch of gravel as footsteps recede, then the creak of his gate opening. The footsteps approach, and the man sits beside him on the porch. "It's okay. Just keep breathing."

Ryn gasps for air as if he's drowning all over again.

His neighbour sighs as if he understands. He tells Ryn to breathe and count to ten and count the shadows of clouds until his lungs return to normal, then he says, "You're young. You're not running out of time any time soon. You can claw yourself out of your sadness again and again and find strength in yourself, and the fight isn't over until you're dead. You're not stuck. Your life isn't over. It's barely even begun."

In a week or so, Ryn will realise that this tough love is exactly what he needed to hear. However, in this moment, his wounds are still bleeding, and his feelings are tender. "You know nothing about me."

"I was you twenty years ago. Ten years ago." His neighbour laughs a mockery of a laugh. "Hell, I was like you last month. And I imagine I'll be the same as you again next year. Your suffering will eat you alive as long as you allow it."

The only thing stopping Ryn from telling his neighbour to 'fuck off' as a panic response is the sound of receding footsteps, and his father's car pulling into the driveway. Ryn retreats to his bedroom and shuts the door before his father has the chance to question him about his visitor.

It's in this quiet moment before he hears footsteps on the stairs when Ryn presses his palms to his surroundings and surveys the full extent of damage in his room, something he's been neglecting to do since the outburst. No mirror. No curtains. No trinkets on his desk. Few clean clothes left in his drawers, and fewer paint fumes left to burn his nostrils.

He kneels beside his bed and drags out the box of art supplies from beneath, feeling significantly lighter than the day he last touched it. The paint tubes have been removed, even the ones he didn't touch, and the brushes, too. All that remains in the box is an unopened packet of printer paper and his waterlogged camera.

His father never mentioned seeing it when he cleaned out the wreckage from the bedroom, but Ryn knows it's not his secret anymore.

Cross-legged on the floor, Ryn holds the camera for the first time since he drowned it. He pries off the lens cap and detaches the lens from the body, wrestling with the salt-crusted seams. He removes the SD card and the battery and fumbles with the strap until each part of the camera is lying separately in front of him.

It feels like a memory. It smells like the ocean.

He sits with the pieces until the feelings wash over him and he feels present once more. Then, knowing the camera is still beyond saving, he puts it back together and holds it in his lap like a child with a teddy bear. He won't ever take another photo with it, but he can see if the photos on the SD card can be salvaged, and he can ask Asher how he can clean it until it looks new and he can save up for a replacement.

Now that he's made the promise to live, even if it's for one day at the time, he's going to make the most of it. He's going to wander the woods and the coastlines with a camera and plaster his walls in photos he's taken and stay in love with the ocean from afar. He may never be able to write a letter again without suspicion, but he can fulfil his childhood dream of becoming an artist, whether or not anyone will see his art.

THIRTY-SIX

Ryn lies on the greenhouse floor, looking very much like the day Asher first met him. Two weeks have passed since the beach and the hospital and the birthday, and Ryn's father has released him from house arrest under the conditions that he messages his location every half hour and doesn't walk home alone, and Asher is trying to figure out how to act around a friend again.

She's not sure how to act around someone who survived.

He remembered her birthday, despite everything else that was going on. An envelope bearing her name—painstakingly handmade, she notes—is neatly placed beside her and the card is yet to leave her hands. Also handmade, the front design a sprawling green line subtitled with the name of a song she hasn't heard yet, the inside a simple message in his neatest handwriting yet.

She cracks open a window to let in the scent of cut grass and the neighbours' barbecue, and then they lay together on the threadbare rug, waiting for something to happen. She looks around at the potting table that's become thick with dust, some cracked terracotta pots, and the rows of garden tools, most of which are now fifty percent rust by weight, and hopes that nothing else ever changes.

"I wish I could be different," Ryn says into the quiet.

Asher knows he might not have wanted her to hear—he's made note of her missing hearing aids and has been told to get her attention before he speaks—and she doesn't know how to say she doesn't want him to change. She just wants him to stop hurting.

"What would you change?" she asks instead.

"Everything," he says, then corrects himself, "Nothing. I would do the entire summer differently. I wouldn't do it at all if I could. I think I just wanted someone to save me."

And Asher would. If she could, that is. Save him from himself over and over again until he eventually believes that he is worthy of the love she thrusts upon him. He could fall apart once more, and she would hold him together with her bare hands and sheer force of will.

She wants to, but she can't anymore.

She wonders if time will ever heal this, or if one day she'll just forget how it hurts.

"I think you'll learn to save yourself in time," she says in the end, and Ryn flinches as if she's hurt him. She turns her head to the side so she can watch his mouth move, wanting to speak but not finding the words. "I'm sorry, but if you're looking for a saviour, it's not me. But I'll stay with you until you figure yourself out. As long as it takes."

He lets out a small, strangled sound, and she tucks her hand into his elbow, propping herself up on her other arm so she can read his lips. "But what if the sadness never ends?"

"Then I guess I'll just have to stay with you for a while."

Ryn rests his head on her shoulder, and she leans in until her cheek brushes his hair, and they lie together watching the sun move across the sky through the greenhouse roof until Ryn's phone lights up with a message from his father asking when he's coming home. He groans as Siri reads the message to him.

"I have to show you something before you leave," Asher says, dragging herself to her feet, then Ryn, then pulling him after her through the garden and into the house and up the stairs and down the hall to her bedroom. She grabs his shoulders and guides him to stand in front of her desk, then says, "Reach out to the wall."

He does. His fingers trail over the mess of letters and pictures and paintings she's pinned to the wall over the summer. He feels the crisp edges of the Polaroids he's signed and the worn ones of his tearstained letter. His hand hovers over the paper as if he recognises it. Looking at him now, Asher forgets all the reasons why she should be angry at him.

He presses his fingers into the indented writing of his tearstained letter like he might be able to feel what it says. "What is this?"

Asher shrugs. "I think I called it a shrine at one point, but that makes it sound a lot weirder than it is."

And then she describes it all to him: the pressed white daffodil and the sticky notes and the pages of coloured lines. She tentatively tells him about how she stole the piece of paper scrawled with Ryn's fear from therapy and doesn't look toward him for his reaction. She's continually added to the wall since crafting the iteration, sticking printouts of low-quality phone camera photos she's taken of them and negative film strips and drafts of letters she's yet to send around the edges of the original shrine.

Ryn's fingers trace the idents on the page from the pen of his tearstained letter. "Why did you do this?"

"Because I love you," she says as if it's obvious, and she can feel it in her palms. "And I had all of this physical stuff to remind me of that, and I'm tired of turning around photo frames of people I love, and I think I just needed to do a crime scene investigation-style pinboard without all the string to work out if you love me too."

Now, she turns to him for his reaction.

Tears soak his cheeks, no longer frothy pink like in the hospital.

"I don't deserve this," he whispers, barely loud enough for her ears to detect unaided, and he leans toward her voice until his head falls against her shoulder. His damp cheek sticks to her skin.

"I don't care," she says matter-of-factly as she buries her face into his hair. It's feather-soft as always and smells like her raspberry shampoo. "I've decided you deserve it."

They walk around the neighbourhood for an hour after they've run out of tears and things to say, which is okay because a lot can be said in silence. They stop at a traffic light, and they wait and wait and wait some more because neither of them wants to go home yet.

At some point, the light changes to green for them to cross, and they stay standing beneath the glow. Ryn sucks the chill of the evening air into his lungs and worries that he'll keep wasting his happiness if he clings on to feelings like he doesn't deserve them. There are so many things that are difficult; why can't he let this one be good?

He's ruined Asher's summer. He's ruined *their* summer, he corrects himself, because he is as much a part of his own life as she is. He's ruined nothing, he corrects himself again, because that's what Asher would want him to think. He's ruined nothing, he's not ruined himself, he's just chosen an unconventional way to work through his feelings and now has to live with the consequences.

Asher brushes a finger against the back of Ryn's hand, snapping him back to their moment beneath the traffic light. "We'll be okay."

"I know, I know," he says, exhausted but relieved she's said it. She's acknowledged that they still have hope after all that's happened between them. There's still a chance that they'll be okay again someday.

And can he just enjoy it? Them, at the end of the summer, four months in and trading stories of the first four weeks—*"Tell me about the first time you saw me? What do you think of me now?"* They walk the same neighbourhood and sit on the same pavement where their friendship started, and Asher had once headed home to watch a hydrangea bloom.

"I decided you were going to become my best friend from the moment we met," Asher says as the traffic light blinks back to red. "I wrote this whole thing in my diary about how that speech you did in therapy made me feel less alone."

Ryn laughs, only to himself, a memory coming to mind. "I told my dad that I thought you were different from everyone else, that I thought you might be just like me."

"Do you still think that?" Asher asks. Ryn hears loose stones on the pavement shift beneath her shoes as she sits on the curb.

He watches a lamppost flicker to life as he sits down beside her. "I think that you're just like me, and that we're both like everyone else in the world."

And, in this moment, Ryn knows that they may not have managed to change the world, but they did change each other's lives.

Silence again. Asher's hand slips into his, her thumb rubbing against his knuckles. A lot can be said without sight or sound. This deep knowing buzzes between them along with the flies above.

They could go on a walk tomorrow. Or they could catch up in a year. Ryn pretends he doesn't know about the mental health inpatient forms waiting on the kitchen table, the 'for sale' sign haunting his doorstep, the boxes lining their living room where his father has started to pack up their life in exchange for a temporary retreat to his aunt's house. He's being taken away from his stretch of the ocean once again, and he's not sure how he's going to find his way back this time.

There is so much to worry about, and Ryn's always been good at that. But he and Asher sitting under lampposts beneath a summer sky? Nowhere new, just the neighbourhood streets cracked and shimmering. And them, on the same path for one more day. If he never gets anything else he's asked for, this will be enough.

"There'll be other summers," Asher says with more reassurance than she feels, because she must know about the forms and the 'for sale' sign and the boxes, and they can't find the words to discuss what it means for their friendship. "There's always next summer. I'll see you when I see you, but until then, take care."

For the last time this summer, Asher walks him home.

Ryn sits on his bedroom floor, notebook resting on his crossed legs, twirling a pen through his fingertips as he thinks. Screwed up balls of paper surround him, a hundred thrown-out speeches he'll never send to anyone. But he will send one of them, as soon as he finds the right words.

He's not sure what he wants to say yet, whether it's an accusation or an apology, a premature postmortem of his past mistakes. Maybe it's a love letter, a desperate confession of feelings before he runs out of time to act on them.

He draws lazy circles in the corner of the page as he thinks. Maybe he'll send Asher a photo and she'll spent an afternoon figuring out if any of the lines resemble a song.

He finally decides on a recipient, and he uses his finger as a guide as he prints their name at the top of the page. Okay. Good. He's overcome the first hurdle.

After the recipient is known and the page is dated—more formal than his previous works—the letter comes spilling out of him, memory after memory pouring onto the page in a semi-coherent mess.

Burgers at one in the morning, fireworks past midnight, spending mundane days in a greenhouse where he platonically fell in love with his best friend, and laughing about how his loneliness can now be a funny anecdote he tells at the end of a long night. *"Can you imagine a world where I didn't know you?"*

He writes through the night. By the time the sun rises, the letter is complete.

This time, he sends it.

ACKNOWLEDGEMENTS

Like all of my books so far, this one is about the horrors of being seventeen: remembering your former friends' birthdays more often than your own, grieving a version of yourself that hasn't existed since childhood, and feeling like everything is going right in your life but still being sick with sadness. Unlike my other books, this one draws significantly more from my personal experience with my teenage years. This book is a tribute to every person who made those years and every following one bearable.

To Han, Bonnie, and Evie, who I tend to write about as if they are characters in a story. The ones who don't write books yet seem to have written this one alongside me for the past ten years (including the seven in the middle when I was thinking about writing more than actually writing) as I steal moments from our lives that I think deserve to be remembered forever in fiction. Thank you for your unconditional love, wide-eyed optimism, and fiery defence of me that makes me honoured to be defined by my role in your story.

To Emma (and Ivy Jean), for getting lunch down by the Lakes as I finished the first draft. And for being the mediator in my toxic relationship with commas.

To the Movellas community who witnessed the earliest incomplete version of this story in 2015 when I would upload unedited chapters as soon as I finished writing them. I have been riding the high from your comments ever since.

To Emily Gwen, who designed the lesbian flag that makes a cameo on the cover of this book. I hope you are eternally fairly compensated for your art and contributions to the community.

To every author who has written a book that I've held until it fell apart and where I've stopped and said, "Hey, that's me!" while reading it, specifically the young adult contemporaries of the 2010s. To every artist who has ever appeared on my Spotify Wrapped for being the defining soundtrack to my teenage years, to every album I've listened to on repeat until my earphones broke, and to my mum for merging her record collection with mine and making me look significantly cooler.

To Jack, who I didn't know personally, but will never forget. I think I had to write this book in order to try.

This book is a love letter to my friends: to song lyrics scrawled across the backs of my notebooks and my hands, to endless summer afternoons beneath the red cliffs, and saturated sunrises captured on film with a finger blurring the lens. It's a love letter to the version of myself who clung to these characters for comfort for so many years. And, most of all, this book is a love letter to the moments that became a supercut of my own eternal blue summer.

www.ingramcontent.com/pod-product-compliance
Lightning Source LLC
Chambersburg PA
CBHW032026180726
48283CB00008B/2831